Jen Wylie

# Broken
# Prince

Untold
Press

# BROKEN PRINCE
## Book Two of the Broken Ones

An Untold Press Novel
First Printing, June 2013

Published by Untold Press LLC
114 NE Estia Lane
Port St Lucie, FL 34983

ISBN: 978-0615838557

PRODUCED IN THE UNITED STATES OF AMERICA

10 9 8 7 6 5 4 3 2 1

# Dedication

To Sean; without your constant 'whip whip!' this book would still probably be a work in progress. You are always by my side in everything I do and I can never say how much that means to me.

## And

To Claire and Amber; thank you so much for all you have done to spread the word about this series. You girls rock! I don't know what I'd do without you!

# Chapter 1:
# Bad Memories

Arowyn looked down, absently rubbing the mass of white scars across the back of her hands. They stood out sharply against her sun-tanned skin. A grimace formed on her lips at the memories they invoked.

No matter how much she wanted to forget the past year, everything remained too clear in her mind. Being sixteen didn't change anything. Age didn't make her wiser or better able to cope with everything that had happened. She wished it would. Her mind overflowed with anger and fear and loss.

When their city across the sea had fallen, she'd been taken as a slave. During the fight, she'd been knocked unconscious and later awoke in a slave ship, alone. What happened to her brothers remained a painful mystery. It didn't hurt as much to think of them now, even though the likelihood of ever seeing them again was small. Most likely they'd died in the fighting or been taken as slaves as well.

She'd made a new family, the soldiers on the slave ship had taken her in, and they'd quickly come to mean as much to her as her own flesh and blood.

Unfortunately, almost immediately, she'd starting losing them. Kendric hadn't survived the dangerous swim to shore past the treacherous rocks and the currents around them. She wouldn't have either if it hadn't been for Prince. Those rocks were what scarred her hands so badly. Prince had taken worse damage trying to protect her from them. Avery's death in the spring from sickness continued to hurt, the wound of his loss still raw and painful. Of the six soldiers she'd befriended, she'd lost two already.

She was so tired of death.

Tearing her gaze away from her scars, she opened her pack to find what had been poking her in the back all morning. Shifting things around, she finally found the culprit; the worn wooden comb she rarely used. Her fingers brushed something soft and she paused a moment before curling her fingers into it. Closing her eyes, she took a deep breath.

A shadow loomed over her and she looked up quickly.

"Having trouble?" Cain crouched down beside her.

Lowering her eyes she shook her head, but pulled the sleeve of a black wool sweater partially out of the pack to show him. Avery's sweater. "I miss him," she said quietly.

He ran a hand gently over the top of her head, his smile sad. "We all do."

She pushed the sleeve back in and closed up the pack. "We going soon?" Her words came out sharper than she intended.

Cain stood, giving her shoulder a quick squeeze. "Shortly. We'll give him a little more time."

She turned and they both looked over to Prince. He sat on the edge of the road, looking wilted and pale.

"I'll take his pack this time."

She nodded and turned to stare off into the fields along the dirt road as he walked over to talk to Prince.

As the days and weeks passed, Prince continued to grow weaker, becoming tired easily. She'd watched his face lose its remaining color, the circles under his now sunken eyes darkening. Forcing him to eat proved a challenge, even though she managed somewhat. Watching him fade before her eyes broke her heart.

# Broken Prince

They did what they could for him, carrying most of his gear, stopping to rest often and traveling more slowly. It didn't seem to help. Slowly he was fading away.

She wished they could afford a horse. The highly valued animals had become more common the further south they traveled, but continued to remain well beyond their means. Her frantic worry for Prince had her to the point she had seriously started to consider stealing one.

She looked away, her eyes finding Kei as he spoke to Bo. Kei wasn't human, but one of the wild Fey. Unlike the rest of his people, he could control his fury, mostly. For some reason she could help, could take the wild madness from him and calm him. Over the last few months he'd started to be able to control it by himself. Now, at eighteen years old, he still looked much the same. A little taller maybe.

Her gaze travelled over his lean and wiry frame. His golden skin complimented his golden eyes. Such windows they were, glowing with his emotions. His anger turned them from yellow to orange to red. Thankfully they weren't glowing now.

Seeing her watching him, he grinned and ran a hand through the light brown hair spiking around his head. It poked past his slightly pointed ears. The sight of them always made her smile.

Kei had become her best friend, her first friend. On the ship simple fey magic bound then together. Hands pressed together, a few simple words, and Kei's power made them friends forever. She looked away, that memory bringing forth another, when they had done the second binding, making them family. She'd been dying then. The sickness that had claimed Avery only days before had almost taken her as well. Kei's magic had saved her.

He always saved her.

Leaving the city that spring to continue their journey to take Prince home had been a relief. Discovering he was in fact an Elf hidden by a glamor had been a bit shocking, yet they'd gotten over it. Learning he was dying proved more difficult to deal with. She didn't want to lose him, couldn't bear the thought of it.

Bo walked over and rested a hand on her shoulder. "Ready to go, pup?"

Nodding, she stood, far from rested but vowing not to complain. Her mind still lost in the past, she quietly joined her boys and continued down the road.

The only road running through these eastern lands, it connected all of the small cities, each ruled by a prince. Back home, kings and queens ruled countries. Why princes ruled cities on this continent, she had no idea. But these lands only became inhabited by humans in the last few centuries, colonized by pirates and slavers. They did what they wanted, even if it was to name themselves the prince of a city.

Bo and Cain walked side by side. They'd grown close, two opposites who somehow found a perfect friendship. Though both tall, Bo's wide shoulders and barrel chest dwarfed Cain's medium build. A few steps behind them, she could barely hear Cain's quiet voice. Bo's loud laugh startled birds in the field next to the road.

Turning to glance behind her, she watched Prince bravely try to keep up. Though tall, his slim frame seemed weak compared to the others. It wasn't, or hadn't been. Few saw past the beauty of his face anyway. Even dying he took her breath away. Had he not been an arrogant, temperamental and impatient prince, he would likely have been a favorite to them all. As it was, quite often the other men barely tolerated him.

The winding road brought them steadily closer to yet another large city. It was situated well back from the sea, the rocky cliff-lined shore preventing any type of port. Stone walls sat upon a wide, low hill, surrounded by a patchwork of fields. Far to the east she could see the forest line. Certainly this had been the closest they had come to it since the previous fall.

# Broken Prince

She regarded the distant trees warily. Humans held the coastline, but Were and Fey ruled the easterly forests.

Drawing closer to the city gates, Kei and Prince adjusted their hats, ensuring their ears remained well hidden. Prince's ears were pointed, too, but much more so than Kei's. She smothered another grin at Prince's floppy hat. It still made her laugh every time she saw it. When the Dragos, Damon, destroyed the rune holding the glamour making him appear human, he'd been forced to adapt and hide.

He had no magic left. At least he could somewhat pass for human by hiding his pointed ears. He still moved more gracefully. However, his weakening condition had started to compensate for that. Keeping his face lowered hid his beautiful face, all planes and angles, sweeping brows over sparkling blue eyes. His black hair hung long and fine down his shoulders.

"Rot." She looked away. Too often, thoughts of him occupied her mind.

Trying to keep them away didn't seem to work, even though she had nothing to offer him. She wasn't beautiful, though Avery had once told her she was. She'd grown some curves, but was too hard and thin from little food and too much walking and weapons practice. Her hair hung to her shoulders, but went wild unless braided. Scars marred her face too, one high on her forehead from when she'd gotten struck by debris in the sea, and she didn't know how many from the slaver attack.

Luckily she'd not seen a mirror in almost a year. Though they travelled through many cities on their journey south, they couldn't afford to rent rooms. Any coin they had went to food. Strangely, she didn't really mind, even though she'd grown up rather privileged. Her family hadn't been nobles, but they'd done well enough.

Her thoughts turned to memories of her lost home and family as she trudged along the dusty road.

Kei stepped up to her side, playfully bumping his shoulder against hers. "No dark thoughts."

"I wasn't–"

"You were." He looked up at the sky, smiling when he saw a few clouds. "Tell me what you see today."

Finding shapes in the clouds proved an easy and amusing distraction. Before long, Kei had her laughing and smiling again.

Entering the city just past noon they immediately headed for the market. They had nearly no coin left and had decided to sell some of their extra daggers taken from slavers Kei had killed. Hopefully they would get a decent price and would be able to afford food for their further travels.

The market teemed with people and she struggled not to lose sight of everyone. She noticed Prince being jostled more than once and moved closer to him. She wasn't certain how much pain, if any, his weakening condition left him in. Though his arrogance had dimmed somewhat compared to when she'd first met him, it certainly hadn't gone away. He always insisted he was fine and never whined or complained.

She worked her way over to him and slid her arm around his.

He glared down at her. "I am fine."

"I know," she said, looking up at him innocently. She thought of Damon then, just for a moment. He had attacked her in a city once, ripping memories from her mind.

Prince sighed and shifted his arm, slipping her hand down into his. "It is unlikely he will be here."

She nodded and ducked her head, more to hide the smile which came to her lips than anything else. Elves could read thoughts and mind-speak. Though he kept out of her mind unless invited, he still skimmed her surface thoughts often enough when they touched.

She wasn't truly worried about the Dragos being here. However if Prince thought she was, he would allow her to remain by his side where she could keep an eye on him.

Squeezing his hand a little, she looked back up at him. "Do you mind? Just in case?"

"Troublesome child. Do as you wish."

She offered him a small smile. "Thank you."

They stood off to the side watching Bo and Cain continue to move from stall to stall looking for someone to purchase their daggers. She adjusted her pack with one hand, wishing it were safe enough for her to remove it. Though she'd grown used to the weight, the day had turned hot and the crowds didn't help the stifling heat.

"We could fill the water skins," she suggested to Prince, looking up at him.

He nodded, his eyes continuing to scan the crowd for possible danger.

Spotting Kei, she waved him over. "We're going to get water. Can you get the skins from Bo and Cain and meet us at the well?" She pointed toward one they'd recently passed.

Kei nodded and slipped into the crowd, disappearing quickly.

Keeping a hold of Prince, they made their way back to the well and stood in line. Kei joined them a short time later, extra skins over his shoulder.

He moved close to them. "People are skittish," he said, keeping his voice very low. "We should go soon."

She looked up at Prince. She hadn't noticed anything out of the ordinary.

Prince stared off into the crowd, a frown on his face.

He continued to watch while the line slowly moved them to the well. When they eventually had their turn they worked quickly. Finding Bo and Cain after a short search, they moved to a quiet spot near a wall to divide up the supplies the men had been able to purchase with the sale of a few daggers.

13

Considering there were five of them, it wasn't much, but it would hopefully get them to the next city where they might find better luck.

They wove their way through the crowded market, carefully keeping track of each other. The mid-afternoon sun beat down and the strange tension within the city had, if anything, gotten worse.

Eventually leaving the market behind, they headed for the south gate, drawing tighter together. The crowds had barely thinned, which was unusual to say the least.

Aro moved closer to Kei, continually glancing over at him while they walked. He didn't notice, his gaze flickering from one thing to another, on constant watch.

The noise of the crowd echoed off of the buildings behind the stalls, making it difficult to decipher anything specific. At least for her.

"Kei, what's going on? Can you hear?"

His gaze darted over to her for a moment before he stopped walking. The others noticed and they moved off to the side, out of the way.

She could tell Kei wished she wasn't there. He wanted to talk to the others, at least at first, before saying anything to her. She scowled at him and managed to keep herself from swatting him. He rarely treated her like a child. Him doing so now both irritated and worried her.

"Tell me," she demanded angrily.

After a moment of silence, and many exchanged looks between the men, Bo answered, "There is an army marching on the city."

She stared at them in shock. *Stupid, stupid men!* "Then why are we still here?" Her voice came out many octaves too high.

"It was just recently spotted. We should have time–"

# Broken Prince

"Rot!" She cut Bo off before he could finish, grabbing Kei roughly by the arm and pushing and pulling and dragging the lot of them to get them moving again.

Panic quickly began winding its way through her. She wouldn't be trapped in a city under siege again. If it happened, and the city fell...she didn't want to think of it, but couldn't help herself. Would they all be killed? Her breath caught in her throat. No, not killed, death would be a waste. They would be sold. Like the last time.

Last time...

She closed her eyes for a moment, fighting the skittering darkness which tried to overwhelm her.

"They're closing the gates!" The fearful panic in the voice of whoever yelled spread through the crowd.

People screamed. Some ran, some stood frozen in shock or terror.

She became one of the frozen, her mind refusing to believe. It had happened, they had become trapped here. An arm encircled her shoulders. She looked up, not surprised to see it belonged to Prince.

"We will be fine," he said softly.

She shook her head wordlessly and let him lead her off the street. They wound their way through streets and alleys until they came to a quiet deserted spot between two old decrepit buildings.

Stopping beside Prince, his arm still around her, she could only stare off blankly into nothing. The fear choked her. The spiraling panic continued to worsen. She couldn't breathe.

"We can leave our gear here," Bo said, removing his pack and tucking it into the shadows. "It would be best if we weren't noted to be obvious travelers and mistaken for spies."

Cain looked over at her. "We'll find a way out. Don't worry."

"Kei, check the main north gate and see if there are any other gates on that wall," Bo said.

Kei nodded. He'd been a scout before, he knew what to do.

"Cain, take the west wall, I'll take the east," Bo continued, scratching the old scar down his face absently as his mind quickly made plans.

She looked up suddenly. They were all leaving her? Shaking her head frantically, words lodged in her throat. She looked up at Prince. *Don't leave me!*

He acknowledged her mental scream with a slight squeeze. "I should stay with Aro."

Bo stared at her a moment before nodding to Prince. He turned to Cain, "We can do the south wall as well, meet us at the gate."

Cain nodded.

Without further discussion they set out. Kei turned to her, pulling her out of Prince's embrace to hold her in one of his own. She held him tightly, struggling to calm down. "Be careful."

He kissed the top of her head. "I will." He ran off, quickly disappearing into the shadows.

Staring after him, a shudder ripped through her. She wrapped her arms around herself, wishing Prince would hold her, comfort her. At the same time she knew better. It wouldn't help. He would say everything would be fine and she would try to believe him. In the end, whatever happened would happen.

She turned when Prince moved and watched him sit down and lean against one of the building walls. Frowning, she hesitated a moment before joining him. He looked so tired, so worn out. Concentrating on worrying about him instead of the fighting she knew would soon come helped calm her panic.

By the time the men returned, the sun had nearly set, staining the sky with pink and red. Kei followed Bo and Cain, making her wonder if he had gone to meet with them at the south gate.

"So what's the word?" She leaned forward, trying to read how things had gone from the expressions on their faces.

"Gates are all too well guarded," Cain answered.

"Even the smaller side gates," Bo added with a scowl. "Men are patrolling the walls. The streets as well. Civilians have been ordered to stay within their homes."

"Rot it," she muttered. It made sense, but didn't help them at all.

"From what we heard there is a small army setting up camp outside the south gate," Bo said. "Kei will see what he can find out tonight."

She looked over at Kei in alarm. "You're not..." She stopped when he shook his head.

"Darkness doesn't hinder my sight much," he reminded her. "I'll be able to see from the walls."

Letting out a deep breath, she nodded.

They ate, the men talking in whispers about the city's few defenses, the soldiers they had seen in the streets and lining the walls. Darkness fell and they grew quiet, resting in the shadows, waiting for the city to go to sleep.

She wrapped her arms around her legs and rested her forehead on her knees. Squeezing her eyes tightly against threatening tears, the sudden urge to hit something rose within her. Knowing she was being irrational didn't lessen her spiraling emotions. Falling apart in such a situation was the worst thing she could do, yet she couldn't seem to stop herself. No wonder they treated her like a child.

A hand settled on her shoulder. Knowing it to be Prince, she shrugged it off and leaned away so he'd understand she wanted to be alone.

Her thoughts circled uselessly in her head. She tried to calm herself, to regain control and be rid of the insane fear and panic haunting her. At some point she drifted off to sleep and dreamed of the Dragos, Damon. He smiled at her, taunting, asking over and over again, "Are you broken?"

When she started awake she saw Kei had already left. Clouds drifted in the night sky causing the faint light of the stars and moon to wink in and out. Leaning her head back against the stone wall, she rubbed at her eyes. Waiting, not knowing if he was safe, left her trembling inside.

Kei returned, his face grim. His appearance didn't help lessen her fears. The others gathered close around him as he sat on the ground beside her.

"There are at least two thousand," he said, getting straight to the point.

She grimaced. Even though the number didn't come close to the size of army which had taken Kingsport, it remained large enough under the circumstances.

"I saw about a hundred horses. Soldiers are geared up the same as the ones here." He raised a hand when Bo and Cain both began to ask questions. "They have a battering ram, were setting up a cover for it by firelight."

The others quickly began questioning him and she stared off into the darkness, listening absently to his responses. The ram changed everything. She hadn't seen the south gates. However, the northern one had been wood. It wouldn't hold long. The men quickly came to the same conclusion. The city would not face a long siege.

She listened to them make vague plans based on assumptions and possibilities. Having nothing to add, she remained quiet until they ran out of ideas and decided to get what sleep they could. Prince and Kei curled up to either side of her and she closed her eyes obediently, wondering if sleep would come, wondering if she even wanted it to.

Prince slipped his arm over her waist. *We are worried about you.*

*I know.*

*We will escape the city. You do not need to worry.*

She sighed and nodded but didn't reply. She didn't really believe him, but didn't want to argue. She didn't want to hear him lie.

Jen Wylie

# Chapter 2:
## How to Escape an Army

Morning brought more clouds and sticky heat. Eating quietly, everyone tried not to look as tired and cranky as they felt. They went through their packs, discarding the few items they didn't need, mostly extra articles of clothing and a few odds and ends. Soon they would need to fight and run, and the lighter their packs, the better.

She clutched Avery's sweater to her chest, not wanting to part with it, irrationally thinking she would forget him.

"Aro."

She looked over at Kei. Sadness clouded his face. He raised a dagger and lightly tapped the tip to his forehead. Avery's dagger. She still had hers, too. Smiling a little, she nodded, hugged the sweater one last time, and placed it onto the pile of items to be left behind.

They each attached water skins firmly to their belts. Packs were put on, tested for balance, sometimes contents adjusted. The skins and packs would be a hindrance in fighting, but they couldn't leave them behind.

"Remember, our first priority is to get out of the city," Bo said, helping Cain adjust a strap.

"And evade the enemy army," Aro added with a grimace.

"Yes, so head directly for the fields." Bo looked at her specifically. "Understood? Don't turn back for anything."

"I know. We've been over this."

"If you are followed then..." Prince looked at her expectantly.

She wished they'd stop treating her like an idiot. Her ears worked, she had been listening. "Run for the woods. If separated, meet there along the boundary."

She didn't like the plan. It was too haphazard, too ripe for disaster. The odds of something going wrong were so high it made her nauseous. Tactics had been one of the subjects in her tutoring. Her brain didn't want to work though. Fear and thoughts of battle drowned everything else out. She simply nodded and listened carefully. The boys were seasoned soldiers after all. She trusted they knew what they were doing.

Kei left to scout ahead and returned quickly, silently guiding them through streets quiet with fear and anticipation for the battles to come. Occasional shouts echoed from the walls to the south, causing them to pause and listen.

Trying to remain calm, she followed slowly, worrying her lower lip. Eventually Kei led them to a narrow alley. They followed him in and then through a broken boarded up door of an abandoned building. Treading carefully on the rotting floorboards, she squinted in the faint light peeking through the boarded up windows. The rooms were empty and the walls in the process of being torn down.

Kei turned and motioned for them to be silent before proceeding up a narrow flight of stairs. The room they entered had little light as well, just enough to make out the gaping holes in the floorboards. Prince drew her aside against a wall and pointed for her to stay there.

The men took turns peeking out the cracks in the boarded up windows. Kei gestured her over. Carefully, she made her way to his side and bent to peek through a crack.

Their building stood close to the outer wall, only one street over from the main street leading to the gate. The window however, gave a view of the main street between the buildings. She could see part of the wall, men patrolling it. Other men were gathered in a rough formation in front of the gate. Waiting.

Something would happen soon. Hopefully they were now close enough to take advantage of it. They continued to watch, and to wait.

Shouts from the walls indicated the attackers were approaching. She smiled a little when she heard the soft whoosh of hundreds of arrows being released, followed by the faint screams of the dying from beyond the walls. The morning dragged on with much of the same; shouting, taunts from both sides, and volley after volley of arrows shot into the enemy ranks. They settled back to wait, listening carefully to orders shouted as the day passed into night.

The next day she heard the first strange noise shortly after noon. Before her mind could make the connection, Bo supplied the answer, "They have the ram at the gates."

Grimacing, she shifted position slightly, getting the cramps out of her legs. She couldn't believe how quickly things had progressed. "How long?"

"Not very," Bo answered. "The gates aren't strong. A dozen or so good rams should take it down." He looked over at her. "You ready?"

"Wither me," she muttered. No she wasn't. She nodded anyway and faked an encouraging smile. It wouldn't help to have them all worrying about her.

Cain stood, watching her for a moment, his forehead crinkled in worry. "Let's move."

They quickly left the building, not bothering to be quiet or to hide while running through the streets. They were on the east side of the city and so met no soldiers along their path to the smaller eastern gate. Nearing it however, they began to meet a growing number of civilians until their path became blocked altogether.

Cain cursed, running a hand through his short hair in frustration.

She took the opportunity to catch her breath and actually look at what had caused the sudden masses to block their path of escape.

Hundreds of people, from the elderly to young mothers with babies, crowded the streets around the closed eastern gate. Soldiers guarded it, others stood upon the walls above. Civilian men fought against all of them. She wasn't certain if the people were aware the southern gates were about to be breached, or merely looked for any chance to escape a city under siege. Either way, it would work in their favor.

Both Cain and Bo continued to curse.

She smiled and smacked Bo's arm. "This is good," she told him when she got his attention. "Let them get the gates open. We'll go with the flow and escape unnoticed."

He grimaced at her, but did stop cursing.

She watched the soldiers resist until it became apparent they were fighting a losing battle that would only end with the loss of their lives. The crowd had quickly grown more restless, more frantic. When the soldiers finally stepped aside, a loud cheer rose up. Men lifted the bars and pushed open the wooden gates, nearly being trampled when the crowd surged forward.

They moved with agonizing slowness as people poured into the main street from side ones. Nearing the gate, she noticed her men had formed a circle around her. Kei walked before her, Cain and Bo to either side, Prince behind with a hand resting against her back.

She rolled her eyes. They continued to protect her. With all the people, she wondered if their plans had changed.

*No. Run for the fields. We will be with you.*

She glanced back at Prince and smiled slightly as they moved slowly forward.

Screams ripped through the air, shattering her tenuous calm. The crowd surged forward then stopped abruptly. She clenched her fists, standing on her toes trying to see, wondering what happened.

"Some are trying to come back in," Prince said from behind her.

She looked back, wondering how he knew, before she realized his height did indeed have some advantages.

His face became grim, his perpetual frown back and dark brows drawn together over his eyes until the crowd moved forward again.

She lowered her head and moved with it, trying not to think about what could have happened to those who blocked the way.

Finally they passed through and she stumbled as the press of people suddenly disappeared. Some ran north, others darted ahead. Others continued to scream.

Someone swore. Excessively.

She turned to Cain and then followed his troubled gaze to the south. Dozens of horsemen bore down on the crowd, not far behind came more men on foot.

"Wither me," she gasped out.

Survival instructs overcame panic. Immediately she took in her surroundings. A long stretch of flat ground before her eventually dropped down into a gentle hill. The fields didn't begin until the ground leveled out once more. The distance between her and the fields actually wasn't too great, unless hundreds of people blocked the way and enemy soldiers pressed to attack.

Everyone drew weapons and moved quickly toward the fields, pushing people out of their way while keeping an eye on the approaching horsemen. It quickly became evident they wouldn't reach the hill before the enemy arrived.

The horses didn't slow, but plowed through the crowd, the riders slashing left and right with their swords, cutting down everyone in their path. Each rider also had bows or

Jen Wylie

spears in cases at their sides. She didn't even want to think of the damage they would cause.

Too slowly, the hill drew nearer. So did the men on foot. The horsemen were nearly upon them. Looking around at her men, she saw them already spreading out around her. Kei's eyes began glowing faintly, already up to orange. No one appeared to notice.

Swords clanged and the screaming took on a different tone as both civilians and the city's soldiers fought the horsemen.

Cursing under her breath, she braced herself for the fight to come, twirling her daggers in her hands. Time rushed forward and the enemy surrounded them. Instinct and training overtook everything else. She fought, spinning and ducking, striking where she could.

A man rushed her, sword swinging wildly in a strike that would remove her head if she didn't move. Bending to the side, she sprang forward to meet him, barely missing the sword. Too close for him to stop her she thrust upward at his chest. Flinging himself back he barely evaded her blow. He failed to see the old man slide an equally old sword up into his back from behind.

Aro nodded to the old-timer before looking around quickly. She'd become separated from her men. She had expected it. However, her gut twisted not knowing where they all were and if they were safe. The horsemen passed, moving on to attack those escaping north. Footmen took their place. Some on horse turned back for another round.

When she finally found a moments respite, she turned, searching for everyone. Kei remained close to her side, eyes red and claws fully extended, covered in blood. Cain fought one man a short distance to her left. She found Prince surrounded by four men, pushed back nearly to the gates. For some reason, she nearly smiled seeing he still wore the stupid

26

floppy hat. Then she noted he wasn't faring well and fear streaked through her.

"Help him! Please," she begged Kei.

He regarded her a moment before nodding once, sharply, and bounding off.

"They'll be fine. Go! Go!" Cain gestured wildly with his free hand, his opponent dead on the ground behind him.

She spun around, searching for Bo. She couldn't see him anywhere. Her heart sank. Cain screamed at her again and with a growl of frustration she sprinted down the hill, dodging those in her path, until she finally entered the corn.

Barely slowing, she looked quickly behind her and saw Cain followed her, slowing only to sheath his sword and glance behind him.

"Run! They're following," he cried, putting on a burst of speed.

She ran, frantically pushing corn out of her way, trying to ignore the sting of the stalks and leaves smacking her face, bare hands, and arms. Glancing back again she saw a rider appear behind them. Cain had closed the distance between them and would soon pass her if she didn't speed up.

She did, panic rising with the thought of the horseman catching them. If he did, he meant to kill them. At least she didn't have to worry about becoming a slave again.

The frantic beating of her heart drowned out the sound of the horse behind her. The absence of sound scared her even more. She didn't know how close the man chasing them was.

Running until her lungs burned and her legs ached she found herself beginning to slow. Gasping for breath, she gritted her teeth against a stitch in her side. *Certainly the horseman had given up by now?*

Cain made a strange sound and cursed behind her. She looked back to see him stumbling, hands grasping at an arrow through his chest.

"Cain!" She skidded to a frantic stop and ran back to him, stumbling in her haste.

Reaching his side, her fingers fluttered hopelessly around the arrow as she searched his face. Avoiding her eyes, he grasped her arm and dragged her through the corn until he dropped to his knees, unable to go any further.

Gasping out curses, she pressed clenched fists to either side of her head, trying to keep calm and to figure out what to do. She'd never dealt with such a serious wound before. Her brothers had never come home from practice or fights with arrows sticking out of them.

"Pull. It. Out," Cain grated through clenched teeth.

"But it will bleed–"

"Out! Now!"

Not hesitating again, she quickly moved around behind him. Taking the shaft in both hands she sucked in a deep, shaking breath and snapped off the fletched end. His body jerked and a hiss of pain escaped his lips. Scrambling to hurry, she knelt in front of him again and grasped the point which had gone all the way through his chest. Bracing one hand on his shoulder, she clenched her teeth and pulled.

He bent over and brought his hands to the gaping wound, coughing blood.

So much blood.

Dropping the arrow, she lurched forward to grab his shoulders. "Cain!"

He straightened suddenly, sucking in a deep, gurgling breath. Coughing, he spit blood to the side.

Blood. Blood everywhere. Everything was turning red.

Shrugging off his pack he tossed it to her. "Run."

Tears welled in her eyes and fell. Shaking her head, she clasped his pack tight to her chest with bloody hands as if it would protect her. It hadn't protected him. The arrow had pierced him just above where it had hung low on his back. If Cain had been a little faster, or the man not on a horse...

28

He forced himself to his feet, drawing his sword. "I'm done." He coughed more blood and looked over at her shocked face. His voice softened, "You know that."

Yes, she knew. He was dead already. Blood soaked his shirt. It dripped from his mouth and down his chin. His lungs were filling with it. If he didn't drown in his own blood he would bleed out. There was nothing she could do to save him.

"No." She didn't want to believe it. Didn't want to lose anyone else. "Rot it all, no!"

"I'll buy you time."

"Cain...John..." Dropping the pack, she stood and moved quickly to his side. Heedless of the blood, she pulled him into her arms, holding him too tightly with trembling limbs. He sagged against her, resting his head for a moment against hers.

"We don't...have...time," he whispered.

She pulled away and leaned in to kiss his cheek. "John," she sobbed, her lips trembling so much so she couldn't speak.

"I'm sorry, Aro." He kissed her forehead, and then bloody knuckles gently caressed her cheek in goodbye. "Go."

"Make them hurt," she whispered.

He nodded and she turned away before tears threatened to destroy her. The horse drew closer, crashing through the corn. Snatching up his pack, she turned and ran, not looking back. She refused to let his sacrifice be in vain by winding up dead from crying.

Later there would be time. She'd cry a million tears until she dried up and blew away. If she survived.

Jen Wylie

# Chapter 3:
# Friend in the Fields

She ran unthinkingly through field after field of corn, each separated by a narrow cart path she quickly darted across. Eventually the corn ran out and she froze at the edge of a field, staring out in despair at the expanse of something else. She wasn't certain what type of crop it was, perhaps potatoes. The problem was the lack of cover. The plants didn't even grow up to her knees.

Clutching Cain's pack to her chest she sank to the ground sobbing and rocking, finally letting the tears fall again. Cain had died. Why did everyone have to die? Why did she lose them all?

Pain lanced through her chest. It was a familiar, dark pain. She'd been torn apart when she'd found herself alone in chains on a slave ship, her brothers gone and likely dead. It had opened further when Kendric, the only person she'd known, had not made it to shore when the slave ship crashed into rocks and sank. Avery's death had opened it again. The long summer months of monotonous travel had allowed it to close somewhat, turning it into a numb, raw wound.

Cain's death ripped her heart out again. Blood covered her chest and hands as if the wound in her soul was real. But it wasn't, it was Cain's blood covering her. So much blood.

Frantically grabbing the water-skin, she fumbled to get it open, spilling the precious liquid and wasting more in an attempt to get the blood off her hands. The worst came off, but too much remained. Choking off a whimper she wrapped her arms about her waist and rocked hysterically.

Chest wracking sobs overcame her. There had been no time for goodbyes. She hadn't told him how much he meant to her, how he'd become family. She hadn't told him so many things.

She cried until no more tears fell and her breath came in little shuddering hiccups. Rubbing at her face and eyes she forced herself to take deep breaths.

She couldn't stay here. She needed to ignore the pain and darkness and reach the forest. If anyone else survived they would be waiting for her there. She went through John's pack quickly, stuffing the food he had carried into her own pack before tossing his aside. Numbness replaced her hysteria. She didn't mind, it was safer, quieter.

Standing on the edge of the cornfield, she adjusted her pack, touched the dagger on each hip to make sure they were still there, and checked the one in her boot. She looked behind her, but all she could see was corn. In front of her the fields of whatever went on and on until corn had again been planted. She was beginning to love corn. She could just barely see the forest ahead, the mountains looming tall and breathtaking beyond.

She didn't want to run across the field before her. A rider spotting her would mean her death. She could run fast, but not faster than a horse. She tried not to think about the spears and bows the riders carried. She tried not to think about Cain.

The low field went on for a good distance in either direction. She wasn't sure what grew beyond to either side. She debated running north or south to see if any cover would present itself. It could end up being a waste of time. She didn't know. Pacing the field's edge in frustration, she weighed her options.

# Broken Prince

"Rot it." She darted out into the field and ran, arms pumping and legs flying, dodging or leaping over plant rows. Her heart hammered loudly in her chest. She glanced quickly to either side of her, saw nothing but fields, and continued to run like her life depended on it, because it did.

When she finally reached the field of corn she skidded to a stop once safely hidden inside. Raising a hand to her chest she struggled to control her breathing, calm her heart. Her legs and chest burned painfully, but she'd made it. Moving slowly, she returned to the edge of field, peeking between stalks, her gaze searching.

The valley had begun to rise again. Now she could see the city in the distance. Smoke drifted toward her from it, they had either set it ablaze, or fires had accidentally been started in the panic of the fighting.

She could vaguely make out bodies scattered along the open stretch around the keep. Hopefully no more of her boys were amongst them. She turned her eyes to the corn and other fields. She could make out movement here and there, people hiding or running. She could also see horsemen spread out through the fields, tracking the people who tried to seek shelter and safety within.

A scream cut through the air. Turning toward it she could see a horseman in the distance off to her left. Relief she couldn't actually see what was happening rushed through her as the heart wrenching screams went on and on. Watching quietly for a while longer she finally grimaced. It appeared the enemy enjoyed hunting down those who had tried to escape.

Continuing through the corn, she struggled to move both quickly and quietly. She ignored the occasional screams of others dying until one suddenly sounded close to her right.

She froze mid-step. Carefully she turned, searching through the corn rows, wishing she could see above them. The sun had begun to set though it would still be light for a good while yet. Crouching down, she listened carefully.

*Yes, there, something moving through the corn.*

Nervously running her fingers through her hair, she shifted, trying to see through the corn in front of her, wondering how much farther remained until she reached the forest.

"Aren't you going to run?"

She spun around and looked up. A man on horseback laughed at her above the corn.

Springing to her feet she bolted, ignoring the laughter behind her. Not bothering to try to hide, she simply ran, even knowing she wouldn't be able to outrun him in the fields. He followed, yelling taunts at her back.

Too quickly she grew tired and her sprint slowed. She pushed on, fighting the pains in her muscles and chest, struggling to breathe. Sweat ran down her face and stung her eyes.

The sound of the horse and rider persisted behind her. She didn't dare to look. He played with her and she knew it. There was nothing she could do but run. Panic and fear gave way to frustration and anger.

She thought of Prince and tried to send her thoughts out to him, screaming them in her head, knowing he wouldn't hear, yet hoping somehow he would. *Where are you? Find me...Please! I can't get away...*

Bursting suddenly out of the corn she stumbled, found her footing, and then lost it again in the freshly turned earth. Pain shot up her leg when her ankle twisted and she cursed out loud. Stumbling to her feet, she paused. Tears of frustration came to her eyes at the sight of the wide empty field before her. Something had recently been harvested, the earth loose and uneven. It would be impossible to run across.

Beyond it was a narrow stretch of weeds and low brush and then...the forest. A stone marker rose not far to her left at its edge. She only had to get into the trees. She would certainly be able to lose the horseman within it, if he even followed.

"You're a pretty little thing aren't you?"

She started off quickly and nearly fell again. Clenching her teeth against the pain in her ankle, she set her eyes upon the trees ahead and pushed herself forward at a limping slow jog.

"I think there's time to play. Would you like to play, love?"

She didn't look at him, merely pressed her lips together and kept moving. His horse walked beside her now; out of the corner of her eye she could see his leg. Her daggers would be nearly useless against a mounted man, especially with her current injury. Still, she moved a hand to clench one at her side. He wanted to play with her first, to do so he would have to get off the blighting horse.

Her heart continued to hammer in her chest, though at least her breathing began to calm. Every step caused pain to shoot through her twisted ankle. She wasn't going to make it. Soon he would tire of taunting her and get off the horse, they would fight, and then...

*Prince! Kei! Where are you?*

No one answered her silent screams. It didn't surprise her. She knew they couldn't even hear her, yet it still hurt. She wasn't used to being alone. She didn't want to die alone. She didn't–

*Get down!*

She dropped to the ground, too surprised at the strange voice in her mind and the urgency of its tone to argue.

Something large and dark passed over her as she pressed herself into the dirt. Ducking her head instinctively, she heard the rider scream and the horse let out a strange piercing whistle. She rolled away when it suddenly went berserk with legs flying everywhere as it tried to bolt and the rider fought for control. The last thing she needed was to get trampled.

Rolling further away she drew daggers as she rose to her feet, ready to help or make her escape. The horse bolted toward the forest. The rider...

She gasped. The rider was being smacked around like a toy by a giant wolf.

Not a wolf, a Were. She'd heard him, like the last time she'd met one in the forest to the north. Had he come to help her? Why? Certainly he wasn't the same wolf, the voice had sounded different. Why were they talking to her?

She straightened slowly, debated sheathing her daggers, and decided better safe than sorry. "I think he's dead."

The wolf stopped playing, sniffed the body and turned toward her.

A quiet, strangled sound escaped her lips. He was huge. On all fours his head came to her chest. She struggled to stand her ground and not run away screaming. Clenching her daggers tightly she forced a small smile. "You helped me."

*I heard you.* He replied in her mind.

Her eyebrows went up. He'd heard... "Oh. Well, thank you."

He walked toward her, ears perked forward. *I will not hurt you. You can put those away.*

Aro looked down at her hands. Her fingers clutched the daggers so tightly her knuckles turned white. Cheeks flushing, she sheathed them quickly. "Sorry. Today hasn't been the best day."

The wolf looked toward the burning city. *No. It seems not.* His gaze returned to her. *I am Garen.*

She smiled again, relaxing slightly. "Aro. Thanks again." She looked around. They stood nearly in the middle of the field. Out in the open. She started limping toward the forest again. Looking over her shoulder at the Were, she forced a small smile. "Coming?"

Ears flicked again before he trotted up to walk beside her.

"I've never really met a Were before. Sorry if I don't do something right. Please let me know if I do." Hopefully that covered any mistakes she might make. The last thing she needed was a Were as an enemy.

His mental chuckle surprised her, but she didn't say anything else. They moved slowly across the rest of the field and through the short stretch of weeds. Entering the shadows of the trees, tension immediately drained out of her.

Stopping to lean against a tree, she raised a hand to her forehead. It shook. She lowered it again.

"I suppose you have to get back to your..." She paused, searching for the word, "to your pack."

*No.*

His simple answer caught her off guard. "Oh. Well, feel free to stay if you like." With a grimace she rubbed her sore ankle against the side of her leg.

*There is a spring not far. You could soak it there.*

"How far?" The sun had nearly gone down. She didn't want to get lost in the forest; not at night, not alone. Besides, she still had to find the others.

*It is close by.*

Though her ankle throbbed painfully, and the thought of soaking it in cold water would be wonderful, she still hesitated. "I need to find my friends," she finally admitted. "We became separated. If that happened we were supposed to meet along the boundary."

*Very well.*

She waited a moment, wondering if he was going to say anything else. When he merely sat and stared at her she turned and headed slowly back to the tree line. Concealing herself behind a tree she peered out, eyes searching the fields and the empty strips of land to either side of her. She saw at least two dozen riders, most scouring the fields. Four of them rode up and down the boundary line. There was no sight of any of her friends.

"Where are you?" She moved back into the shadow of the trees. Closing her eyes, she tried to calm the panic and fear swirling within her. Sucking in a very slow breathe, she clenched her fists so tightly it hurt. She hadn't lost everyone again. They were alive. They had to be. They likely hid from the horsemen, probably waiting until dark to move. She let out a deep breath. Yes, certainly they would find her later.

She turned to look at Garen. "Where is this spring?"

He regarded her for a moment before turning and heading further into the trees. *This way.*

She followed, relieved to see he moved slowly, always staying within sight. They did not walk far before he stopped beside a thicket. *In here.*

Moving carefully to avoid a few thorny bushes, she found a small depression filled with water. The plants had been trampled around it; apparently the wildlife used it often. Sitting at the edge she removed her boot and sock, wincing at the swelling already visible.

Sticking her foot in the water she gasped at the sudden cold. Immediately the throbbing dulled. Closing her eyes she tried to empty her mind. She had to calm down and think more clearly. She needed to figure out what to do now.

All she could see was Cain with an arrow through his chest. With a gasp her eyes snapped open again.

*Are you well?*

She nodded and blinked back tears. "One of my friends died," she told him quietly.

*Are you hurt? I smell so much blood on you, is any yours?*

She looked down at herself. Blood spattered her clothes and stained her arms and hands. Some of it belonged to Cain. Clenching her teeth, she fought the choking despair building in her chest. She had to stop thinking about it. Now was not the time to break.

Looking up she saw the wolf staring at her, head cocked slightly to the side.

"No. None of it is mine." She didn't want to talk any more.

Her foot had begun to tingle from the cold water and she pulled it out. She crawled forward to the head of the pool where the water flowed quickly and refilled her water skin. More tears threatened as she washed her face and watered down blood dripped from her hands. She'd washed away Cain's bloody kiss.

Fighting rising hysteria she pushed herself forward and dunked her whole head in the freezing water a few times. It shocked her enough the numbness returned. Numb she could deal with.

Garen circled before lying down and resting his head on his paws to watch her. *You are a strange girl.*

She raised her eyebrows and dug out some food and forced herself to eat a little.

"Have you met many humans?"

*Some. Are you human?*

Choking on a bite of food she stared at him incredulously. "Of course I am!"

*You smell strange. For a human.*

Just what she wanted to hear. She scowled at him. "I assure you, I am." She wondered suddenly what he looked like in human form. Had he not changed because it wasn't safe? Or perhaps he didn't want to be naked in front of her. Or did they change with clothes? She had no idea. "I'm sorry we don't have any extra clothes. If you wanted to change I mean." She grimaced at her floundering.

*It doesn't matter.* He stood suddenly and circled the pool. *We should go. Animals will want to drink and they will not come with me here.*

"I'm almost done." Drawing her daggers she cleaned them quickly, but well. After drying them on a mostly clean edge of her shirt, she sheathed them again.

Biting her lip, her swollen ankle captured her attention. It should be wrapped but she had nothing to wrap it with. Prince had all the bandages in his pack. She packed up her sock and forced her foot back into her boot. It hurt, but she didn't have any other options.

She rose and donned her pack. Limping along carefully, she followed Garen out of the thicket and through the trees. He moved very slowly. Darkness had fallen. The branches overhead hid the stars and moon, severely limiting her sight. She cursed under her breath at the pain in her ankle. She could hardly put any weight on it. Perhaps if she could find a large stick to use as a crutch, it wouldn't be so bad.

Garen stopped suddenly. *Rest here. You will be safe. There is nothing dangerous in the area.*

She bit her lip in dismay. "You're going?"

*You cannot walk. I will search for the horse.* He walked up and pressed his nose to her hand. *I will return soon.*

She smiled in relief and resisted the urge to pet him. "Be careful."

His laughter filled her mind. *I am a Were. Very little will harm me.* He turned, his laugh still echoing in her mind while he disappeared into the night.

Positioning herself with her back to a large tree and facing the fields she tried to make herself comfortable. It didn't feel safe enough to sleep, even though she felt dreadfully tired. The fear of someone or something finding her asleep kept her awake and skittish. So did the fear of the nightmares which would certainly come if she closed her eyes.

Staring off into the darkness she concentrated on identifying what created each little sound; the wind, bugs, an owl.

Something suddenly brushed her shoulder and she screamed, fingers scrambling for a dagger.

A hand covered her mouth as she turned her head…and saw a pair of orange glowing eyes. The scream died abruptly and she swatted the hand away. "Rot! You scared the life out of me!"

Kei chuckled.

Pulling him close, she buried her face in his neck and hugged him tightly. "I was worried about you."

His arms tightened around her. "Me, too. About you." He leaned back slightly. "Where's Cain?"

She drew back and looked away. Words caught in her throat. She didn't want to tell him, didn't want to say the words. "He didn't…" She shook her head and drew in a deep breath. Her hands started shaking again. Tears filled her eyes and slid down her cheeks. Very quietly she told him what had happened.

His eyes changed to red while she spoke. He pulled her close again, holding her head to his chest and tucking it under his chin.

"Cain," he whispered, his voice choked. They sat in silence, just holding each other and sharing their misery and grief.

She could have stayed there all night. Kei understood.

His arms tightened briefly and then he leaned back to look at her face. "Are you angry? At me. For leaving."

She forced a small smile and ruffled his hair. "Stupid Fey. No, I'm not. I asked you to go help Prince," she faltered and looked away. "Is he..." She couldn't say the words.

"We made it to the fields."

"What happened?"

"We split up." He added, "To look for you."

She nodded. "So he's not hurt?" When Kei didn't answer panic seized her chest. "Kei?"

"He got cut. I tended him." He grimaced. "Fighting did him no good. He was exhausted."

She bit at one of her fingernails for a moment before suddenly standing. "Let's go find him."

Kei rose and reached out to steady her when she swayed. "You're hurt!"

"I twisted my ankle. I'll be fine."

He opened his mouth to say something and suddenly froze, eyes darting about, searching the darkness.

She turned but he pushed her back. Swearing under her breath, she wondered what he had seen or smelled. Another curse left her lips; she'd forgotten to tell him about Garen.

Thinking of the Were brought him forth, a blur of darkness and fur which leapt from the night's shadows directly at them. He landed on Kei, knocking him backward onto the ground.

Growls and snarls from both echoed around her.

"Stop it! Both of you! Stop!" Heedless of accidental injury, she threw herself at them, grabbing a handful of Garen's fur and trying to pull him off of Kei. "Stop it! He's my friend!"

Garen ceased his growling and attack so she pulled harder on him. *He's one of my friends!*

The Were growled once more before springing away. *You failed to mention one was a Fey.*

She dropped down beside Kei. "Are you hurt?" He had fallen into a full fury, eyes blazing, teeth and claws extended. "Kei! He's my friend. Calm down." She took his face in her hands and started pulling the power of his fury into her.

He surprised her by pulling her hands away and sitting up. "I can do it," he whispered.

She nodded but smiled a little when he wrapped his arms around her and rested his forehead against hers. His deadly claws rested gently across her back. She wasn't afraid. Kei was someone she'd never fear again.

Quickly he began to calm himself. She felt the wild power within him recede.

Garen whined, startling her.

*Please move away, Aro.*

Kei leaned back and scowled at her. His eyes had gone down to a light orange, his teeth had returned to normal and she could feel the claws against her back retracting. "You didn't mention him."

She sighed and sifted position to rub her ankle. Kei arms fell to his sides. Garen paced around them.

"I'm sorry, boys. Kei this is Garen, he helped me earlier today. Garen, this is my friend Kei." She glanced back at her Fey. "As you can see, he's not wild."

*Your scent is a mix of fey and human,* the Were muttered in her mind. *No wonder you smelled strange.*

She laughed and Kei looked at her strangely. *Can you speak to Kei?*

Garen stopped pacing to look at her. *Not easily. It is difficult for Were to speak to others not of our kind. Without the power of a pack it is nearly impossible.*

She opened her mouth and then closed it again. Had he just implied he didn't have a pack?

"Aro..." Kei began.

She shushed him, mind racing, trying to decide if she should ask or not. Why not? "Do you not have a pack, Garen?"

He looked away, ears flattening. *No.*

She bit her lip and looked back at Kei. "He said no."

"And this is important?"

She felt it was. She had one more question to ask, "Are you in trouble with them?"

*No,* he said again. *They leave me alone. I am...solitary.*

Their meeting had been chance, however she felt like something important was about to happen. She liked Garen, he had saved her, helped her. "Do you want to stay with us," she asked impulsively. "We can be your pack?"

"Aro," Kei hissed.

She turned and grimaced at him. "Garen helped me. He saved my life." She looked back to the Were.

"He can't replace Cain," Kei whispered harshly.

She snapped her head around to glare at him. "I know that!" She stared him down until he only pursed his lips and looked away, shaking his head.

*Aro?*

She turned back to Garen.

He was staring at her, ears twitching back and forth. *Do you mean this?*

*Of course. Obviously we aren't a normal bunch, but we stick together. We're family.*

*Family.* His voice echoed in her head, amazed, surprised, afraid.

She had no idea what he was thinking, how he felt. She couldn't understand what his posture or actions meant.

Uncertainty overcame her. Perhaps she'd been too impulsive. She did have a problem with that sometimes. However, for some reason a feeling of rightness filled her. She didn't understand, but it was better than the overwhelming darkness threatening to claim her again.

She reached out and took Kei's hand, giving it a tight squeeze.

After a moment he sighed and squeezed back. "We need to go." Kei stood and helped her up.

Garen still hadn't answered her. Perhaps his silence was answer enough. However he hadn't left either.

"We're going to look for our other friends," she told him. "Both are men; one human, one an Elf."

*Elf?* His incredulous laughter filled her head. *You are a strange pack indeed.* He paused. *I think I will join you. It will be...interesting.*

She related this to Kei who sighed and shook his head again. He seemed resigned to the situation. At least he wasn't fighting with her.

Reaching for her pack, Garen's voice stopped her again.

*Wait. I found the horse. I will bring it now.* He darted off into the darkness.

"What is he doing now?" Kei growled in exasperation.

"He got me a horse," she said with a grin. She laughed out loud at the look on Kei's face.

Garen returned, the horse's reins in his mouth. Strangely, the steed did not seem afraid of the giant wolf leading it. She loaded her pack and Kei's behind the saddle and Kei helped her up.

"Thank you," she said to both of them. "Let's go find our friends."

Jen Wylie

# Chapter 4:
# The Pack

They walked for a while in the darkness, Kei and Garen moving silently so only the sound of the horse could be heard. To be cautious, they kept just within the trees. They weren't sure if riders still roamed beyond.

She couldn't see a thing and began to wonder what good continuing to look would do. Her ankle continued to burn and throb and exhaustion kept pulling her eyes closed.

A hand on her leg startled her. She hadn't realized she'd drifted off.

"Garen seems to want to stop," Kei whispered.

With a tired nod she guided the horse further into the trees, following Kei until he stopped. He helped her down and she hobbled a few steps before collapsing to the ground with a weary sigh.

*There doesn't appear to be anyone near.*

She looked over at Garen sitting not far from her. Kei tended to the horse. "We should stop looking I guess. Get some sleep."

"We'll find them in the morning," Kei said.

She nodded vaguely, staring off into the darkness. She hoped Kei was right. He finished with the horse and came to sit beside her.

"We will find them," he said quietly.

Tears welled in her eyes and her lips began to tremble.

He took her hand and they both shifted to lie down. She closed her eyes, knowing he watched her. Knowing he worried.

*Is he your mate?*

She choked and raised her head, looking over at the Were. *What?*

*He doesn't harm you when he's in a fury. He protects you and sleeps by your side.* When she didn't answer he asked again, *The Fey, is he your mate?*

*No. He is my friend.* She lay back down with a grimace. Kei raised his eyebrows questioningly. "Garen asked if you were my mate."

Kei snorted and chuckled. He squeezed her hand. "She is my family."

*Strange girl.*

Her lips twisted in amusement before she closed her eyes and with a deep sigh, slipped into sleep.

She felt absolutely horrid. Nightmares had haunted her sleep. The swelling in her ankle had gone down somewhat, but it still hurt. They ate quickly, discussing which way they should travel to look for Bo and Prince.

*Perhaps we should split up?*

Biting her lip, she turned to Kei and repeated.

Kei grimaced. "I would agree, however you don't know Bo. There were a lot of humans running around out there yesterday."

She rubbed at her forehead. Prince wouldn't be a problem. His elven heritage would make him easy to identify. Garen felt certain he would be able to talk to him even from a distance. Probably.

She sighed. *I don't suppose you can look in my mind and see him?*

# Broken Prince

*I...could. You would allow this?*

From the tone of his mind voice she could tell her offer shocked him. She grinned, if it worked, problem solved. She turned to Kei, "I'm going to picture Bo in my head and Garen is going to try to see it."

Kei frowned. "More people in your head?"

"It will be fine."

She grinned at Garen's obvious surprise at their exchange. "Do you need to touch me?"

*No. Just think of him.*

Closing her eyes she pictured her fortress and herself standing outside of its towering walls. They needed to meet outside of them. She didn't even let Prince inside her inner walls.

Opening her eyes she found herself within her own mind again. It didn't frighten her. She had done this many times with Prince while he taught her how to strengthen her mental barriers. Her fortress rose tall and mighty behind her. For a short distance all around lay barren, dark earth. The sky rolled with darkness and abstract thoughts. It wasn't pretty. However, it was her.

Turning, she glared into the darkness made of anger, fear, panic, and everything else dark and broken within her. She wished it would go away, turn into sunlight. She doubted it would happen, not for a long time at least.

*This is your mind?*

She turned again at the sound of Garen's voice, grinning because he sounded so surprised. She froze when she saw him.

He wasn't a wolf.

He looked human, thankfully clothed in simple pants and shirt, though his feet were bare. A very sweet, innocent and handsome human. She blinked a few times trying to smother her thoughts when she realized where they were.

Too late. A flush crept across his cheeks and a cute half grin appeared. He looked down at himself, holding out an arm, turning it over. He looked back at her. *Am I acceptable?*

She rolled her eyes. Stupid men. *Don't be getting any ideas.*

His grin cracked into a full smile. He looked beyond her and it faded. *How did you do this? Why did you?*

*I travel with an Elf,* she answered flatly. *And I've had some problems with a Dragos.*

His eyebrows went up in surprise.

Before he could ask for the story she brought them back on topic. *You wanted to see Bo?*

She pulled forth the memories, spreading her arms to release the images to float around them. At least he paid attention and looked, finally nodding when he had seen enough.

He bowed slightly in her direction. *Thank you.* He gestured around them. *For sharing with me.*

She shrugged. *I don't mind if you want to come again. Prince is here a lot.*

Surprise spread across his face again before he turned thoughtful. *I suppose the Elves are different. Were rarely go into other's minds. We usually don't have need to, since we can mind-speak so freely.*

She smiled a little. *Well, you can discuss it with Prince, once we find him.*

He took the hint and left her mind. She followed.

They made plans to meet. Garen would go alone, she would stay with Kei. They still had a problem with Garen not being able to communicate with Bo while in wolf form. So she peeled some bark and scratched "Aro sent me. Follow" onto it. Garen would be able to carry it easily and hopefully Bo would read it and not attack the wolf.

They set out before the sun rose over the mountains, though its light filtered through the shadows so at least she could see enough not to ride into a tree. She and Kei headed north. Kei quickly bounded across the section of plowed field to search the fields beyond while she kept to the tree line, keeping watch within the forest and also the cleared sections.

The rider slowly moving out from a corn field caught her attention first. She quickly pulled on her horse's reins until it stopped and they both froze under the shadows of the trees. She turned, eyes searching frantically for Kei.

What was she supposed to do? Biting her lip, she looked back at the horseman, trying to figure out what he was doing. He had a spear out, pointed down, and moved very slowly.

She noticed the man on the ground then, crawling, pulling himself valiantly forward despite the armed, mounted man at his back. Leaning forward she squinted, trying to see better.

*Prince.* Her breath caught in her throat and she quickly searched for Kei again. Seeing him suddenly peek from within the crops across from her she waved her hand and pointed. He nodded.

Cursing under her breath she looked away, trying to decide what to do. Kei apparently knew about Prince. However, what exactly they were going to do about it she had no idea.

Watching Prince crawl through the dirt brought tears of anger and frustration to her eyes. She couldn't watch, couldn't let him go through this. He was a prince, her prince. The soldier would not kill him, not in front of her, not if she could save him.

Kicking her heels into the sides of the horse, she pulled the reins to the side, steering it out of the trees and directly at the horseman. The horse thundered forward and she struggled to keep her seat. Growing up in a city, she'd had very few experiences riding. Her brothers had made sure she'd learned the basics, but she'd never ridden full out before.

Her only thoughts centered on saving Prince. There was no time for tactics or planning. Other than that, she had no idea of what she was doing, or what she would do. It scared her. For once, she didn't care.

The man looked up at the sound of the approaching horse and turned, but she was too close for him to move out of the way. He tried to raise his spear but didn't have time. Her horse veered slightly, trying to avoid his, but still it crashed into the front side of the other mount. With a scream she threw herself at him, vaguely realizing she hadn't even drawn a weapon.

Her momentum took him off his horse and they landed heavily on the ground while the horses bolted. Luckily she landed on top of him, breaking the worst of her fall. Even so, fury and anger still boiled recklessly within her as she shifted and sat up to straddle him.

She automatically drew a dagger with each hand and attacked, screaming and stabbing while he tried to push her off and defend himself. Anger took over everything else. She'd lost Cain. He would have killed Prince. Loss after loss was destroying her. Someone had to pay. She couldn't take it anymore.

He died…at some point. Kei's cry brought her out of her fury, distracting her.

She stopped. Bloody daggers raised, she turned her head to see him and Prince sitting together a short distance away, both staring at her in complete shock. Looking down she saw the bloody mess beneath her. She stood quickly, keeping her weight on her good foot, hands dropping to her sides as she stood over the body.

Her chest heaved and she tried to control her frantic breathing and calm the wild anger within her. It had felt good, killing him. It probably shouldn't have, but one like him had killed Cain. How could she feel guilty for having her revenge?

There was no trace of guilt or remorse within her. She felt strangely better, freer.

She crouched down and wiped her daggers clean on the dead man's pants before sheathing them. She wiped her bloody hands as well. The actions gave her more time to calm herself.

Sucking in a deep breath she stood and faced her friends again. The feeling of being alone struck her suddenly, a sharp pain in her heart. Embarrassment at her wild attack heated her face. Not for what she had done, but the messy and uncontrolled way she'd done it.

Hands slid gently down her arms, and she looked up at Kei, wondering how he'd come to stand before her.

He looked searchingly into her eyes, his full of confusion. "Ar-ro?" Her name came out a quiet stutter. "You–" His hands came up to gently wipe spattered blood off of her face. "Aro." Kei shook his head slightly. "Are you hurt?"

She shook her head and glanced past him to Prince.

His pale face looked more tired and haggard than she had ever seen him. Blood stained his clothes. She didn't know if any belonged to him.

"So you do know how to fight," he said quietly.

She smiled weakly. Did they think she had gone insane? "That wasn't fighting," she murmured.

Kei cupped a hand to her cheek. "Vengeance."

She nodded and locked her gaze on the ground. The image of their shocked faces wouldn't leave her mind.

"Aro," Kei whispered.

She met his eyes again. They shined with an orange glow. A small, encouraging smile crossed his lips for a moment. "We have to talk…later."

Despite his words, his tone filled her with relief instead of worry. She nodded. Kei understood.

"I'll get the horses." He glanced over at Prince. "We could use two now."

She watched him dart off across the field in the direction the mounts had gone.

Prince sighed and shifted, his shoulders slumping. She noted his pack was missing and held in a curse. Maybe Kei could find it. Limping over to him she dropped down to her knees. "I was worried about you."

He glanced over at her and shook his head. "I am fine."

"No. You're not," she said with a frown. He barely looked alive. She wished she knew what to do. What to say. They sat in uncomfortable silence for a moment. "How far back did you drop your pack?"

He grimaced. "Not too far."

She nodded. "Kei can find it, when he gets back." She worried her lip in the silence which came again. "So... I made a new friend. A Were. He's helping look for you and Bo."

Prince raised his eyebrows and frowned. "Lovely."

She forced a smile. "You are a troublesome Elf. I hope you know that."

He glared over at her. "Where's Cain?"

She froze. Turning her head away she tried to fight the pain within her. "Dead."

He sucked in a startled breath. "Aro..."

"It's like you said. People die to protect me. I understand." She clamped her mouth shut over her stiff and angry words.

"That explains–"

"My mindless killing?"

"Arowyn." He leaned forward and reached out a hand to her. When he swayed suddenly, she scrambled closer and caught him, holding him against her. "You're not fine," she whispered. He turned in her arms so he rested on his back, looking up at her. His blood and dirt streaked face looked so broken and weary she clenched her jaw to keep from crying.

*I am sorry.* His voice whispered through her mind.

# Broken Prince

*I know. We'll have you home soon. The horses will help.*

*Aro, I do not...*

She squeezed her eyes closed and held him more tightly to her. "Shh..."

Feeling his hand on her cheek she looked down at him in surprise, blinking back the tears in her eyes. *Don't leave me. Don't die.*

He smiled faintly as he looked up at her. *I am trying not to.*

His wry reply forced a small laugh from her. "Stupid prince."

Closing his eyes he sighed again. "The things I do for you."

"I know, living and all. Such a hardship," she replied blandly.

His lips curved up slightly. She couldn't find it within herself to smile.

"I'll get you home," she whispered. "I promise."

*You have saved me enough already.*

*As you've saved me. It's what friends do. I won't ever stop. Don't ever ask me to.*

*Aro, you do not–*

Despite the fact he spoke to her with his thoughts, she pressed her fingertips to his lips. "Hush. You need to rest."

She looked up and saw Kei returning quickly, having found both of the horses. "We have horses."

As Prince mounted she stood next to her horse for a moment, taking in a deep, shuddering breath and closing her eyes.

While holding the beautiful, broken man in her arms, acceptance had suddenly flooded through her. He was her friend. Her family. More than that, she finally understood she truly was in love with him. Months of trying to deny the feelings, to hide and ignore them, had failed. The emotions he created within her would not go away. She just had no idea what to do about them.

"Wither me."

She and Prince moved quickly back into the trees. Kei went in search of the lost pack. Heading south again, Prince followed behind her. Once certain he wasn't going to topple off the horse, she closed her eyes and pictured Garen.

*Can you hear me?* She waited a moment, and then tried again, thinking of the human form he'd shown her and attempting to push her thoughts out further. *Garen? Are you there?*

*Yes. I have not found your friends yet,* he finally replied.

Relief flooded her he had answered. *We found Prince. We're heading south again now and still looking for Bo.*

*Very well.*

"Aro, what are you doing?"

"Talking to Garen," she replied. "Letting him know we found you." She turned in the saddle to look at Prince when he didn't answer.

He was staring at her incredulously.

"What?" She frowned, wondering what she had done now.

He shook his head. "You should not be able to talk to him."

She shrugged. "I've had a lot of practice. With you, with Damon."

He opened his mouth and closed it quickly again before looking off to the side and shaking his head. "Troublesome child," he muttered softly.

# Broken Prince

She turned back around, keeping her eye out for Bo. Kei would be pacing them within the fields and doing the same. She hoped they found him soon.

She and Prince made their way south slowly, stopping a few times to rest. Kei checked in on them occasionally, tying Prince's pack onto his horse on the first visit. They met again at noon to eat a quick lunch, fill their water skins, and do a quick wash at a small stream.

The new horse drew her attention when they stopped. She'd noticed it had a small pack. It didn't take her long to go through it. She found some food, a small knife, and other odds and ends they could use. The best discovery was the sword. They'd only had two, and John had carried one of them.

"Is it any good?" She set the sword in Prince's lap.

"Where did you get this?"

She shook her head. "It was on your horse. How did you not notice it?"

He looked down, his brow furrowing. She'd been teasing. However her comment seemed to hit him hard. He wasn't doing well at all, and he knew it, too.

Pulling it out of the scabbard he then tested for balance and looked briefly at the blade and hilt. "It will do. I can sharpen it for you later." He looked up again. "Or did you want to give it to Bo?"

Prince carried the other sword. Kei had his claws when needed. She bit her lip, wondering who could use it better. "We'll give it to Bo. I'm quick enough with my daggers. They will do for now."

He handed it back to her and she went and put it back on the horse. She spent the rest of their stop trying not to stare at Prince and worry about how awful he looked. At least her thoughts distracted her from thinking about Cain.

They had started packing up again when she heard from Garen.

*I found your human.*

Grinning, she quickly told the others. *Is he hurt?*

*He is being very troublesome. I dropped your note for him. He threw it at me. I'm not an over-sized dog.*

She burst out laughing at the mental picture his words brought to her mind.

*Can he even read?* Garen's mind voice sounded extremely annoyed.

She paused. She had assumed he could. She knew Kei and Prince could read. So could Cain. During the long winter he had picked up books now and then from somewhere and read to them all. She closed her eyes for a moment, the memory of her lost friend bearing down heavily upon her heart. Letting out a long, slow breath she got back to the problem.

She couldn't once bring to mind ever seeing Bo actually reading. *Rot it all. Apparently not.*

*What would you like me to do now? He won't follow me.*

*I'll send Kei. Where are you?*

He told her and she quickly relayed the information to Kei who set out immediately. She grinned at Prince. He had a rare smile on his face. She just didn't know if it was from Bo being found, or from what he had done to the Were.

The way his smile made her heart pound and face flush irritated her. Now wasn't the time to think such thoughts. Being happy Bo lived, she could deal with. Anything else just felt wrong. She hurried him along so they could meet up with the others quickly.

They rode silently for quite some time, keeping within the trees, until she spotted Kei ahead of her further in the forest. He beckoned her on and she turned her horse to follow him to the others.

# Broken Prince

A smile of relief spread across her face when she spotted Bo washing up at the edge of a pond. He truly was alive. Pulling the horse to a stop she slid off, carefully minding her twisted ankle. Kei took the reins and she quickly limped toward her friend.

Bo grinned and came to meet her, pulling her into a tight embrace. "I'm sorry, pup," he mumbled into her hair.

Nodding against his chest, she held him tightly and fought back tears. Kei must have told him about Cain. She had been trying so hard not to think about him. There wasn't anything she could have done. She couldn't have saved him. He had died, like Kendric and Avery, and there wasn't anything she could do about it.

Despite wanting to stay in his big, strong arms she squeezed him once more and pulled away. "You hurt?"

"Nothing major, and all far from my heart," he said with a crooked grin.

She forced a smile, blinking away tears. "Good. We'll get you taken care of–"

Something thumped behind her and she turned quickly when Bo cursed. Her eyes first found Kei where he stood a short distance away, tending her horse. Just beyond him Prince's mount shifted beside a prone body.

"Prince!"

She and Bo raced for Prince. Surprisingly, Kei reached him first, dropping to a knee and bending over him.

Her ankle burned with pain from the short run as she dropped to the ground beside Prince, her hands reaching out for him. "What's wrong?"

Kei shook his head, his brows creased with worry.

*Your Elf does not fare well.*

She glared over at Garen. "I know."

Prince moved beneath her hands, bringing her attention back to him. He had collapsed onto his stomach and she quickly shifted her hands under him, either to help him turn over or sit up.

Tears threatened again when he turned and his arms came up. With her help, he pulled himself up against her chest, his head falling weakly against her shoulder.

"Prince," she whispered, bowing her head over his and wrapping her arms around him. He felt so light, so thin, like he had truly started to fade away into nothing. He didn't move within her arms, his breath came slow and shallow against her neck. She wasn't sure if he had lost consciousness or not.

"Prince?" She gently shook him. "Wake up, you have to wake up." Her hand shaking, she gently brushed hair from his face. "What should we do?" She looked from Kei to Bo, hoping one of them knew.

Bo ran a hand over his face, shaking his head slightly. "We'll not be moving tonight I think." He glanced over at Kei. "We should set up camp, maybe start a fire and have some decent food. Maybe that will help him."

She nodded and looked over at Garen. "Is a fire safe here?"

The wolf cocked his head slightly to one side, considering. *Keep it small. It should be safe. We mustn't stay long however. Other Were may come to investigate.*

She nodded and relayed the information to the others, grimacing slightly at the inconvenience caused because they couldn't hear Garen. Bo took the Were's sudden addition to their family without comment. Kei must have introduced them while they waited for her and Prince.

Kei frowned down at Prince, though it was different than normal. It wasn't directed at the man, but the situation. "I'll get his pack."

She remembered Prince had been wounded in the fighting. How badly had he been hurt? Nodding at Kei as he rose, she tried to see where the injuries were.

# Broken Prince

Bo moved to quickly set up a small fire pit near the pool while Kei took Prince's horse away to tend to it and unload all of their packs. She remained where she was, holding Prince. She didn't know what else to do.

Kei brought the pack of supplies and a skin of water over and helped her treat and re-bandage the wounds Prince had taken. None would normally be life threatening, but in his weakened condition, she didn't know how serious they would affect him. She held him to her again when they finished, wishing she knew if he would get better or not.

Kei watched her silently.

"Can you help treat Bo? Please," she asked quietly.

He squeezed her shoulder as he rose and gathered the supplies.

The frustration of it all began to tear her apart. They had come so far, were so close to his home, surely only a few more weeks at most, yet she didn't know if he would make it. Tears ran down her cheeks and she bent her head over him again, gently rocking and mumbling a quiet children's tune.

After a while, Garen's voice came tentatively into her mind. *He is very weak...*

She nodded, not looking up, trying to hide the stupid tears. *Do you know how long it would take to get him home?*

*To Rivenward?*

*What?*

He snorted. *Has he told you nothing? That is the name of the Elven lands.*

*He doesn't talk a lot about his home. How long?*

*Riding hard, as the crow flies, maybe five days. However you are not crows and the northern border is warded. There is only one entrance and it is south. With the fighting going on, I do not think you would make it through. Best would be to keep moving south along the forest boundary until you reach the wardwall and then head west. Two weeks perhaps, now that you have the horses.*

*I don't think we have enough time.*

*No,* Garen agreed. *You do not. He is very far gone.*

Squeezing her eyes tightly together against a sudden torrent of tears, she sucked in a shuddering breath. They weren't going to make it. Prince was going to die.

Just like Cain had died.

She gritted her teeth suddenly. "No." Looking over at Garen she shook her head. "No, I won't let him die. There has to be a way."

Garen rested his head on his paws. *He needs power. That is the only way. Elves are bound to their land. They need its magic to survive.*

She thought a moment. *The slavers took his amulet.*

*He has been too long without it. Too long from home.*

She stared down at Prince. Garen's words made sense, but didn't really help. Where was she supposed to find power? "Elven power?"

*I imagine any would do at this point.*

"Where do I get some?"

Garen snorted and raised his head off of his paws. *It's not as easy as that. It's not like any of us can simply give it to him. With the Fey and the Were, we don't practice magic, it is part of us.*

"You're not really helping," she complained.

He sighed. *If he was part of a pack, he could draw some small power from it. How the Fey might share power, I don't know.*

Frustration started to overwhelm her. They weren't Were, they weren't a pack, so a packs' power would not help. She looked over to Kei. "Kei, is there any way you can share power with Prince?"

He looked up from collecting wood and shook his head. "No. Not that I know of." He grimaced at his words, reminding her he didn't know all of his heritage. His parents had taken him across the sea when he was little. They had died when he was ten. She imagined it frustrated him as much as it did her.

"What about…" She looked at him knowingly. He had done some sort of magic with her, a fey binding which bound them together as friends and later again as family.

Kei shook his head. "He would never agree."

She grimaced. "True."

"It is not an exchange of power either."

Also true. Holding Prince to her, she struggled to think, to come up with anything at all.

"So," she said finally, raising her head to look at Garen. "A pack. Does it only work with Were?"

He stared at her. *I would assume so.* He paused and cocked his head to the side. *I don't know.*

She nodded once, determination suddenly filling her. "Boys! Come here!"

*What are you doing?*

She didn't answer him, waiting for Bo and Kei to come over. When they did she looked up at Bo. "Take Prince. We'll do this by the fire."

"Do what?" Kei looked at her questioningly, moving forward to help her up once Bo had easily picked up Prince's limp form.

She raised a finger. "I've an impulsive and insane plan!"

He rolled his eyes and helped her over to the fire. She sat again and beckoned for Bo to pass Prince back to her. She held him to her again, his head against her chest. "Sit close, everyone. You, too, Garen."

They sat around her and she let out a deep breath, sorting out her thoughts. "Prince is fading away. Dying. The only thing which will help him is power. I don't know how to get any for him." She looked at each of them solemnly. "We are already friends, a family. I want to try to make us a pack.

Like the Were are. Garen says packs have power. Maybe it will help."

Bo shrugged. "If it will work."

Kei frowned and shook his head. "I don't like this."

"But–"

"Magic is dangerous, Aro."

"I know that!"

"No. You don't."

She pressed her lips together tightly to keep from screaming as she glared at Kei. Fine, she didn't know anything about magic. But he didn't know everything either.

"It might work," she said quietly. "We just lost Cain. I-I can't…" A sob caught in her throat and she shook her head violently, hugging Prince tightly to her. "I can't lose him, too. I just can't!"

Kei wilted under her emotional plea and looked away. His face looked haunted, defeated. He closed his eyes and took a deep breath.

"Please. Please let me try," she whispered desperately.

He looked back at her, his golden eyes staring into hers for what seemed like forever. Finally he nodded and then lowered his head, staring at his hands.

She reached a hand over and squeezed one of his. "Thank you, Kei."

She looked over at Garen. *Well?*

The Were sat and let out a sound which sounded like a snort. *You're insane.*

*Probably. I doubt it will work. But it just might. I…Sometimes I can do things I shouldn't be able to. I have to try.* "You in or not? I'm thinking it has a better chance if there's an actual Were involved."

*Very well.*

She smiled.

Bo raised his eyebrows. "He up for it?"

"He is. So..." She let out a deep breath, trying to think of how, exactly, one created a pack. *Do you know how to do this?*

*We simply are. So...no. I don't.*

His words weren't what she wanted to hear. *Tell me about your magic.*

*Magic is everywhere. It's all around us. We live and breathe it. We are born from it, we return to it when we die. It simply is and always has been.*

*This is the same magic the Elves use?*

He cocked his head to the side. *Yes. Magic is magic, Arowyn. It is everywhere. The Elves have bound themselves to the magic within their borders to make themselves stronger there.*

Hope sputtered within her. It might actually save Prince, if she could figure out how to make them a pack. She held out the hand which wasn't holding his limp body to her. "Everyone touch."

Bo and Kei rested a hand on hers. Garen hesitated before standing to move closer and then raising a huge paw to place on top of theirs.

"Hopefully this works." She closed her eyes, fighting off sudden nervousness. She had no idea what to do. If she failed, Prince would die. The odds of her succeeding were slim. She had to try…she would. She would make it work. The magic Kei had done with her came to mind. Perhaps something similar would work again?

"All of us come together now, wishing to become a pack. We are friends. We are family. Forever we wish to be bound together as such." She paused, searching for more formal words. "As a pack we will stand together, fight together, live together, love together. Though we are not all Were, we wish to be bound as such, together, so we can support each other, help each other." She squeezed her eyes closed, pulling Prince more tightly to her chest. "Whatever power exists out

65

there, please hear me, hear us. Make us a pack. Bind us together. Help us help each other."

She waited, afraid to open her eyes, wondering if anything had happened.

*Very good, little one.*

She opened her eyes, looking over at Garen. The howling started suddenly, sounding very far off, yet still echoing through the trees. Garen raised his head and howled along with them.

She looked at the others, allowing her hand to drop. Bo and Kei both were staring at Garen. "Did it work?"

"I...I heard him," Bo said finally.

Kei nodded. "Me, too."

Garen stopped howling suddenly to look at both of them. *You hear me?* They both nodded again, speechless. *Well that is an unexpected benefit.*

Prince shifted in her arms, gaining her attention. He opened his eyes, slowly locking onto her face as they came into focus. "Arowyn," he whispered. His fine, dark brows drew together. "I feel...strange. What did you do?"

She laughed, so relieved he seemed better, that it had worked, more tears came to her eyes. "I made us a pack."

He stared at her a moment before sighing and closing his eyes again. "I am just going to pretend I did not hear that."

"You woke up, and you're talking." She smiled down at him. "You can pretend anything you like."

# Chapter 5:
# Admitting the Truth

A good amount of light remained in the day. Content Prince wouldn't suddenly die in her arms, she helped him to the pond's edge to clean up. After doing a quick wash herself she set to work making a good hearty dinner for him, digging small pots out of one of the bags and carefully adding ingredients from their combined packs.

Thankfully Garen took it upon himself to teach them how mind-speech worked. He and Bo seemed to have struck a quick friendship which made her both relieved and happy. Of them all, Bo had been closest to Cain.

*Speaking with your mind is much like using words. Gather your thought and then release it.*

*This is not easy!*

*No need to shout, Bo. We're right here.*

Aro smiled. *It gets easier with practice, Bo. Garen, how far does it work? Distance I mean?*

*Quite far. Though the further away, the harder it is.*

*If I was in Franua now could you hear me?*

*It would be difficult,* Garen admitted. *Possibly not. Packs stay within their territory and rarely are far apart. Our pack is small, and so has less power. The king travels the forests and can speak to all, but he is much stronger than all of us.*

*Does he know? What we did?*

Garen remained silent for a long moment. *Yes,* he thought finally.

He didn't say more. Aro didn't ask any more questions. She was afraid to find out how much trouble her impulsive actions had gotten them into.

She glanced over at Prince and a small smile tugged at her lips. It was worth it.

An occasional mental shout from Bo kept her smiling while she worked.

Kei listened in quietly while he gathered more wood. She watched her family while puttering about the fire. Though for the time being they were safe, she knew it probably wouldn't last.

Worry gnawed at her stomach. Prince looked better than he had in months, however he was very quiet. She didn't know how long the power of the pack would sustain him. Hopefully it would be long enough to get him home. Even so, she waited for him to start yelling at her for what she had done. Certainly there would be consequences, she wasn't an idiot. He was an elven prince now part of a pack of misfits.

The sun eventually set and they ate silently around the small dying fire. Though summer was drawing to a close the weather remained warm enough they did not need its heat, even at night.

Bo had finally gotten his volume under control.

*You've done well, all of you,* Garen commented. *You have been speaking with the pack as a whole up to now. Let us work on sending thoughts to specific people.*

Bo groaned and put his head in his hands.

*It is not so difficult. Think of…ropes…connecting us. Picture the person or persons you wish to speak to. Again, mind your volume!*

Bo and Kei both spoke to her and she practiced with them for a while. Prince drifted off to sleep. She didn't wake him for the lessons. With his Elven heritage and mind speech so common she was certain he knew what to do. Of course the looks of annoyance and distain he'd worn all evening rather let her know, too.

When weariness overcame her she moved to the pond to do a better job at washing. Stripping down to her underclothes she slid in, grimacing at the muddy bottom as it squished around her toes. She scrubbed herself, her hair, and clothes as quickly as she could before returning to the bank to work more on her shirt and pants. She knew the blood would permanently stain her clothes, but at least wanted the worst of it out. The constant reminder of where the blood came from hurt too much.

She hung her wet clothes over a branch before returning to the fire. The boys didn't stare. They'd seen her half-dressed too many times to take notice any more.

She'd forgotten about Garen however.

Bo laughed out loud. *She always does that.*

She turned and saw the wolf staring at her. "What?"

*Nothing,* Garen said quickly.

Putting her hands on her hips she shook her head. "Don't look if it bothers you."

He stood and walked off into the trees. *Bother isn't exactly the correct word...*

Her cheeks flushed suddenly and she ducked her head, moving to sit with the others, pulling her knees up and wrapping her arms around them. After a few tense moments of silence they all began to talk quietly, making plans to head out the next day. Conversation quickly slowed however; they did not have a lot they needed to plan.

Garen returned quietly after a while and settled down next to Bo.

She yawned into her hand. "Good night, boys."

A quiet chorus echoed her and she smiled faintly. Kei moved over beside her and she curled up on the ground facing him, as always. She heard Prince get up and walk into the woods. A short while later he returned and settled down behind her. She held in a sigh. He'd hardly said a word all night. She wondered how angry he was with her.

Everyone settled down quickly. Not surprising, they were all exhausted. Her twisted ankle throbbed with a low annoying burn.

She closed her eyes...and saw Cain, surrounded by darkness, the arrow sticking through his chest. Blood spurted everywhere. Gasping, her heart suddenly racing, she opened her eyes quickly.

Squeezing her eyes closed, she tried to fight the tears. Cain appeared again and she opened them quickly once more.

Kei shifted closer to her and she instinctively reached out her hands. He took them both in his, holding them between his own. A tearful shudder passed through her and she fought the sobs wanting to escape. A small whimper made it past her lips and she cringed.

Kei gently removed one of his hands and a moment later his fingers touched her face, brushing tears from her cheeks.

"Shh..." he whispered. "I'm here."

She nodded, holding in more sobs. Kei was always there, always helping her. She heard him shift again, moving closer.

Suddenly she felt a cool hand slip around her bare waist. Strong fingers curled around her, pulling her back, away from Kei. Her mouth opened in surprise. Not that Prince would try to keep her from Kei, the two very rarely got along, and never had. It was some stupid Fey and Elf thing, and also a soldier and nobility thing, and who knew what else.

Her surprise came because she had thought him angry with her. He hadn't spoken to her all night. He hadn't immediately rested a hand at her waist when they went to sleep like he usually did.

# Broken Prince

Kei growled softly as Prince pulled her away. However he didn't try to hold her and the growling was nothing new either.

"Go to sleep, Kei," Prince whispered harshly.

Kei seemed as shocked as her at his words and tone. Shocked enough he actually let go of her other hand, which he never did. Prince pulled again, until her body curled up against him. She stiffened, unsure what exactly was going on. Was he angry with her or not?

*I am not.*

She frowned and tried to turn over to face him but he held her in place. "But–"

*Use your mind, Arowyn.*

She had the urge to snarl herself suddenly. *Fine. La la la la...*

*You are–*

*Do not call me a child again.* She remained stiff in his arms, watching Kei across from her. The Fey stared at her, obviously unhappy. She didn't like him unhappy so made a funny face until he smiled and shook his head a little.

*There are things we must discuss.*

Prince's words frightened her, though she kept such thoughts locked away from him. *Such as?*

*First of all, you are giving me a headache.*

She stiffened. *What are you talking about?*

*The way we speak, and the way the pack does, are two very different things. You needn't use both, only one. Both at once creates…an echo. It is rather disturbing to listen to.*

What he said made sense. She took a moment to distinguish the two ways of speaking in her mind. Once she had them clearly sorted out, she left the Were mind speech alone and just spoke to him as they had always done before. *Is this better?*

*Much, I thank you.*

*Was that it? Can I go to sleep now?*

*No. We must speak of what happened.* He paused. *Arowyn, I understand why you did what you did. I don't understand how exactly you did it, however I've learned you always seem to do the impossible. You are such a troublesome...*he paused a moment...*girl.*

*So you tell me. You are rather a pain yourself.*

*You do point that out quite often.*

*Because you are.* She grimaced, not wanting to fight. *I'm going to get you home. We are,* she amended. *So stop trying to die all the time.*

*Arowyn, even given the power you granted me with what you did, I do not believe I will make it home. Do you understand?*

She gritted her teeth together and let him sense how angry his words made her. *Stop it! If you need more, then I'll find you more. I won't let you die! I–* She stopped, not letting the words out, not letting him know. "I won't," she whispered quietly instead.

*Aro, I know this is difficult...*

Difficult wasn't quite the word. She'd just lost Cain. How could she even consider losing Prince? *I'm tired. I'm going to sleep now. We are not discussing this anymore.*

He didn't answer for a long moment. *Sleep well.*

She doubted she would, but didn't say so.

Mornings, as always, came too early. The only good thing was her ankle felt much better. She guessed another day or two of riding and she'd been able to at least walk on it all day again.

After eating quickly and packing up, they set out. Time had become their enemy. Garen and Kei left first, they would be scouting and hunting, being able to move quickly through the woods and undergrowth. Bo walked while she and Prince rode, the two of them keeping an eye on the Elf, ready to stop quickly if he suddenly took a turn for the worse again. Bo seemed the only one happy, but then she'd remembered to give him the sword. He'd probably be up all night sharpening it once they stopped.

They did not move quickly or travel far. At least not enough for her. They stuck to the woods, Kei and Garen having continued to see humans in the fields. Travel had been slow since they could only go as quickly as their slowest member, which at the time was Bo, who remained on foot. Had they not had so many packs he could have ridden behind her, but the last thing they wanted to do was overburden the precious horses. Having to stop frequently so Prince could rest didn't help either.

She tried not to grind her teeth when they finally stopped for the day. She, Bo, and Kei set up camp while Prince rested and Garen watched them all. Her temper grew shorter. She knew her worry for Prince caused it. She feared they were moving too slowly, and wouldn't get him home in time.

Cooking a small dinner, she resisted the urge to scream. Tears threatened again, which didn't help either. She had grown sick of crying, sick of feeling so helpless. Spooning out their dinner onto crude thin wooden plates, she then passed them out to everyone. Taking one for herself and Prince, she went and sat beside him.

"You better eat all of that," she said crossly.

Prince raised his brows in surprise before a faint smile came to his lips. "I will."

She nodded once, annoyed with herself and the foul mood which wouldn't go away.

Garen sat beside Bo. He'd caught a rabbit or something earlier and had already eaten. He watched everyone. Constantly.

She jerked her head in the Were's direction. "Why does he keep watching us all so much?"

73

"I believe he is trying to figure out the pack dynamics."

"What?"

"You made us a pack," Prince said, tilting his head slightly, not quite admonishing her. "Wolves follow a sophisticated group hierarchy. Every member of a pack has its place. It is led by the Alpha male and female, with a Beta wolf or wolves as second in command."

She stared at Prince, wondering how he knew all of this. "I see."

"Unfortunately, we are not wolves. I imagine he is trying to determine his place within the pack, and we are not making it easy."

She understood, sort of. Her gaze went to Garen again, wondering where he thought he fit in. Wondering where she did. The Were certainly lived differently than humans. She remembered how Garen kept asking her who her mate was. She glanced over at Prince and away quickly. She finished eating in silence, her thoughts wandering.

Prince ate all the food she'd brought him and she smiled a little as she collected his plate. "Good boy."

He frowned up at her, making her laugh. That was the Prince she knew.

The Prince she loved.

She turned away quickly, her smile vanishing. Finally admitting the truth to herself meant nothing. It certainly didn't do her any good. She loved him, but he didn't love her. Yes, he protected her, cared for her, but only because he thought her a child. He was a prince and an Elf. She had to remember those things. It might help in the end, when she got him home and finally had to leave him.

She looked down at the pile of dishes she'd collected and started cleaning them quickly, pushing her frustration into her work. Idiot, idiot, idiot. She wished she could change the way she felt. She wished she could love someone else. Or no one at all.

## Broken Prince

It would be so much easier if she didn't care.

She closed her eyes for a moment and took a deep breath. Thinking wasn't helping. Thinking made it worse. Whatever would happen, would happen. She couldn't change anything.

Jen Wylie

# Chapter 6:
# Family First

The next day they made slow but steady progress again. Though they no longer saw soldiers in the fields, they decided not to continue their travels along the road. Though riding the forest border had its dangers, it also provided food and wood for fires. As long as they were careful, they could forage the fields as well. Their decision pleased Garen immensely and she felt horrible she'd never considered he wouldn't want to travel in the human lands when she'd asked him to join them.

Her temper remained short. She'd tried walking, and had been able to for a time until her ankle began hurting again. Frustration overwhelmed her so much she wanted to hit something. It did not help the days had seemed to drag by so slowly. Nothing of interest happened. They rode. They rested. No one talked very much. There wasn't really a lot to be said. Perhaps her bad mood had started infecting the others, or perhaps they were simply staying out of her way.

They found another of the many small streams which ran from the mountains down to the sea and started setting up camp early. Kei and Garen both brought back a number of small birds and game.

Bo started getting a fire going while Kei went off to clean their dinner. She collected firewood, thinking it sad they were all rather excited over the large meal they would be getting. Once she had never been hungry. That had been over a year ago though, before their city fell. It had also been the last time she'd slept in a real bed, not a pile of blankets like they'd used in the room they rented. The last time for so many simple things.

She glanced over at Prince. He never complained, which surprised her. He'd snap at her about her manners or speech, but not whine over being dirty or hungry.

Leaning against a tree, he had his eyes closed now, resting. Black hair spilled around his beautiful face, making it appear paler than it actually was, highlighting the dark circles under his eyes. Sadly, he'd looked worse. She tried to picture him when she'd first met him, but that really didn't help. He'd been under an Elven glamor at the time. Though even with it he hadn't looked well. He'd been dying even then.

Even sick, he still took her breath away. *Stupid.* She turned and picked up another fallen branch. She had to stop this. She was only making it harder on herself, and making everyone else miserable, too.

Walking over to the fire she dropped her pile of wood and went back amongst the trees to search for more. She didn't go far, she'd learned her lesson the hard way last fall when she'd gotten lost and attacked by slavers. The sun remained high enough in the sky to light the woods enough for her to see well. The area of woods they had entered did not have a lot of underbrush, for which she felt thankful. Brush only slowed them down. Had they needed to hide, it would have been good, but speed had become their aim now.

She did not hear Garen move behind her, his large paws somehow silent on the forest floor. She did hear his sudden growl just before he bounded past her. Staring at him in shock, she froze as he stopped directly in front of her, hackles raised, ears flattened back against his head. He snarled, his lips pulled back from his huge teeth.

"What is it, Garen?" She stepped up beside him, resting a hand on his back.

*Run!*

She looked down at him. His voice in her mind had quivered with fear, as if he'd struggled just to get that one word out. Yet he didn't look afraid, he looked ready to take on an army.

"I see you have made a new friend," Damon said, walking into her view.

She pursed her lips and glared at him as she stepped forward, putting herself between him and Garen.

The Dragos was dangerous. He also had no qualms about hurting her friends. The last time he'd come Kei had attacked him, so had Prince. Neither had hurt him, he was simply too powerful.

She glanced back at Garen, *Do not attack him. It won't do any good.*

He growled in response, but his head lowered slightly, which she took to mean he'd actually listen to her. Hopefully the others didn't know Damon had come. If she could keep them out of it, she would. They tended to try to protect her too much. She didn't want them hurt at her expense again.

"Hello, Damon," she said, struggling to make the words come out calmly.

A smile spread across his handsome face as he stopped a few steps in front of her. "Arowyn. It's been a while."

"Not long enough." She forced a smile, trying to make light of her words. She had to be careful. He could get angry so quickly.

He chuckled. "Now, now. Last time I believe I was quite helpful to you."

Yes, he'd come back, and answered some of their questions, mostly concerning Prince, who had left them. But Prince had only left because Damon had torn his glamor away and shown them all he was an Elf. This was of course after

Damon had ripped through her mind, destroying all of her inner defenses, nearly destroying her.

She didn't like him. Of course, she didn't understand him either. Though he mostly looked human, he wasn't, his true form being a monstrous dragon.

He cocked his head to the side, his strange iridescent eyes with their vertical slits seeming to swirl. "I take it you didn't miss me?"

"We've been busy," she said quickly. "Trying to get Prince home." She bit her tongue. She shouldn't have mentioned the others.

However Damon merely nodded. Perhaps he actually remembered. He stared at her intently. "You seem stronger."

She tensed, waiting for him to invade her mind, waiting for the pain of it. It didn't come, not yet, however she didn't know what to say.

His gazed went past her, back to Garen. "You have them all now. Perhaps that is why."

She had no idea what he was talking about. Not really. She guessed he referred to her friends being from all of the races, human, Elf, Were, Fey. However she didn't know how that could be important. She hoped there hadn't been something about them in the stupid prophecies he liked to prattle on about all the time. She doubted she'd be so lucky.

"You're very quiet this time," he said, breaking her thoughts.

"I don't really have a lot to say."

"You just never know what I want you to tell me."

She clenched her fists, trying to stay calm, trying not to say something sarcastic or stupid which would cause problems. "You should ask then, if you have a question."

He smiled. It was a little smile, he was not amused. "That takes too much time, you don't say everything. I like to see for myself."

"Stay out of my mind," she said sharply. The edges of panic crept over her. She knew what was coming, knew she couldn't stop it. No one could. She wanted to run, but knew he'd catch her. He'd probably love that, some extra excitement. She shifted slightly from one foot to the other, waiting.

"You…" he paused and looked over one shoulder then the other.

She looked as well, confused, until she saw all the others come forward out of the trees, even Prince. They had circled him. Idiots. She ground her teeth, furious they had come.

She carefully focused a thought at Garen. *Did you call them?*

*Yes. I felt him to be a threat. Was I wrong?*

She tried to stay calm and to not yell at Garen. He didn't know. She'd never gotten around to telling him about Damon, about what the Dragos had done to them. *No. It's fine. Just be careful. He's very dangerous. Try to keep your thoughts well-guarded.*

Damon looked back at her, apparently heedless of her conversation, and chuckled. "You've all been spending too much time with the wolves. You're starting to act like them."

She stared at him and then she understood. He didn't know. He didn't know they had worked Were magic and become a pack.

She wanted to keep it that way. She smiled a little. "They have some good ideas."

"So they do," he answered. He turned to regard Prince. "You are holding up well. Under the circumstances."

Prince gave him a faint nod, somehow managing to stand tall and straight and not look like he would collapse at any moment. Maybe the Were magic had done more for him than she'd thought.

Damon cocked his head to the side, pursing his lips for a moment in thought. "Do you honestly think you will make it?"

A small smile crossed Prince's lips and he looked over at her. "Aro seems quite determined I will."

Damon turned his attention back to her, which she didn't really appreciate. At the same time, relief flooded through her that he had turned away from Prince. The Elf was in no condition to deal with any sort of fighting right now. "And so I imagine you will. She is a remarkably strong girl...for a human." He smiled that little smile she hated so much, like he knew things she didn't. It was a cruel, patronizing smile. It fit him perfectly.

She wanted to ask him what he wanted, but was afraid speaking would cause something horrible to happen. Keeping her mouth shut seemed to be a much better idea.

Damon frowned and then pointed a finger at her. "One of you is missing."

She closed her eyes for a moment, sucking in a deep breath. Of course he'd notice. "Cain."

"Where is he?"

"He died."

"How?"

She swallowed roughly. "Arrow. Through the chest."

"Ah. How ironic."

She flinched.

Damon continued to regard her thoughtfully and then gave a little shrug. Like Cain's death meant nothing. That he'd meant nothing.

She wanted to kill him.

Instead she clenched her jaw and forced herself to stay still, to stay calm. Somehow she managed. Maybe she was getting stronger, growing up.

Damon took another step closer and smiled again. "I have discovered more about you. Would you like to hear it?"

"No," she said promptly.

"But it is quite interesting. It mentions in fact, all of you." He paused and then smiled again. "Well, perhaps not. Things do change of course and any one of you could be replaced. Prophecy is always so vague. Still, it is most interesting you have filled the requirements already. It's almost a shame really."

She was having trouble following what he was saying. "What?"

He grinned and shrugged. "You are too young yet. You will not be Queen for some time."

Before she could stop herself she rolled her eyes and sighed.

"You don't believe me?"

"Does it matter?" She tried to cover her reactions. Why couldn't she act more responsible? This wasn't a game. She knew it, knew it so very well. Yet she couldn't seem to stay out of trouble. So far, she'd thought she'd done very well, but she had to be better. Lives depended on her.

Damon apparently found her amusing. He laughed and shook his head. "Not at all, of course. Do you really not want to know?"

"No," she said firmly. "I don't."

"Not anything?"

She shook her head.

"Not even where you will rule? How it will happen? Who will rule by your side?"

"Most definitely not."

He seemed disappointed. "Perhaps I should tell you anyway."

"Maybe that will change things." She smiled sweetly.

He snorted, his mouth twisting in an ironic half smile. "Possibly."

"Is that what you intend?" She had wondered if he was trying to help, or to hinder, the prophecy he so liked to talk

Jen Wylie

about. Honestly she had no idea. Of course she only knew the one line he'd told her about herself, and the one about Kei. Perhaps the prophecy said she would kill him. She almost liked that thought.

He smiled again, which was no answer at all. Not with him. She glanced quickly at the others. Everyone had been so still, so quiet. It surprised her, but she certainly wasn't going to complain. So far they had avoided fighting, and having Damon in anyone's mind.

Damon continued to regard her silently, as if waiting for her to speak.

She didn't want to. Her mouth tended to get her into trouble with him. Counting her heartbeats she waited, staring at him, watching his strange eyes swirl.

He smiled again suddenly, and took a step forward. She tensed. He had moved close enough now, he could touch her. In the past he had always done so just before he invaded her mind.

Damon lifted a hand, but didn't touch her. He looked down, behind her.

Garen whimpered.

Turning quickly she saw her friend had lowered himself, his back arched, tail tucked between his legs and his ears flat against his head.

Even as a wolf she could see how frightened he was. Whirling around, she stepped forward and smacked Damon's outstretched hand away. "Stop it!"

The Dragos looked away from Garen and turned his attention to her. He wasn't impressed.

Clenching her jaw she fought back her fear and prepared to fight.

He laughed. "What is this? Do you think you can stop me? I could kill you all with a thought."

"If you wanted to kill us you've had plenty of chances," she said levelly. A strange calm came over her. This was important, standing up to him.

He raised his eyebrows, clearly surprised.

"You will *not* hurt my family," she continued. "No more of this. I will fight you if need be and I will fight until I die."

"Aro, stop."

She ignored Prince, keeping her eyes locked with Damon's. Placing her hands on her daggers she spoke firmly, "Do you understand? I will fight for them, and I will die for them."

Damon tilted his head to the side, no expression on his face. She couldn't tell how angry she'd made him. She raised her chin, staring back at him defiantly even though her heart pounded frantically in her chest. She meant every word, and knew he could see that.

"Aro!"

Clenching her teeth she glanced over at Prince, then to Bo. Both had drawn their swords. She looked to Kei, whose eyes glowed orange, almost red. Carefully channeling her thoughts she put as much command and power behind them as possible. *All of you stay out of this!*

Tightening her grip on her daggers she looked back at Damon. "Do you wish to fight? Now?" His silence increased her anger. "If not, I need to start cooking our dinner."

She wasn't overly surprised when he burst into laughter. "Very well. I shall leave you to your cooking then, little queen. Today is not a day we will fight."

Nodding her agreement, she took a step backward. She didn't relax, not yet. She wouldn't until he was gone.

"If you keep moving, and stay near the forest boundary you should be able to avoid the Were." He turned slightly, looking at Bo. "They do not allow humans in their woods. They will kill you if they find you here." He turned and began walking away. "There is a human army massed north of the entrance to Rivenward. Do take that into consideration when you make further plans."

She didn't thank him for the information as he disappeared into the trees. Removing her hands from her weapons she did let out a deep relieved breath.

The others rushed up to her, gathering around and talking all at once, reprimanding her.

"Enough!" She glared at each of them in turn, Bo and Kei and Prince. "I am not a child. Stop treating me like one. I've had enough of it!"

"Aro..." Bo began.

She shook her head vehemently. "Why can't you understand you're my family? You're all I have. I know you'd do anything for me, some of you have..." the words choked her and stole away her anger. "Some of you have died for me. I am not weak. I am not a child. Stop treating me like I am."

They stood in shocked silence at her tirade. She turned and quickly headed back to the camp to cook dinner, escaping while she could.

# Chapter 7:
# The Story of the Queens

Due to Damon's unexpected and unwanted arrival, dinner was delayed. At least the meat hadn't been set to cook before he came, likely it would have been charred and ruined.

While she prepared the meal she mulled over what Damon had said at the end. The human army could be a problem, but wasn't an immediate threat. The Were, however, most certainly could be. The forest was their territory and humans knew well to enter it meant death.

"Garen," she said suddenly. "How likely is it the Were will find us?"

He took a moment before answering. *It is possible. Few other than patrols travel this close to the border. I think one of us would sense their approach. Contrary to what the Dragos said, many will give a warning first. You being with me, and a Fey and Elf, would cause them to hesitate as well. Only humans are banned.*

"If they come, just cross the border as quickly as you can," Prince said quietly.

Looking over at Bo, she nodded when he did. "We'll stay close then? Not go too far in?"

"You and Bo won't, no."

She didn't like that, but certainly didn't have any reason to fight it.

Eventually they all sat down to eat and rest. She worried everyone remained so quiet. Perhaps she'd said something wrong, but she'd meant every word. They were her family. They did mean everything to her.

She looked over at Garen, worried Damon had hurt him. He'd gone to do a quick scout of the area while dinner cooked and just returned. *Did he hurt you?*

Garen raised his head off his paws. *I'm fine now.*

She frowned. *I know what it's like. He's been in my head before. He's hurt me, torn down my defenses.*

A growl rumbled from the wolf.

*There isn't anything we can do. We can't fight him. We've tried. He's a Dragos, the most powerful of creatures there is.*

*He would be wise not to return.*

She smiled a little. *We're never so lucky. We just have to be careful. He gets angry easily.*

*He seems most interested in you.*

She nodded, and then told Garen of their previous meetings. How Damon thought she and Kei were someone special.

*What are these prophecies?*

She answered out loud, as the others had started to look at her curiously. "Mine is: find the broken arrow carved of stone, stolen from across the sea. It will heal the Fey and they will rise again."

*That doesn't make much sense,* Garen said.

"I know." She shook her head in frustration.

Kei shared his, "Your son will make the Queen and he will remain by her side bound to her by three."

*Your son?*

"His grandmother was the Fey Seer."

"There are more, a whole book of them. But he's never told us more than that. He just keeps calling me a queen. Of the Fey," she added, just to be clear.

"I think he's just insane," Bo surprisingly cut in with a half-smile.

She snorted her agreement. She looked back at Garen. "Across the sea, we have countries ruled by kings and queens, and nobles under them. How do the Were work?"

*The forests from the Elven lands of Rivenward north to Franua are split into pack territories. Each pack is led by its Alpha pair. We have a king who governs us all. His queen died long ago, before my time. He has never taken another.*

Good information to know, considering they currently traveled through the Were's forests. She glanced over at Prince, who was actually awake and paying attention. "The Elves have kings and queens right?"

He nodded. "Yes, my parents."

Her mouth opened and closed but nothing came out. Why did she often forget he was truly a prince sometimes? Flustered she scrambled for something else to say. "Well I hope the Fey queen doesn't hear about Damon's rambling."

*The Fey don't have a queen. Not anymore.*

She stared at Garen in shock and then turned to Kei in surprise. How had she never heard this?

"Her death caused most of us to go wild," Kei said, looking away from her. The pain on his face broke her heart.

"I don't understand," she admitted. "How?"

Kei simply shook his head. She turned to Garen, however it was Prince who answered.

"The Fey have always been ruled by a queen. No king. If she took a mate, he became merely her consort. The Fey queen was very powerful, powerful enough to keep the fury of her people in check."

"If she was so powerful then how did she die?"

"Garen?" Prince looked to the Were.

*You may tell it, if you wish.*

"Tell what?" She looked back and forth between the two.

89

"The story of the Queens."

"Very well," Prince frowned for a moment. "First I should point out it was known the Fey queen controlled her people. Precautions were in place to protect her, and also she always had a named Heir, who could take her place immediately should something happen.

"Centuries ago all our people got along well. The Queens would on occasion meet in secret. No one knows what they discussed. At their last meeting, the Fey queen also took her new heir, presumably to introduce her to the other queens. No one knows what happened at their meeting. Only that they all were killed."

"Wait. All of them? All the queens?"

Prince nodded solemnly. "Yes. The Fey queen and her heir, the Were queen, and the Elven queen, my grandmother."

She blinked in shock. "That's...horrible."

Prince looked down at his hands. "Yes. It heralded a horrible time. None knew where the meeting took place. It is still not known. There was no way to discover what happened or trace who could have committed the act."

"How did everyone find out then?"

"The Fey knew immediately," Prince answered. "Their fury overtook most of them. Only the strongest remained sane. Thousands died in the rampage which followed. Their city was nearly destroyed and later abandoned. They blamed the Elves and Were. We too knew of our queens death by magical means, we blamed the Fey and Were."

*And the Were, being telepathic, knew of our queen's death as well.*

"Many died before all sides understood all the queens had been killed."

"Wither me," she muttered, picturing the destruction and death which must have occurred.

"My grandfather died in the fighting," Prince revealed, his voice quiet. "Thus my parents inherited the throne."

They all sat in silence for a moment. She simply didn't know what to say.

"That's why it wouldn't be a bad thing," Kei finally said, his voice quiet and tentative.

"What wouldn't?" She turned to look at him in surprise.

His cheeks flushed in the firelight. "If we had a queen, we'd be whole again."

"Oh." She didn't know what to say to that. Did he truly want her to be his queen? How insane was that? Maybe they'd all lost their minds. She'd begun to wonder about hers. Another thought came to her and she reached out to take Kei's hand. "But it doesn't have to be me. You know I'll do whatever I can to help the Fey heal. I think…what Damon's been saying, what the prophecies are saying, is that it will happen soon though. I'm here, we're all here. Things are in motion now."

Kei pulled her forward and held her tightly. "You're right," he mumbled, tears choking his words. He buried his face into her neck, hiding it from the others.

She held him and stroked his hair. "Soon, Kei."

He nodded against her. *Even if you aren't my queen, I will still stay with you. I meant it when I promised you forever.*

Her breath caught and she smiled slightly, tears forming in her own eyes. *Or I'll stay with you. We'll figure it out when the time comes.*

Her heart sang with joy. She might lose Prince, but she would always have Kei. Though her love for him was different, she did love him, and knowing he would always be by her side made everything suddenly better. She would never be alone again.

Jen Wylie

# Chapter 8:
## More Human than Human

"You healed fast," Kei noted as she jogged next to him through the trees.

Frowning, she glanced over at him. "I'd only twisted it."

His answer was a faint, worried smile she didn't understand. She let it go and focused instead on keeping an eye out for dinner.

She'd spent two days on and off the horse. By the third, her ankle had healed enough she could not only walk, but dart about and even run for a while. That had suited her just fine. Now Bo could have her horse and they could travel faster.

Prince seemed the same. He hadn't gotten any better, but he hadn't gotten any worse either. She could deal with that. It was one less thing to worry about anyway. She had too many things on her mind. Would they get him home before he faded away? Which route would be fastest? What would they do about the human army? When she wasn't worrying about all of that she struggled with her feelings for him. Kei's talk of it being a good thing she might be the Fey queen didn't help her nerves either. Her mind had turned into a chaotic mess.

Running felt good. Running with Kei felt right. She glanced over at him, smiling to see he looked so free and happy. The sun and shadows played across his face and spikey hair as he ran amidst the trees. For a moment she thought how perfect it would be if they could just run forever and have no worries at all.

*We still need to talk.*

She raised her eyebrows and looked over at Kei. He rarely used mind speech if he could talk instead. She slowed and then stopped. They were alone. She assumed he meant he wanted to talk now.

She hadn't forgotten how Kei had said they needed to talk after she had killed the soldier attacking Prince. Kei didn't like to speak a lot, so she'd let him bring it up when he was ready.

He stood in front of her, squinting up into the trees and looking decidedly uncomfortable.

Her stomach tightened in worry over what he wanted to talk to her about. "What is it?"

His gaze moved to the ground, some of his light brown hair falling over his face. Biting his lip he shook his head slightly.

"Kei? You're scaring me." She took a step toward him.

"Don't take my fury anymore."

She blinked at him in surprise and waited silently for him to say more. He didn't. "Why?"

A pained looked crossed his face and he glanced up at her, his beautiful golden eyes glowing faintly. "When you attacked the soldier...you were so...furious." A frustrated growl rumbled from his chest. "I'm afraid. Of what it's doing to you."

She shook her head in confusion. "But I didn't–" She stopped. The night before she had taken some of his fury into her. She'd forgotten about that. "It wasn't very much," she continued. "I don't mind–"

Kei growled again and grasped at his hair, turning from her to pace angrily. "You don't understand! You get so angry sometimes. It's not like you."

"But–"

"You're not Fey!"

His sudden outburst left her at a loss for words. She just shook her head, trying to figure out what he was talking about.

He rushed toward her, stopping to grab her shoulders roughly and lock his eyes with hers. "You're not Fey," he repeated more quietly. "Yet you are healing faster. You run faster and fight quicker. For some reason you can speak to Were and build walls in your mind. Even Fey don't do that. You can take my fury. You somehow made us all a Were pack. Do you understand? You are human. You aren't meant to have our power. I don't know what I've done to you. What my power has changed in you...I don't..." His choked words stopped and he leaned forward, resting his forehead against hers.

His fearful, frantic tone sent a chill down her spine. Put into words and all together, the little changes weren't so little anymore. Garen's question suddenly echoed in her mind; Are you human?

Kei's arms wrapped around her, pulling her tightly against him. "Please, Aro."

Resting her head against his, she held him just as tightly. "I'm fine. I am."

"Promise me."

She hesitated for a moment. "I promise I won't unless you need me to."

His growl shuddered through his entire body.

She pulled back to look at him. "I won't risk losing you again. If you can't break free, then I'll do it again."

"I can control it now," he insisted.

"I won't promise never to do it again. I won't."

His eyes flashed to orange. "I can't lose you either," he whispered.

The words tore at her heart. She understood. Knowing he felt the same way for her as she did for him meant more than she could say. "We'll be careful. Everything will be fine." She smiled slightly. "At least I can keep up with you now, and I'm not nearly as breakable."

"This isn't a game."

"No," she agreed. "But what's done is done and I don't regret any of it."

Her words clearly startled him and he stared frozen at her for a long moment before the light in his eyes suddenly dimmed and a brilliant smile lit his face instead. He held her tightly again, nearly crushing her. "My Aro."

She squeezed him back as hard as she could. "My Fey."


*Aro? Kei? Garen?* Bo's voice called faintly.

*Yes? What's wrong?*

*Nothing. Time to stop and rest. Meet at the rocks by the river.*

She glanced up through the trees, surprised to see the sun high in the sky. After their emotional talk she and Kei had continued with their scouting. *On our way!*

She heard Garen and Kei also confirm and with a small smile to the Fey they turned and headed back to the river they'd passed earlier. It had been one of the largest they'd come across yet. She wondered if it had fish in it.

When they returned they found Garen resting in the sun by the tethered horses.

"Where's everyone else?"

*Bo is using the bushes. Prince is by the river. He seems tired today.*

She nodded and frowned, turning to look toward the rushing water. She couldn't see Prince, but perhaps the many trees lining its shore hid him.

She and Kei rummaged through the packs, finding some cooked corn on the cob left over from the night before and some summer berries collected that morning to serve as a meal.

Bo rejoined them. "We've eaten, but take your time." He glanced toward the river.

She fought to finish eating despite her sudden lack of appetite. Was Prince fading again?

"We could try fishing," Kei said into the silence. He and Bo, and even Garen, began discussing where to look for fish, and what other food they might find near the river.

Choking down the last of the berries she licked her fingers clean. "I'm going to see how Prince is doing."

"Have a rest, too," Bo told her. "You don't want to injure that ankle again." He rested a hand on her shoulder. "We've made good time."

She nodded and headed for the river. She didn't see Prince so went to the water's edge and carefully washed her hands and face. If she had berries smeared on her chin he'd be certain to admonish her for it. The thought brought forth a smile.

A noise downstream startled her and she jerked up, head snapping toward the sound.

Prince was not resting by the bank as she'd supposed, but knelt at the river's edge, cleaning up in the crisp waters. Frowning, she walked over to his side and stopped.

He glanced up at her, but then went back to scrubbing his bare arms. He'd tossed his shirt next to him beside his floppy hat. He didn't wear it now, alone as they were in the woods, but he kept it near just in case.

Her eyes, however, were drawn to the scars on his back. Though fully healed, they stood out sharply on his fair skin. Covering from shoulder almost to his waist, more also streaked down the outsides of both arms to his elbows. Most looked new and pink, some were darker grooves in his skin, others lighter ridges.

When the slave ship had crashed into rocks and sunk they'd had to swim to shore. The rocks in the waters had not been kind. Her eyes skipped to the scars she had on the back of her hands, they were much like his. The only reason she had so few was because he'd held her in his arms, keeping her safe from the rocks and from drowning altogether. Other than her hands, her only other scar was a deep one high on her forehead when she'd been struck by a piece of debris.

She reached out a hand, wanting to trace the marks down his back, but then stopped and pulled it back. "Do they bother you?"

He looked up, water dripping from his hair into eyes. Brushing it away he frowned, and then noticed her staring. "No. It was a necessary sacrifice at the time."

She blinked, opened her mouth and then closed it again, unsure what to say to that.

He'd gone back to scrubbing dirt off his hands. "Since the slavers took my amulet, I knew I had to conserve what power I had left. Healing my broken arm was more important, so I allowed the scars."

"I see," she said quietly. Her mind turned that information over and about, trying to make sense of it. "Wait, you can heal like the Fey?" Kei healed quickly, very quickly, and with no scarring.

He glanced up at her again, his brows drawn down in confusion. "Of course. As do the Were." When he noted her confusion he continued, "It takes power to do so."

She dropped to her knees and grabbed his shoulder, roughly turning him to face her. Her lips hardened into a thin angry line when, as she'd suspected, the wounds he'd taken fighting to escape the besieged city were gone.

They were quite simply not there. Her eyes lifted to meet his. "Why did you do that?"

His brows rose. "Heal my wounds?"

She nodded and sat back, crossing her arms.

"I had the power to do so."

"I don't know how much we gave you!" She shook her head, trying to keep her sudden fury contained. "Are you trying to kill yourself? We have no idea how this Were power works, how much you'll have or for how long. How could you waste it like this?"

"Waste it?" He brushed water off his arms and stood angrily. "They pained me, and were draining. I did not want to risk infection and having to deal with sickness."

"But the scars–"

"They were few and small. It did not take a lot of power to be rid of them."

She scrambled to her feet. "And you are a prince."

"That has nothing to do with it."

She raised her chin. "What will your people say, seeing you scarred like this?"

"Very few will ever see them," he said calmly. He shook his head slightly. "What is making you so angry?"

His words were like a slap. Kei's worry about her growing anger, about her changing, came back to her. "You don't seem to want to make it home," she finally whispered. "Are you intentionally sabotaging our efforts?"

Laughter sprang out of him, startling her so much she took a step back.

"Oh, Arowyn. You do have the strangest ideas."

"I don't understand you sometimes," she muttered.

"You are not an Elf," he said in amusement.

She had no idea what he found so funny. His reminder she was merely a human twisted her gut. Her cheeks warmed slightly and she looked away. "The boys have gone upstream to fish, should you want to join them." Before he could answer, she turned and walked quickly away.

Jen Wylie

# Chapter 9:
# Stormy Weather

Walking around the general area calmed her down. She took her frustrations and confusion out by stomping and muttering to herself. It wasn't at all a mature reaction, which made her even more frustrated. Being stuck between a child and an adult made her want to scream. She didn't, if only because she didn't want to attract any attention to them.

They traveled in woods ruled by Fey and Were. Humans were forbidden on pain of death. Despite Garen and Kei's comments, she was still human, and so was Bo. Meeting the inhabitants of the forest was the last thing they wanted to do. Garen had been clear on that, and so had Prince. They'd kept as close to the forest border as they could.

She found a few edible plants and collected them to add to their supplies. Keeping close to the forest's edge helped with their supplies at least. Kei or Garen often made runs to the edge to see what crops they were passing. If it hadn't been harvested already, they grabbed as much as they could.

Bo called her back, later than she'd have thought if they were going to set out, but there was still a lot of light left in the day for foraging if they were going to stay and make camp.

"What's the word?"

"We're heading out again." The way Bo wouldn't meet her eyes worried her.

"What's wrong?"

"Storm coming," Kei said quietly, jerking his head in the direction of the sea. Before she could open her mouth again he added, "Bad one."

She nodded once and put what she'd collected into the packs. "Is there shelter nearby then?"

Garen sat next to her. *It has been a very long time since I was this far south and I am not very familiar with the land. I do remember it gets rockier very quickly. There will be outcrops, cliffs, ravines. Perhaps we can find a cave.*

She supposed that would have to do. It wasn't like they'd come across a small house. "But what if we can't find something? Wouldn't it be better to use the time to make a shelter now?"

"The storm comes quickly," Prince answered, pulling himself up onto the horse. "We are moving further into the forest."

"What!" She turned sharply to look at Bo. "You know that's not safe for us, right? We're lucky Garen is the only Were we've met."

Bo grimaced and scratched at the long scar on his cheek. "I know, pup. But Garen and Prince say the further we head toward the mountains, the more likely we'll find decent shelter."

"Come, Aro. We need to get moving."

She glared over at Prince. "Just for the record, I don't like this one bit."

"Understood," he said sharply, clearly beginning to lose patience with her. "You can ride with me or run, but we need to go now."

Pressing her lips tightly together to keep from saying something she shouldn't, she turned on her heel and took off toward the west.

*This way.* Garen quickly bounded ahead of her, and a moment later Kei ran by her side.

# Broken Prince

*What's wrong?*

She didn't glance over at Kei, they were running quite quickly through the trees and she didn't want to trip. The trees were large here, and though much of the area was in shadow and free of thick undergrowth, some places weren't and fallen branches were always something to be careful of.

It took her a while to decide what exactly she wanted to say. Kei didn't push. At least he had some patience. *I'm worried about going deeper. What if the Were find us?*

*They won't hurt you. I won't let them.*

His thought made her smile for a moment. *But there might be fighting. Someone could get hurt.*

*Don't worry. They will be taking shelter from the storm. The rain will wash our scent away. As soon as the storm passes we'll head out.*

Leaping over a branch, she held in a grimace. *But–*

*You should be worrying about the storm.*

*Getting wet won't kill us. We've been through storms before.*

*Not like this one.*

That put a stop to her rambling thoughts. Apparently they weren't about to get a summer shower. Kei was right, she should be thinking about the storm; what could go wrong and how to avoid stupid mistakes.

Weather could kill just as easily as a man could.

After running west for a time, Garen led them southwest. She was happy with the change. They were sort of still on course.

Prince and Bo pushed the horses as quickly as they could. Once the ground began to turn rocky, their pace noticeably slowed. Quickly enough the terrain turned even rockier.

*Spread out,* Garen said. *Search for caves, overhangs…anything that can provide shelter.*

The speed the storm moved in rather shocked her. They hadn't been searching long when the first buffets of wind began. Grey and black clouds soon rolled in the distance, moving quickly enough she ran more haphazardly from one outcrop to another.

Stopping a moment to catch her breath, she jumped as thunder cracked in the distance. Someone cursed in her mind.

*Will the horses bolt? Should we each get our packs?*

*Good idea,* Bo answered. *We'll put ours on now. If you or Kei see us, come and collect yours.*

Her mind murmured with everyone's agreement. She shook her head slightly. When everyone spoke at once it still got confusing.

Thick clouds turned midday dark as evening as they continued to search for shelter. Rain started to spit down, not hard, but the now driving wind made navigating between rocks and trees more difficult.

Half a dozen times she stopped herself from asking if anyone had found anything yet. They'd let her know when they did. This pack mind speech turned out to be rather helpful.

*I found a cave!* Kei's excitement made her trip. She barely managed to steady herself against a tree.

A grin split her face, and then she winced as everyone tried to get a location from him. She moved south, raising a hand to shield her eyes from the rain as she searched for anyone else. Visibility continued to worsen.

Worry began to knot her stomach as the rain fell harder. Finding the others might be harder than she thought. They didn't know the area and landmarks were almost useless. The few they could use now they couldn't even see because of the storm. Maybe splitting up had been a very bad idea.

Her clothes were soaked through already, her hair a tangled dripping mess. Over and over she wiped water from her eyes. The rain fell harder and she had to bow her head against it as she trudged along.

*Boys, I've no idea where I am, or where you are.*

*I see Bo and Prince,* Kei said. *As soon as they're here I'll come for you.*

*I've the horses scent. For now.* Garen's annoyed growl echoed in her head. *I don't think I'm far behind though.*

She directed her thoughts to Kei only. *How will you find me?*

*I can always find you. Look for me with your heart and soul, Aro.*

His words made her stop in her tracks. They could find each other? Is that how he had tracked them last fall when the fury had taken him? Perhaps. Of course they hadn't tried to hide either.

She frowned. How did she look with her heart and soul? Kei spoke of the Fey magic they had done. Twice. They were friends, they were family. The Fey had a third binding, of mates, though she didn't have any inclination to do that one. What she and Kei had done wasn't really magic, at least not compared to what the Elves could apparently do. Fey bindings involved promises of intent. They were heart and soul magic. Whatever that meant.

Standing against a tree, trying to stay out of the driving wind and rain, she closed her eyes and thought of Kei. Other than the pack mind link, there was nothing. She couldn't get a direction from it either.

*I can't find you.*

*I'm coming. The others are here.*

*You should have told me about this before. We could have practiced!*

*I thought you knew. I'm sorry.*

The strangely sad undertones to his thought made her sigh. Shivering, she sniffed and got water up her nose. "Rotting rain!"

The tree proved to be less and less of a break against the storm. Grumbling in annoyance, she carefully struck out again, moving in the direction of the next outcrop of rock she'd seen. If she moved to the other side, at least it might block the raging wind.

Lightening lit the sky in the distance, but the worst of the storm hadn't even hit them yet. Finally she found some shelter behind a rock and hunkered down to wait.

*I hope you all are nice and dry,* she muttered at the others.

*Wait until you see the cave,* Bo answered. *It's huge, we even got the horses in. Someone has used it before. There's wood, and a fire pit. Even some–*

Kei's thought interrupted Bo. *I'm almost to you.*

Despite feeling like a drowned rat, and quite miserable, she smiled in relief. When he appeared out of the rain directly in front of her she still jumped and swung.

He caught her hand with a laugh and pulled her into a wet embrace. "Easy!"

Even with his mouth to her ear she could hardly hear him over the wind and rain. Squeezing him tightly to her for a moment, she then pulled back and slipped her hand into his. *Let's go get dry!*

He nodded and set off slowly, pulling her gently behind him.

*Is it far?*

*Not very. Terrain gets much worse though. Watch your steps.*

Proving his words, the ground quickly became rockier. Her legs started to ache as they went up and down increasingly steep and slippery slopes. Despite struggling up and around the rocks, she kept a hold of Kei's hand. For now, just having one free helped her enough.

*We're almost there.*

*Good! I'm freezing.* At least her mind voice wasn't affected by her chattering teeth.

*Just over–*

Kei's thoughts stopped abruptly. Before she could even blink her hand jerked and the ground collapsed beneath her feet.

Their wet hands slipped apart as the slope disintegrated beneath them into a muddy and rocky sliding mess. Screaming, she scrambled for something to hold on to, anything.

*Aro? What's wrong?*

She didn't have the concentration to answer Prince. Rocks and branches moved along with her as she continued to twist and slide. Just as a full blown panic began to set in she slipped to the left and stopped.

"Kei!" He didn't answer. *Kei!*

*Are you hurt?*

*I don't think so. Are you?*

*I'm stuck.*

*I'm coming!*

Spitting mud, she tried to wipe it from her face. Her eyes stung and she tilted her head up, raising her hands as well to let the downpour clean the mud away. Rubbing her eyes clean, she twisted and turned, trying to free herself from the mud and debris.

"Wither me," she grumbled, finally getting free and staggering to her feet. She collapsed again as pain shot up her leg. "Rot it all!" She'd hurt her ankle again.

Gritting her teeth against the pain, she stood again, keeping her weight on her good foot. She saw Kei not far from her and took a step toward him. She sank into the mud up her knee and fell again.

Prince's panicked voice startled her. *Aro! What's wrong?*

Letting out a sigh of frustration, she gritted her teeth for a moment. *A slope gave way and we got washed down. Kei's stuck in the mud.*

*Can you get him out?*

*I think so.*

Giving up on walking, she crawled over to Kei. His eye's glowed orange, little beacons of light. She found him pinned between a branch and a rock, one arm stuck behind him, the other trapped to the side by the branch. With some grunts and curses she managed to free him quickly enough.

*Thank you.*

*Anything broken?*

*No.*

She smiled in relief. *Silly Fey. You shouldn't play in the mud.*

*Not funny.* His lips twitched as he held back a smile.

With a jerk, she helped pull him upright and they both started crawling toward the sloped they'd just fallen down. Once they reached the bottom she looked up and laughed.

A very wet and bedraggled Prince stood at the top, hands on his knees as he stared down at them.

*Need help up?*

She glanced over at Kei and raised her eyebrows.

*You didn't answer him quickly enough. I told him where we were.*

Kei started to climb up the bank and then turned and offered her his hand. Limping and gritting her teeth, she managed to make it up. At the top Prince reached down, grabbing her other hand and pulling her all the way up.

*You hurt your ankle again.*

*It will heal.*

She sputtered a bit when he slipped his arm around her, forcing her to lean on him and take weight off her ankle.

He frowned down at her but didn't comment.

Kei led the way and she pressed her lips together in annoyance to see, though he wasn't really limping, he was walking stiffly. He might not have any broken bones, but he was certainly at least badly bruised from the fall.

She felt pangs across her whole body as well. However, the burning in her ankle distracted her from them for the most part.

Prince shifted, slipping his arm around her more, taking more of her weight. Resigned to being coddled, she didn't complain. She would have done the same for him.

She fell, so quickly she didn't even have time to scream. The drop was much shorter this time, but she hit so hard her breath whooshed out of her. Everything abruptly disappeared.

Jen Wylie

# Chapter 10:
# Wake Up

*Wake up. Wake up. Please, wake up. Wake up...*

The words filtered into the calm darkness surrounding her. Wake up? Had she fallen asleep? She didn't remember...

Opening her eyes, it was startling to see a fortress before her. Her fortress, the one she'd built in her mind. Rebuilt actually. After the Dragos Damon had torn down the first one. Over the long summer months Prince had stayed true to his word and helped her rebuild her defenses.

It was an impressive sight now, and even she was amazed at how large and daunting it had turned out. She frowned at the dark rolling sky and bleak barren landscape around it. How would she ever change that? If only she could find some happiness, if the people she loved would stop dying...

*Arowyn!*

She twisted around quickly. *Garen?* Blinking at him in surprise, she shook her head in confusion. *What are you doing here?* He hadn't been in her mind since the time she'd needed to show him what Bo looked like.

*Please, forgive me for coming uninvited.* He bowed slightly, but not before she caught the worried look on his young, handsome face.

He looked older than the last time, or perhaps she just wasn't remembering right? One day she'd have to ask him how

111

old he really was. At first she'd thought near her age, but she doubted that now. Getting to know him, she'd realized he spoke like someone much older. He knew too much.

*You need to wake up,* he said quietly, walking toward her.

*I don't understand.* Again with the waking up. She turned her head to the side, listening. As if from very far away, she could still hear someone repeating the words over and over. *Do you hear that?*

His brows drew together and he frowned. *Hear what?*

She shook her head and looked away. *Nothing.*

*Please, wake up. We need you. We need our alpha. Everyone is worried. Prince is...* He paused a moment. *He's falling apart.*

Alpha? Prince was falling apart? Her mouth opened in surprise as she turned back to face him. She didn't understand. Words finally made it to her mouth. *I don't know what you're talking about.*

His face was so full of sadness it tore through her heart.

*Why didn't he come?* Garen looked away. She knew he understood she spoke of Prince. *Garen?*

*He is...too distraught. He won't let you go, he won't stop calling you. Wake up, wake up now.*

Before she could answer he faded away.

*Garen, wait!*

He was gone.

She looked back up at her fortress and then the darkness surrounding it.

*Wake up. Wake up!*

That voice continued to repeat itself. Was it really Prince?

Closing her eyes once more she concentrated on it, trying to grab ahold of it and pull herself closer.

# Broken Prince

Pain flared in the darkness as consciousness returned. Perhaps waking up wasn't such a great idea. The darkness didn't have this pain.

*Wake up. Wake up...*

The litany continued, pulling her forcefully into wakefulness. A groan whispered from her lips and she squeezed her eyes more tightly together. Her head hurt so much she thought she might be sick.

The faint sound of a sharply inhaled breath caught her attention. What happened? Her senses returned suddenly. She smelled wet wolf and smoke. Something heavy covered her, keeping her warm despite her soaked clothes. The sound of the storm was loud, but muffled. Closer to her she heard the crackle of a fire and murmured voices. Her head was pillowed on something that shifted beneath her.

Opening her eyes, she saw an arm and blinked rapidly, trying to focus beyond it.

Her vision finally began to clear and she tilted her head to stare up at Prince's worried face. Heat warmed her cheeks as she realized her head rested in his lap. Very gently, his fingers brushed along her cheek over and over again. Her brows drew together as she noticed the arm next to her face led to a hand pressing against the side of her forehead.

*Aro's awake!*

Garen's voice startled her and she winced as pain ripped through her head again.

"How do you feel?" Prince moved his hand from her cheek to stroke her hair, his touch feather light, yet...shaking?

"My head hurts," she whispered. "What happened?"

Someone took her hand and she turned her head to see Kei kneeling beside her. "You fell."

"I fell?" She didn't remember falling.

"Actually, I fell," Prince said gravely. "You went down with me and hit your head on a rock."

113

That made more sense at least. She raised her free hand, her fingers gliding up Prince's arm to rest over his hand.

"You hit hard," Kei said quietly.

She tried to pull Prince's hand away.

"No, Aro. You are still bleeding. I need to keep pressure on it."

"Is it bad?"

"You'll have a new scar next to your other one."

Closing her eyes, she let out a resigned breath. "Wonderful." Just what she needed, more scars.

"The cut is higher," Kei said quickly. "Your hair will still cover it."

"Once the bleeding slows we'll clean you up and take care of it."

She blinked as her vision blurred again. "Are you hurt?"

Prince smiled slightly. Was it just her imagination his lips quivered before the smile quickly faded? "Just a few bruises. Nothing to worry about."

Her eyes closed on their own. She was so tired. Her head pounded and nausea twisted her stomach.

"No sleeping," Prince said quickly. He pulled his hand back from her head and she gasped at the blood soaked cloth. "It is slowing. Sit up, slowly."

Kei helped her and she gritted her teeth against the urge to vomit. Spots danced in front of her eyes.

Prince placed the cloth back on her head. "Hold this." He got up and moved through the cave, gathering items from one of the packs. She watched him quietly as the room spun around her.

Bo brought over their small pot filled with water. "How you doing, pup?"

She forced a small smile. "I'll be fine."

"Good girl."

Kei took the pot and another cloth, motioning for her to lower her hand. Bo took the bloody piece and Kei started cleaning her forehead. Closing her eyes, she held her hands fisted in her lap and concentrated on taking small, even breaths.

By the time he finished Prince returned with a small bowl full of a purple paste. She almost smiled, remembering how he'd made it to treat their cuts when they'd washed up on the beach.

"We should get her cleaned up, before you put that on," Kei said.

Prince paused and then nodded. They all regarded her thoughtfully for a moment.

She took in her soaked and mud covered clothes. "Help me up," she said to Kei, holding out her hands. He did, and she managed to stand without throwing up. Little breaths. "It'd be easier to wash up in the rain."

Kei paused and looked at Prince, after a moment he nodded. His arm around her, Kei slowly walked her to the cave entrance. The ground seemed to tilt and move beneath her and she leaned against him, clenching his arm tightly. Leaning against the stone mouth of the cave, she stood patiently while he undid and then removed her boots, followed by her socks. The stone felt wet and cool beneath her bare feet.

"How's your ankle?"

She blinked down at him in surprise as he carefully felt around the area.

"It's not swollen."

Now that he mentioned it, there was a dull ache, but it didn't hurt nearly as bad as the first time. "It hardly hurts at all."

Her eyebrows went up as he stood again and regarded her warily. A small, rough laugh escaped her before she could stop it. "Boys." She pulled her arms out of her shirt. "Help me get it over my head?"

Kei nodded and did as instructed. He let her hold his arm as she shucked off her pants, leaving her just in her underclothes. Shivering in the cool, stormy air, she looked down at the pile of muddy clothes.

"I'll clean them later."

"Thanks. Help me outside?" Warmth spread across her cheeks. "I'm feeling a bit dizzy."

He was at her side again in an instant. She latched onto his arm and he led her out into the pouring rain. It didn't take long to clean off the remaining mud. Kei struggled to hold her at arm's length and still keep her upright. Though he helped swish the mud off her arms and legs he didn't touch anywhere else. She checked that the ties on the wide band of cloth across her chest remained secure. The last thing she need was it falling off. Once finished, Kei quickly guided her back into the cave.

Prince met them just inside and tucked a large fur around her. Bo had set up a pile of furs by the fire and gestured to them as they approached.

"Where did they come from?"

"They were here. We might as well use them. They seem fairly clean."

Kei settled her down and draped another of the furs around her shoulders. The heat of the fire began to warm her immediately. She hoped her underclothes dried quickly.

Prince knelt in front of her. His eyes searched hers for a long moment.

"What are you doing?"

A frown crossed his lips and then he shook his head. "How is your vision?"

"Fine?"

He nodded and then pushed some wet hair away from her face. Some fell back over her wound and he scowled at it. She watched in amazement as he got up and moved to sit behind her. Fingers slowly worked through her hair, getting the worst of the tangles out. It felt…strange. Strange and good.

She kept her eyes on the fire's dancing flames, hoping everyone thought the heat rising up her neck and across her face came from it.

A smile played across her lips as he carefully pulled back her hair and started to braid it. She found it difficult not to make a comment, yet somehow managed. Could he hear her heart thumping away in her chest?

He finished all too soon and returned to kneel before her again. It didn't take long to apply the purple paste. She watched his face as he did, resisting the urge to reach out and touch those lips so firmly pressed together in concentration.

His eyes met hers and his shaky smile appeared for a moment before he turned away. "We need to get cleaned up as well. If you want to…" He made a turnaround motion with a finger.

Carefully, she shifted herself back from the fire and turned to face the wall. Garen padded over and flopped down in front of her.

*I will keep you company.*

She smiled. *Thank you.* It would be some time before the men were cleaned up and their clothes dried by the fire. She wouldn't be turning around for a while. Too much skin tended to make her blush like a stupid girl. So did Prince, for that matter.

She only hesitated for a moment before asking, *What's wrong with Prince?*

Garen shifted slightly and then looked over her shoulder. It took him a while to reply. *He feels responsible for your injury. Despite us all telling him it was merely an accident. He said, since the beginning he had promised himself to take care of you, yet has done a poor job of it.*

*That's not true at all.* She let out a soft sigh and resisted looking behind her. The sounds of the men stripping and cleaning up by the cave mouth were enough to deter her. *He has strange ideas sometimes. I really don't understand him.*

Garen turned his gaze back to her. *He couldn't wake you. There was so much blood. Kei nearly went into a fury. We were all worried.*

*I'm sorry.* She worried her bottom lip between her teeth. *Is he angry with me?*

*You truly do not understand, Aro. It is rare for Elves to show such emotion. Particularly an Elven Prince.*

Despite the throbbing pain, she could only shake her head slightly. The motion made her wince. She didn't understand. With Prince, it seemed like she never did. One moment it seemed she meant more to him than just a friend, the next she was just an irritation. Constantly, he both lifted her heart and dashed it to pieces.

He cared about her, she knew that. But was it only the caring for a child? Had he yet noticed she wasn't a little girl? If only he would let her know how he truly felt about her. She would have to wait and hope. She didn't have the strength or confidence to ask him. Unfortunately she knew time wasn't on her side.

# Chapter 11:
# Uninvited Guests

The boys returned to the fire and she heard someone moving about cooking. She hoped they'd put some clothes on. Since she wasn't invited to turn around again, she doubted it. Men were impossible.

She talked about nothing with Garen for a while until a plate of food suddenly appeared over her shoulder.

"Thanks," she managed. Not looking. Not looking. "You boys almost dried off yet?"

"Soon, pup," Bo answered with a chuckle.

She picked at her food. Though the nausea had finally settled, she feared it would return. She hated being sick to her stomach and preferred to avoid it. Eating slowly helped to pass the time as well. Once she did finally finish, long after everyone else, she set her plate to the side.

"The leathers are mostly dry," Kei called.

Waiting patiently, she listened to the sounds of leather pants being slipped on. Garen chuckled in her mind, watching her flaming cheeks. "You're not helping," she muttered.

His ears flicked back and forth. *It is safe now.*

"Finally! You all decent?" She wasn't sure she wanted to trust the Were. Hearing assent from them all, she turned and wiggled closer to the fire.

Prince sat next to her spot, watching her carefully.

She stared back at him, watching the firelight flicker across his face. "What is it?" She ran a hand over her chin. "Do I have food on my face?"

He smiled faintly and looked away. "No."

Pain lanced through her head and she closed her eyes. Her stomach rolled and she clenched her teeth, taking shallow, even breaths. She shouldn't have eaten so much.

Kei settled down next to her on the other side. "Head still hurt?"

"Yes," she grumbled. "I think I ate too much, too."

"You should get some sleep."

"No. She shouldn't sleep," Prince snapped.

They all looked over at him, surprised at the vehemence in his voice.

"Why shouldn't I sleep?"

"You hit your head very hard."

"She's in pain. Rest will help," Kei said.

"What do you know? No. She might not wake up again if she does."

Her eyes widened. "I might not wake up?"

"You're scaring her!"

"I'm trying to protect her! What will you do if she goes to sleep and won't wake? Bind her again?"

*Bind her?*

The fighting stopped abruptly at Garen's question.

Prince sighed and shook his head. "Kei and Aro are bound together with one of the Fey bindings."

Garen looked from Prince to Kei and back again. *She is human. It's not done. Why would you allow this?*

"She was sick. It was the only way to save her. We'd already lost Avery and..." Prince pressed his lips together angrily. "Kei offered. It was the only way to save her."

Aro stared worriedly at Prince. Did he realize he was repeating himself? Was he trying to convince Garen or himself?

# Broken Prince

Garen turned his gaze to her and Kei. *That explains much. Do you know what you've done?*

"Yes, and I'd do it again," Kei answered firmly.

*I don't think we should mention that was the second time,* she said only to Kei.

His faint smile was slightly pained. *No. I told you no one would understand.* His fingers found hers and curled around them.

*I do. That's enough.*

*Yes. It is.*

"Can I sleep or not? I'm exhausted and my head is killing me."

"If we check on her often, that should do," Bo said into the silence. "She'll have to sleep sometime."

Prince relented and she thankfully drifted off quickly into a deep sleep. It seemed like someone woke her constantly. They'd make her speak for a moment and then, apparently satisfied she still had her wits about her, would let her sleep again.

The next day the storm continued and she spent most of it sleeping, waking up fully only a few times to dress, eat and do the necessary.

The absence of sound woke her. Staring up at the ceiling of the cave, she listened carefully as her mind struggled to wake up. The storm had stopped raging. Yes, that was it. She could hear dripping, but the wind had calmed as well. The fire crackled. One of the horses shifted. Panic tickled up her spine for a moment until she felt the warmth of a body to either side of her. They hadn't left her alone. From across the fire, Bo let out a loud snore.

Rolling carefully onto her stomach, she looked out the cave mouth. She rubbed at her eyes, trying to clear her blurry vision. It wasn't dark out, but the sky remained grey. Perhaps the boys had decided to get rest while they could, or boredom had gotten the better of them.

The pain in her head hadn't gone away. Gingerly she reached up and touched where she'd hit. Her fingers found a huge raised lump. No wonder her head hurt so much. Wine or ale certainly started to sound good. She'd rarely been allowed to drink much, but she knew it could dull pain good enough.

The clattering of rocks outside caught her attention and she turned toward the cave mouth again. A giant wolf bounded inside.

Garen?

Another followed, and then another. Either that or she was seeing double...triple. No, there was another.

"Wither me."

The Were had found them.

She hunched back into the furs as they lined up in front of her, hackles raised and teeth bared. Fear froze her in spot. All she could do was stare at the horrifying scene before her.

Garen bounded over her, landing lightly before her, facing the other Were. Kei and Prince scrambled out of the furs to either side of her, instantly alert and grabbing weapons.

She sat up, furs sliding off her shoulders, and immediately fell to the side. Catching herself on her forearm she grunted in surprise. Apparently her balance was still off.

Using her arms, she pulled herself around and saw her weapons by her feet. With a push, she got closer and reached, but her hands couldn't find what her eyes saw. With a curse, she tried to pull herself forward.

"Aro!"

She turned her head to see Kei glaring at her.

"Stay back."

Shaking her head sent a lance of pain through her brain and she groaned, lowering her head to her arms. This wasn't happening. They needed her!

If the Were spoke she didn't hear them. If the boys spoke through their pack bond she didn't hear that either. The thought choked the breath out of her and she forced her head up to look over at them all again. Searching her mind, she couldn't find the link. What was going on? A whimper slipped through her lips. Why was it gone? She needed it! How would she talk to Garen?

Everything blurred and she blinked her eyes frantically. They had started fighting, the cave filling with echoing shouts and growls. The horses panicked. Their terrified whinnies and the clacks of their prancing hooves on the stone added to the clamor.

The chaos of sound sent painful vibrations through her head. Squeezing her eyes closed, she gritted her teeth. Sweat beaded on her forehead and trickled down her back. Someone shouted in pain.

She needed to get up. She needed to help them.

"Rot it all," she muttered and tried to push herself up again. Her arms refused to work and she flopped back down onto her stomach.

The noise of snarls, snapping teeth and claws on stone and metal overwhelmed her senses. She made it up onto her forearms and looked up again…right into a snarling face. The Were stood so close she could feel each breath on her skin.

Eyes widening in terror, she could only stare at the massive teeth dripping spittle onto the stone.

As suddenly as it appeared, it was gone. With a blink of surprise she watched it fly to the side and crash into a wall, Kei, in full fury, attached to its side.

Prince dropped down beside her. "Get up, Aro." He yanked the fur still over her legs off in one swift motion and then held out his hand.

She reached for it, or tried to. Her arms and eyes still didn't seem to agree. Embarrassment heated her cheeks and she glanced up at Prince. "I…I…can't seem to…"

He stared at her, his eyes widening in shock. With a slight shake of his head, his brows drew down in worry as he tried to catch her flailing hand. He opened his mouth to speak, but before words left his lips one of the Were let out an ear piercing howl.

Aro gasped as the sound blasted through her head. Her body jerked and–

She opened her eyes, surprised to find herself in Prince's arms, her body across his lap. The taste of blood filled her mouth. Blinking she turned her head. Everyone still fought.

"Waz hap?" What happened? But those words hadn't come out of her mouth. Her eyes grew wide in horror and fear.

"You had a seizure." Prince choked and held her tightly, rocking her gently back and forth. "I am sorry. I am so sorry. Please forgive me. Forgive me."

She didn't understand. "Rince?" Her lips trembled and she blinked as he became blurry and then back into focus.

"I am sorry." He continued his quiet litany, bowing his head over her.

She remembered then, he thought her injury was his fault. Somehow she managed to raise her hand. Grasping wildly, it found one of his. He looked down at it as she squeezed it tightly and drew it up to her chest. She tried to tell him it wasn't his fault but the sounds that came out made no sense.

A tear slipped down his cheek as he shook his head. His whole body trembled. "Arowyn, Arowyn…"

Pain of a different kind overcame her. Her sight blurred again, this time from tears. She tried to raise her hand to wipe his tears away. She'd broken her prince.

A blast of wind wiped through the cave. The ground rumbled beneath them. Dirt and small rocks fell from the ceiling. Prince quickly bent over her, shielding her from them.

Turning her head, she watched a monstrous head enter the cave and let out a bellowing roar. The fighting stopped, the force of the sound sending everyone scattering to the cave sides.

Prince gripped her tighter as she stared. She knew that head, that roar. "'aym! N-n-n. D-d-d…" It was impossible.

"Damon," Prince whispered.

She blinked, amazed he'd understood her. Yet he wasn't looking at her, he watched the dragon. Perhaps he knew what Damon looked like in dragon form, too.

The head retreated. Damon walked into the cave a moment later, looking extremely displeased. The Were backed away, coming together near the cave entrance, but not leaving.

She watched them closely. Whatever was being said, she couldn't hear it. Until it was gone, she hadn't realized how much she would miss the mind speech.

The Were apparently dealt with, he regarded the rest of them. Again, if more was said she couldn't hear it. When his eyes found her she felt nothing. His brows drew together. A laugh almost twisted her lips. Had she entirely lost her mind? Was there nothing there for him to find and invade? He took a step toward her and the others sprang into action.

They didn't attack…they ran to her side, taking up positions around her and Prince.

She held out her free arm, grimacing as it flopped in the air. "K-k…" Though she could barely make the first sound of his name, her eyes found him and pulled him to her. Kei took her hand and crouched by her head, his arm reaching around her shoulder.

"I'm here," he whispered.

For some reason his voice brought a strange calm and her rising panic began to subside.

Damon knelt before them.

"Will she get better? Will she…" Prince's voice trailed off.

Her eyes locked on Damon's face as he regarded her thoughtfully. His hand came up and she flinched as it rested on the top of her head. No pain came. She felt…nothing. If he tried to speak to her, she couldn't hear him.

"No," he said finally. "There has been damage to the brain. There is bleeding and swelling inside."

Prince's cry startled her, almost as much as the sudden clutching of his arms around her. "Can you do anything," he choked out. "Please, I am responsible. I cannot…I will pay–"

Damon chuckled. "It is not your life that needs saving." He stared at Prince for a long moment. "I see." He shook his head. "Perhaps I was wrong and she isn't the one. I read so few pages of the book." He turned to Kei.

"No," the Fey said. "I don't remember."

"Pity."

"Dragos, I beg of you," Prince began again.

"The Elven prince begs, and for a human. How very far you have fallen." He looked down at her again.

Blinking up at him, she tried to get her scattered thoughts to work. She'd barely comprehended what he'd said past the inference she was dying. The words sent an icy chill through her body. Terror crawled through her, speeding her heart. Sweat broke out on her forehead and all she could hear was her increasingly frantic breathing.

Kei startled her, leaning forward over her to press a kiss to her forehead. She tilted her head back, trying to see him.

"I'm with you."

Damon's fingers brushes her cheek, drawing her attention back to him. "Do you wish to live, young Arowyn?"

Words refused to pass her lips. Somehow she managed to nod. She didn't know what the cost would be, certainly there would be one. Right then, she didn't care. Rot it all, she wanted to live!

"Very well." He regarded her thoughtfully for a moment. "Dragos rarely heal others. I do know the magic, but it is difficult. Your story has barely begun. I find I would actually attempt it, just to see what you might become and how it will unfold."

He sat back and gestured to the pile of furs next to him. "Lay her down. This will take some time and I'll need no distractions."

Prince carefully set her amongst the furs, arranging her arms so her hands rested on her chest, tucking stray locks of hair behind her ears. Leaning forward, he rested his forehead for a moment against hers.

"Get well, Arowyn."

Bo appeared next, smoothing the hair back on the top of her head and squeezing one of her hands. "You can do this, pup."

Garen pressed his wet nose against her temple. If he spoke, she didn't hear him.

Kei pushed the wolf aside and took her face in his hands. His eyes glowed with that strange orange inner light. Tears streaked down his cheeks. Despite the awkward position he leaned down and held her close for a moment. "Remember our promises," he whispered in her. "I'm always with you." He choked on a sob and squeezed her tightly again. "I love you," he whispered fiercely before quickly pulling away.

She wished she could speak. More than anything, she wanted to tell him she loved him, too. She wanted to tell all of them she did. Tears filled her eyes and slid down her face.

Damon knelt beside her and turned her head to look at him. "I will do what I can," he said. "However I can't guarantee it will work. I have never tried to heal a human before. Understand?"

She managed a faint nod and pressed her quivering lips together.

He glanced up and gestured the others away. "Stand back and be silent." His eyes found hers again. "Don't fight me this time, little one. Fall into my eyes…"

Blinking once more to clear the tears away, she tried to do as he asked. Damon's eyes were strange enough she found it not difficult to stare. They had vertical slits and no whites at all. The iridescent color was a wash of blue-green with streaks of gold and red. The colors began to swirl, making her dizzy as she tried to watch them. A comforting thrum emanated from his chest, soothing her as his power wrapped around her. Her thoughts drifted into nothing.

# Chapter 12:
# The Price of Life

"How do you feel?"

Aro watched the swirling dark clouds for a moment longer before turning. Damon leaned against the stone of her mind's fortress, arms crossed and a satisfied smile on his handsome face.

"Nothing hurts," she said finally. Memories returned and she quickly tried to discover if she truly was better. She felt no pain. She didn't seem muddled and...she was back in her mind. Looking around quickly, everything appeared to be in order.

"Despite my doubts, the magic worked surprisingly well. You are completely healed."

She bowed her head to him. "Thank you," she said solemnly, meaning every word. He smiled in response and they stared at each other in silence. "I assume you are here to discuss the price," she said finally.

He chuckled and slowly clapped his hands. "You always surprise me, Arowyn. It may be the time is sooner than I thought. You are growing up so quickly." He tilted his head to the side, regarding her thoughtfully. "Perhaps that is the human part of you, you live such brief lives."

"Perhaps," she agreed vaguely. She didn't want to anger him, or get him started on the prophecy nonsense again. "The price?"

His strange eyes swirled. "What is your life worth?"

"I have no idea." She frowned, wondering what he game he played now.

"I know you don't believe in the prophecies. You don't need to, for them to come to pass. This does not concern me. Events will happen as they are meant to. I believe you will become the new Fey queen. With that title will come power, a great amount of power. Enough even, to rival my own."

"Is this why you won't leave me alone?"

He nodded slightly. "In part. You are in debt to me now. I have given you your life so you can become what you were meant to be. In return, you will one day grant me a favor."

"One?"

"Yes, just one."

"What, exactly, will you ask of me?"

He shook his head. "That I do not know."

Crossing her arms she looked away, thinking furiously. Finally she turned back to him. "I won't hurt anyone, or kill. Directly or indirectly."

His laugh was joyous. "Very good! That is acceptable. We are agreed then?"

She nodded. "What if I die before you collect?"

"Then I have lost my favor."

"What if I don't become queen?"

He shrugged. "Perhaps I will find something useful you can do for me. If not, I am not concerned."

"Then yes, I agree." She paused. "Do we need to make a written record of this?"

He laughed again. "No. You have given your word. You will honor it."

"I suppose I should wake up now. The others must be worried."

"I've told them it was successful, but yes, they do still worry." All trace of humor faded from his face. "Take care,

Arowyn. Others will learn of you soon, and you will gain enemies. Not everyone wishes the Fey to rise again."

She grimaced. Enemies were the last thing she needed. She had a hard enough time staying alive as it was.

"Don't stop being yourself. Your friends may call you troublesome and impulsive, but it is natural instinct that guides you. Because of this you have survived. You are young and full of life. Live that life to its fullest."

Looking at him strangely, she forced a smile and nodded. Why did he speak as if he were her father?

"It is time for me to take my leave once more. Are you ready for my parting words of advice?"

"Oh, yes," she said dryly. "I always love those."

He chuckled at her sarcasm. "Yet still I give them to you, in case you ever care to listen. Your prince is fading again. The remorse of almost losing you is breaking him apart. He still feels responsible. Take care of him, if you can. Be wary of the Were. I would get out of their territory as soon as possible."

She nodded, the last made sense at least. As for Prince, she didn't know what she could do to help him any more than she had. Her options had run out. "Is that all?"

"The human army has moved north for now. If you move quickly, you should be able to travel along the border to the gate undisturbed."

"Thank you," she said, again meaning it. That information she could use.

"We will meet again, little one. Until then, safe travels." He withdrew from her mind, his form disappearing. "Wake up!"

Despite Damon's parting mental shout, she did not wake up immediately, or so the others told her. She slept peacefully for some time, waking only when darkness had

131

fallen and dinner was ready. After too many hugs and coddling, they teased her about that. It didn't really bother her; she lived, and had her family around her.

"So what's the word?" She looked around the fire as she chewed. "What did I miss? Was anyone hurt?"

"We're all good, pup," Bo answered. "Those Were certainly gave us a good fight though."

"What were they saying? I couldn't hear anything at all." She grimaced and turned to Garen. *I missed hearing you.*

He lowered his head. *I as well. It was a shock, when you never answered.*

*I'm sorry.*

*You can hear me again. All is well now.*

"What did they want?"

"The usual," Bo replied again. "We're trespassing, breaking laws, the humans must die."

She snorted.

*They were shocked, finding us all together,* Garen added.

"I imagine they were. It didn't stop them though?"

*No, which was strange. They did not even question me, they simply attacked.*

"And then Damon showed up. I remember that."

Kei bumped her shoulder from beside and she turned to look at him. "You saw him as a dragon?"

She nodded and grinned. "Impressive."

"Very," he agreed. "We saw a real dragon."

*It was my first time as well. Hopefully my last,* Garen said wryly.

"I wish he would have a waited a little longer," Bo said with a wicked grin. "I needed a bit of a fight." He cracked his knuckles.

"Don't do that!" Aro pointed at finger at him. "Your joints will swell."

He did it again, his grin widening.

"Men," she muttered. "So did you hear what Damon said to them?"

The others shook their heads and she ground her teeth. "That would have been helpful. Next, what happened to them after Damon healed me?"

"Nothing," Kei muttered.

She laughed and raised her eyebrows.

*Damon threatened them to leave us be and told them to return to their pack. They left without a backward glance.*

"Strange."

*Again, yes.*

"Damon told me not to trust them. Maybe he thought something was off, too. He said to get out of their territory as quickly as we could."

"We'll head back to the forest border at first light," Bo said. "If you're feeling up to it?"

She nodded. "I feel great."

"Aro and Bo should ride," Kei said. When they all looked at him he added, "No scent trail then."

They made plans to shift their supplies around and she would ride with Prince. Kei collected her empty plate and rose to start cleaning up.

She glanced over at Prince where he sat slumped on the other side of her, staring at his plate. "Prince?" She waved a hand in front of his face. "Eat your dinner."

He jerked and looked over at her slowly. She wondered if he had heard a word of their whole conversation. His blue eyes met hers. Such sorrow filled his pale face her lips suddenly trembled. His brilliant blue eyes were dark and haunted. He reached over and trailed the back of his fingers across her cheek.

"I failed you, my child," he whispered. "I…I am so sorry."

She took his hand and squeezed it tightly. Words caught in her throat. Taking a shaking breath, she squeezed his hand again. His sad eyes tore at her heart, almost as much as his words. "It wasn't your fault. Please, please," she quietly begged, "stop blaming yourself. I don't blame you at all. Understand? And I'm well now. You don't need to worry anymore."

He looked away and shook his head. Kei walked by and Prince raised his full plate.

Suddenly furious, she reached out and pushed his arm down. "Eat it!"

He sighed. "I am not hungry."

"I don't care," she snapped. "Stop acting like this." She sent her thoughts directly to him. *I need you, Prince. You have to keep up your strength. We have a long way to go yet.*

His gaze returned to the plate and slowly, he started to eat. She watched him, arms crossed, until he finished.

# Chapter 13:
# Dark Thoughts

She stumbled about the cave with the others, packing up. Garen woke them up before dawn and she still felt groggy. They tried to leave everything as they'd found it, except for the wood supply being severely depleted. There wasn't a lot they could do about that. They didn't have time to chop wood.

She yawned into the back of her hand as Bo put out the fire. The horse shifted beside her so she patted its neck. Hopefully Prince would break out of his solemn mood soon. He'd been quiet the rest of the night, and had tossed and turned beside her. She wished she knew what to say to make him understand her fall had been an accident. Maybe she'd be able to talk him out of it during their ride. If not, she didn't relish the quiet ride they'd have together.

Everyone finished their chores and Bo led his horse out. She followed and quickly mounted once outside. Prince silently pulled himself up behind her.

*Kei will scout. Follow me. Quickly now.*

She smiled at the urgency in Garen's voice. After Damon's display, she couldn't see the Were bothering them again on the off chance the Dragos would return.

Garen took off at an angled route, heading south and west, leading them carefully through the rocks. They returned to the trees and the Were picked up the pace, pushing the horses as quickly as possible.

135

The group let out a collective sigh of relief when they broke out of the tree-line to see fields stretching out before them. It wasn't yet noon, and the horses fared well enough they didn't stop to rest.

Prince remained her silent companion, even though she tried to speak with him a number of times. Eventually she gave up. The horses made such good time she stayed mounted. She worried about the time they'd lost because of the storm and her injury.

They stopped at noon to eat and rest the horses. Kei raided the fields and Garen brought back a rabbit. Bo gutted it and strung it on his horse to add to their dinner.

She'd had enough of Prince's silence and ran with Kei for the rest of the day.

Despite running with Kei, after they'd stopped for the evening, set up camp, and eaten, she found herself full of nervous energy. She paced around the camp, messing with the fire now and then.

Bo slapped his thighs. "Come on, pup. Let's do some training."

"Yes!" She jumped at the idea. Perhaps she'd be able to tire herself out enough to sleep.

"Get out your daggers." He drew his sword and then gestured Kei over. "I've been talking with Kei. He can extend his claws without being in a fury of course. Since we don't know if we'll come across any Fey wild enough to attack us, let's practice fighting one."

She nodded, but his words made her hesitate.

Kei extended his claws and then cocked his head to the side. "What is it?"

"I don't know if I could hurt a Fey." She pressed her lips together for a moment, trying to find the words. "You're Fey," she finally said quietly.

A rare brilliant smile lit his entire face and then he laughed. "All Fey aren't like me. Just like all humans aren't like you."

"Yes, but…it's not their fault, is it?"

This sobered him quickly, and he nodded, glancing over at Bo. "We will teach to subdue?"

"Good enough." Bo shook his head as he looked over at her. "You know how to kill a man. The same will work for Fey."

Kei crouched, readying himself to attack her. "Avoidance is important." He sprang, claws slashing toward her. "Block with your blades. They aren't strong enough to cut."

She did, and then stepped back and recovered as he deflected a dagger. "It won't cut through your claws?"

Kei shook his head and attacked again. He barely held back his speed.

Aro grinned. She would definitely get a good workout.

When she finally plopped down beside Prince she let out a groan and then sprawled back on the ground. Every muscle burned.

"Do not overdo it," Prince said as she stretched and wiggled to find the least uncomfortable spot.

"I didn't." She rolled over onto her side to look at him. "How are you doing?"

He frowned. "I am fine."

"No, you've been all sullen and miserable."

A very small smile curved his lips for a moment. "I have." He rolled onto his back and looked up through the branches.

"Do you want to talk about it?"

"I want to go to sleep."

She huffed in irritation. At least he was talking, and she'd gotten a little smile out of him.

Kei settled down beside her and she rolled over onto her side facing him. She started to count and got to eleven before she heard Prince roll over and then felt his hand on her waist. Smiling again, she closed her eyes.

*Can you help me for a moment?*

*I thought you were going to sleep, Arowyn.*

*I am. Can you check my walls? I want to make sure everything is as it should be, after...what happened.*

Prince remained quiet for so long she wondered if he'd fallen asleep.

*Yes, I will look.*

She pushed herself inward, into the spot in her mind where she'd build her fortress around her personal thoughts and memories. Opening her eyes, she quickly looked around the barren landscape.

Prince stood to her left, staring up at the towering walls. He'd shown her how to build them, so she stood quietly for a while, letting him look them over.

*They seem fine. Have you noticed anything wrong?*

*You mean other than it still being very depressing here? No.*

Prince glanced up at the dark clouds. *It will clear up one day. You've dealt with so much loss and pain. It will take time for you to come to terms with it all.*

Grimacing, she turned her face away. *Is your mind as dark?*

*Sometimes,* he said quietly.

She turned back to him. *Is it now?*

He averted his eyes and nodded slightly.

*You'll get better, too. All sunshine and rainbows.*

His sudden laugh was bitter. *I have never had those.*

# Broken Prince

Impulsively stepping up to him, she gave him a tight hug. *I want you to have them. You know I'm not at all angry with you? It was just an accident. And you took care of me.*

His frown returned but he briefly returned her embrace.

*Please talk to me,* she whispered.

*I am just tired. Watching everything slip away, not being able to hold on, becoming a shadow of myself. It is frustrating.*

*What do you mean?*

*This is not who I am, Aro. I used to be strong, fast, powerful. Not this weak thing I have become. Other than healing myself, I've done no magic in almost a year. It is...painful.*

She held him tighter. She'd never really thought about what Prince would be like if he had his power.

*This weakness, it is not me. Yet I can do nothing about it. I just watch it become worse.* He shook his head and sighed. *I apologize.*

*For telling me what's wrong? Don't,* she said firmly. *You'll be home soon. We're almost there! Then you'll be yourself again.* She tilted her head to look up at him.

He smiled faintly. Such a sad smile, it matched the look in his eyes. *Yes, you are right. I will remember that.*

*I want you to be happy, Prince. I don't know what to do when you're not. I don't know what to say to you.*

A deep sigh escaped him. He kissed the top of her head.

*I need you, you know.*

*I know.*

She gave him one last squeeze and stepped back. *Let's get some sleep. So you can be all bright and cheery in the morning.*

Prince shook his head, but he chuckled and that made her smile.

Aro grinned as she helped Kei raid a field of beans and carrots. Not wanting to get caught, they moved quickly and tried to stay low to the ground. It didn't take long to each fill a pack they'd emptied earlier. Darting back into the trees, they ran again until they met up with the horses.

"We need to wash the carrots at the next stream," she told Bo as she tied her bulging bag to his horse. "Maybe Garen will get some meat and we can have stew for dinner!"

"Stew without bread?" Prince shook his head in mock horror.

She laughed up at him, thrilled to see he'd broken out of his sullen mood. The last three days he'd come out of it, slowly, but he had. Perhaps it had something to do with how close they'd come to getting him home. Even though they'd lost time with her sprained ankle, and then the storm, Garen assured her they were now maybe a week away. Prince could count the days on his fingers. She wondered if he would grow happier the closer they got.

Her chest tightened and she turned away. Even though she wanted Prince to get home so he could get well, she didn't want to lose him. Quite likely, once he passed through the Elven gates she'd never see him again.

Looking up at the sky, she took a slow breath to calm herself. "Kei, let's go look for a place to set up camp. It will be dark soon." She forced a smile and waved at Bo and Prince. "We'll let you know when we find a spot."

Kei followed as she ran through the trees. Running usually calmed her thoughts; one step in front of the other, breathe, navigate the terrain. It took moderate concentration and allowed her to not think of other things.

*Slow down.*

She forced her legs into a brisk walk. Kei joined her side a moment later, ducking a branch and then looking over at her worriedly.

Concentrating on where she walked, she refused to look at him.

"What's wrong?" When she didn't answer he pressed. "Prince is doing better."

"I know," she answered. "He's still not sleeping well though, even if he's seemed to have broken out of his dark thoughts."

"Is that what's bothering you?"

Grimacing, she shook her head. "We're almost there."

"Ahh." They walked in silence for a while. "Just be yourself."

Startled by his words, she jerked her head around to look at him. "I am."

"Then you'll be fine."

She frowned at him. "I just, I don't know what to do. He'll be gone soon."

Kei smiled wryly. "Do what you need to. Live your life. Be true to the person you are. Follow your instincts."

"You're just full of vague advice, aren't you?" Ducking a branch, she resisted the urge to smack him. He wasn't helping.

He laughed and shrugged.

"I suppose you'll be happy when he's gone," she muttered.

"Prince annoys me," he admitted. "I don't care if he stays or goes. I can live with either." He reached out and took her hand. "It's you I need."

His words made her smile and she squeezed his hand as they walked side by side. The warm glow of knowing she was loved filled her. "I'm not planning on going to Rivenward, if you're worried about that. I don't think that world is meant for me. Being surrounded by arrogant Elven nobles who consider me a pet would not be pleasant."

He chuckled. "No, it wouldn't."

She smiled over at him. "I'll be fine."

"I know." He paused and stopped walking.

"What?"

"If you do go. I'll come with you."

She rolled her eyes and pulled him over for a hug, and then messed up his wild hair. "Idiot. Like I'd do that to you. I think the Elves hate Fey more than humans."

He laughed. "True." They wrestled while he tried to get revenge on her hair. Eventually he won.

Laughing until her sides hurt, she sprang out of his reach. "Enough! We need to find a place to camp. I want stew tonight!" She tried to pull her hair into some semblance of order but gave up once she hit the knots. "You're combing this mess for me tonight," she grumbled.

He grinned and nodded.

"Rotten Fey." She couldn't help smiling the rest of the afternoon. She was so lucky to have such a perfect best friend.

# Chapter 14:
# How to Shock an Elf Speechless

Aro handed out carrots when they stopped well before noon. The boys grimaced, but took them. They'd eaten well the night before, devouring the stew she'd made. Even with the lack of ingredients or any spices, it had tasted wonderful. They ate every spoonful and talked about what they missed most.

She wasn't surprised everyone had been quiet all morning. Remembering everything they'd lost, all the things they didn't have, was hard.

They came across another large river and stopped again. Garen ran along the banks to find the easiest place to cross with the horses. Kei took the horses to be watered and to find a spot they could graze. Bo wanted to try fishing again. She followed him down to the bank.

"Where did Prince go?"

Bo gestured further down the river. "To wash up." He stopped when the ground abruptly cut off where the river had eaten at the bank. Carefully navigating the drop off, he stomped the ground. The river, though still deep and large, had receded and left a muddy shore.

"It's pretty solid." He held out a hand and helped her down. "Do you want to fish?"

She shook her head. "I'm going to see if I can find anything else for dinner. Catch lots of fish!"

He laughed and winked at her. "Of course. I always do. If there are fish to be caught, they will soon be ours."

Finding a place on the bank that wasn't too muddy, she crouched down and washed as much of herself as she could. Running wet fingers over and over through her hair calmed it down a bit. She debated asking Kei to cut it short again. Hanging just past her shoulders, it got in her face and never wanted to stay in a braid.

As clean as possible without a bath and lots of soap, she stood and looked up and down the river. It curved in each direction. She couldn't see Bo or Prince.

Spying some overhanging bushes downstream, she headed toward them. Drawing closer she found familiar orange berries. Prince had pointed them out last fall in the northern woods as being edible. With a grin she plucked one and carefully tasted it, the mix of tart and sweet assaulted her tongue, just like she remembered.

She picked the bushes clean of ripe ones, popping a few into her mouth as she worked. The sweetness lingered on her lips. The boys would be thrilled at her find. Once the pouch she'd made of the front of her shirt was full, she climbed the bank and returned to where they'd left everything. After she'd put them in one of the packs, she checked her worn shirt, happy to find the thick skinned berries hadn't left any stains.

Returning to the lower river bank, she headed downstream again, hoping to find more berry bushes. After following the curve of the river, she found Prince instead.

He sat propped against a large boulder sticking out of the river ledge. His silly hat pillowed his head and his hands rested in his lap. She took in his closed eyes and the way his head tilted slightly to one side and smiled. He was finally getting some sleep.

Quietly picking her way over to him, he didn't hear her faint footsteps over the sound of the river. She crouched beside him, smiling as she watched his sleeping face.

# Broken Prince

Her eyes followed the planes of his face, the dark shadows around his eyes, the way his long lashes rested against his pale skin. Her fingers itched to brush his long dark hair back from his face, to tuck it behind his pointed ears. He was so beautiful her breath caught in her throat. She loved him more than she was willing to admit, even to herself. Just watching him sleep made her heart race. Imagining crawling into his lap to rest her head on his shoulder sent a rush of warmth to her cheeks. She just wanted him to hold her, to stroke her hair and kiss her gently, and tell her that he loved her.

The knowledge that he never would rested heavily in her heart. He didn't know she was in love with him. To him, she was just a child, not a woman at all.

Shifting forward to kneel closer, she focused on his lips. Slightly parted, they looked so soft and inviting. Waiting. Her eyes jumped to search his whole face. He hadn't moved, his breathing continued slow and even.

"Prince," she whispered softly.

He didn't stir.

She worried her bottom lip between her teeth for a moment. Her heart pounded in her chest. How could he not hear it? She knew she should get up and walk away. Her traitorous heart didn't want to listen.

Bracing her hands on her thighs, she leaned forward. Lips almost touching his, she hesitated. She could stop. She could come to her senses. The problem was she didn't want to. She wanted to kiss him, just once. Her first kiss. If he slept through it, that was fine.

Heat warming her cheeks, she brushed her lips across his. Feather light, barely touching, but still a tremble rolled through her body as she pulled back. He still hadn't moved.

Closing her eyes, she leaned in carefully once more and again softly set her lips to his. She didn't move this time, just so very gently placed them there. With her eyes closed, all she could feel was that touch. So soft. So perfect. She couldn't stop her lips from pressing a little more, moving over his, caressing them.

For a brief moment his lips moved beneath hers. She didn't notice until they suddenly stopped and a sharp breath was inhaled.

Jerking her head back, she snapped her eyes open.

Prince stared at her, his lips slightly parted, his blue eyes wide with shock.

A shudder ripped through her as she returned his startled look. With a horrified gasp she flung herself backward away from him. Before he could speak, she flipped around and scrambled to her feet.

Her heart raced again, but for a different reason, as she ran away as quickly as she could.

What had she done?


She plopped down next to Kei where he sat watching the horses graze. "I'm an idiot."

He looked over at her, eyebrows raised. "What did you do now?"

She sighed. "Kissed Prince."

He choked and gaped at her and she actually found herself smiling.

"Why?"

Good question and not one she wanted to answer. "I don't know. I'm an idiot?" She gently touched her lips. "I just…maybe I just wanted to see what kissing someone would be like."

He surprised her by suddenly laughing. "You should have said so. I would have volunteered."

It was her turn to gape at him.

His cheeks flushed slightly and he grimaced. "I don't mean...I..." He growled. "I don't want you to think I'm in love with you. I love you, but not like that."

She let out a little sigh of relief. Kei being in love with her was not something she wanted to deal with. "I understand. Me, too. With you."

He let out a deep breath. "Awkward."

"A bit," she said with a chuckle. Unfortunately curiosity got the better of her. "So why would you want to kiss me then?"

His blushed again. "I am a man, and you're pretty."

"I am?" She bit her lip, trying to decide if he was making fun of her.

"You are." He grinned suddenly. "Even if you are human."

She scowled at him. "Stupid Fey!" She threw a rock at him and he laughed.

"So, tell me."

She made a face, knowing he was talking about the kiss. "It was short. I just leaned forward, pressed my lips to his. Then he woke up and his eyes got really big and he looked really surprised so I ran away."

"He woke up?" His lips twitched as he struggled not to laugh. "And you ran away."

She nodded and closed her eyes as she sighed.

"So…you don't know if he's mad…or not."

"No idea. I'm wondering if I pretend it didn't happen if he'll be fine doing the same."

"Probably. I doubt he's mad. He'll likely lecture you. About growing up."

She groaned. Kei was right. She probably had nothing more than that to worry about. Well, other than she'd made a fool of herself and made her feelings for him obvious. "You want to do some scouting for the rest of the day?"

"So you can avoid him?"

147

"Exactly."

He chuckled. "Sure."

They sat in peaceful silence for a while until Garen told them he'd found a good crossing point. Bo excitedly shared he'd caught a few fish.

Her stomach clenched and rolled as she helped Kei catch the horses and walked them back to where they'd left their things.

She kept a careful eye out for Prince, ready to bolt and leave Kei to tell the others they were both going scouting if necessary. However she didn't see him, so assumed he was still sitting where she'd left him. She didn't know what to make of that. On a good note he hadn't immediately gone and washed his mouth out with soap. Not that they had any.

They told Garen and Bo their plans. After filling their water skins and strapping on their packs they headed out quickly. She was pretty sure Prince hadn't seen them come or go, and that made her perfectly happy. Unless something went wrong, she wouldn't have to deal with him until they stopped for the night. The thought made her grimace. For once she wasn't looking forward to curling up next to him. How was she going to be able to do that now? Maybe he'd avoid her altogether; otherwise they'd have to talk.

# Chapter 15:
# Words and the Tears They Bring

She had a wonderful day running around the woods with Kei. Somehow she managed to not think constantly about Prince. Mostly.

When they returned in the evening to help set up camp she couldn't stop herself from continuously glancing over at him.

He didn't ignore her. However he wasn't making an effort to speak with her either. The few times their gazes met he looked merely...thoughtful.

What did that mean? At least he didn't appear to be angry with her.

Dinner turned out rather crispy due to her lack of concentration. The boys didn't comment about it though. They chatted around the fire while they ate and then Kei helped her clean up.

"He say anything?"

She shook her head and concentrated on cleaning the pot in her hands. "Not yet."

"You're both acting strange," Kei whispered.

Biting her lip, she closed her eyes for a moment, trying to keep her stupid raging emotions under control. "I hate feeling like this."

"Aro." Kei bumped his shoulder against hers. "What happens, happens. Stop worrying."

149

"I'm trying."

He grinned over at her. "You always have me. Don't forget."

No, she couldn't ever forget that. Even if Kei didn't melt her heart, she loved him. He loved her.

This full out crazy love thing wasn't something only she had ever felt. Everyone did, at some time or another. Some people fell in and out of love all the time. Kei was right. Prince's reaction was beyond her control. Whatever the outcome, she'd be fine. Eventually.

After cleaning, she and Kei returned to the fire. Kei threw on another piece of deadfall and she went to the packs to put everything away.

Once done she turned and stopped abruptly, finding Prince standing directly before her.

"Will you walk with me a moment, Aro?"

Her heart lodged in her throat, but she managed to nod and plaster a small smile to her face. There was no excuse not to, the sun had started to set, but light remained. As long as they didn't talk too long she didn't have to worry about being away from the fire in the dark.

She followed Prince quietly, clenching and unclenching her hands, trying to control her sudden nervousness. She knew what he wanted to talk about. The kiss. She also knew the conversation would likely not go in her favor. Apparently her wish for the whole thing to be forgotten had not been granted.

She wondered what it sounded like when your heart broke. Glass shattering? The thundering roar of falling mountains? Or maybe the squishy rip of a real heart?

Prince finally stopped and she did, too, keeping a few steps back from him and trying not to look like she was about to be sick. She sucked in a deep breath as he turned to face her. He wasn't smiling. Not a good sign.

"Do we have to have this conversation?"

He raised his brows, clearly startled. "Yes, I believe we do," he said solemnly after a moment.

She turned her head away, waiting for the worst.

"You must not do that again," he said finally. "Kiss me."

Her jaw clenched. Idiot. Like she didn't know what he was talking about. She lowered her head, allowing her hair to fall over her face. It hid the rising color spreading across her cheeks. She concentrated on trying not to cry like some fool girl.

It was hard to do. She had been rejected. Deep down she'd known she would be, but would have much preferred to not actually have it happen.

At least she knew what the sound of a heart breaking sounded like. Nothing at all. It just hurt. Deeply, painfully, like someone had stuck a dagger in her chest and twisted. It became hard to breathe, impossible to speak.

"Do you understand why?"

She nodded once, still not looking at him. It took a moment for her to gain control, however he patiently awaited her answer. "You're a prince. I'm not...I'm not anything." She grimaced at her mangled words.

"That is part of it," he agreed. "There are so many different reasons."

His words hurt, even if she knew they were true. "I know," she whispered. "I'm sorry."

He sighed. "I care about you very much. I hope you do know that." She nodded. "You should be with someone human," he said gently. "It would be best for you." He paused a moment. "What about Bo?"

She raised her head and stared at him. Not only because he'd given her a suggestion on who to love, but the person had he chosen. "Bo?" She said the first thing which popped into her mind. "He's old!"

Prince stared at her, eyebrows raised as he made his point.

She realized then the trap he'd set. The Dragos had mentioned Prince had been gone from Elven lands for decades. Decades. Rot it all!

"I am much older than Bo," he said after a moment. "Very much older. That is why you will always be a child to me. I am immortal, Aro. Do you know what that means?"

She set her lips stubbornly and looked away again.

"All of us, the Were and Fey and Elves, we age until we hit our prime. Then we stop. We do not grow old. We do not die of old age. We also rarely get sick, and never from the hundreds of different human diseases. We are not frail creatures such as you. Your lives are but brief moments to us." He paused and sighed. "This is why we do not interact with humans much. It is too hard on them, on us."

She grimaced. "Kei doesn't mind." Again, she knew immediately she'd said the wrong thing.

A dark look crossed Prince's face. "Kei is just as much a child as you are. He also knows little of what he is. Had he been given proper guidance he would never have even considered binding himself to you."

She shook her head in denial. No. Kei would have. He knew what he had done. He knew she would die one day. He didn't care. Or if he did, he was content to be her family for the time they would have.

"Aro..."

"I understand," she said firmly, not wanting him to start again. She gathered what dignity she could and looked up at him. "I apologize. It will not happen again."

He didn't look happy. He looked...pained. Hurt.

She didn't really care. "I would like to be alone now."

He winced and lowered his head. "I am sorry. I–"

# Broken Prince

"I know." It became a struggle to hold back the tears. She just really wanted him to leave so she could cry. "I'm not angry. It's not like it's your fault. So...it's fine."

He took a step toward her, clearly distressed, reaching a hand out to her.

She stepped back, avoiding him, but not looking away. He needed to know she was serious so she looked him in the eyes. "I'm fine. However I don't wish to discuss it anymore. Or ever again. And I would like to be alone right now."

He lowered his hand and nodded, dropping his gaze again to the ground. "Arowyn, I am so sorry," he whispered so quietly she could barely hear him.

She wished she hadn't. His pity for her made her furious. It wasn't her fault he was an idiot and didn't love her back, didn't want to accept her love for him. Fine. She would move on. She would add this to the rest of her messed up emotions and memories. She would learn and grow stronger. She'd survive it and be fine again. Eventually.

Since he seemed to not take the hint to leave she turned and walked away.

Though they hadn't spoken long, the sun had slipped below the tree-line. Darkness quickly hid her from view and she began to run. Little light from the moon and stars made it through the canopy, barely enough to see by. She didn't go far before she slowed and dropped to her knees. She couldn't see. Tears blurred her vision and streamed down her cheeks.

*Aro? Aro? What's wrong? Where are you? Aro?* The voices of the others rattled through her head.

She ignored them.

Clenching her teeth didn't quite smother the scream of frustration, of anger and hurt and embarrassment. So many emotions coursed through her she didn't know what to concentrate on first.

She heard Kei coming long before he crouched down in front of her. "You're noisy." Wiping her eyes, she sniffled.

153

"I was worried." Leaning forward, he reached out and brushed new tears from her cheek. "Didn't go well."

A short, rough laugh cracked through her lips and she shook her head. "No."

"Did he hurt you?"

"Of course not. He didn't touch me."

Kei grimaced. "That's not what I meant. Was he cruel? Should I kill him?"

Her laugh came out easier this time. "No. He wasn't really."

"I'll tell the others then. So they don't."

Startled, she looked up quickly. "What?"

"You didn't come back with him. You didn't answer us."

Groaning, she put her face in her hands. "Everyone knows?"

"I'm sorry. Prince said…" His words trailed off at her horror stricken face. "I'm sorry."

The tears started again and she wrapped her arms around herself. She looked up at him through blurry eyes. "I hate this. It hurts so much."

Kei moved to sit beside her and pulled her against him. She cried against him for a while. He truly was her best friend. Her brother. After a while she leaned back and pulled a rag from her pocket to blow her nose.

"Better?"

"No," she admitted.

"Are you sure he wasn't cruel to you?" He tucked a piece of hair behind her ear. "I don't like seeing you cry, Aro."

"I don't like crying."

He smiled slightly. "Do you want to talk about it?"

"I…I..." She shook her head, but then the words bubbled out of her, everything Prince had said.

"Wait. Stop."

She sniffled again and rubbed more tears from her face. Had she been talking too fast? No, she'd gotten to the part where Prince said Kei was foolish for binding himself to her. She should have known Kei would take offense to those words.

"That's not true," he said stiffly.

"I know," she whispered, lowering her head.

He grasped her shoulders and peered to look at her. "Do you? Do you know why?"

Well, maybe she didn't really. She shrugged, not meeting his gaze.

"Then you will listen." He pulled her back to his side, putting an arm around her. "Those first days, you amazed me even then. Here was a girl, dressed as a boy, who'd lost everything. You were hurt. Alone. But you tried so hard to be strong. You were so brave, Aro. I respected you. Then I found out you were Commander Mason's daughter. Have you understood how much he meant to me? He saved my life. He had died, but there you were. That first time, I bound myself to you willingly because of your strength, and who you were. Honor demanded I protect you. I knew you were human. I knew what it meant. Even then, I was prepared to protect you and be by your side for the rest of your life. Your father gave me this life. It was the least I could do to take care of his daughter."

She'd never, ever, heard him speak so much. Staring at him in shock, his words slowly sunk in. Leaning forward she hugged him tightly. "Thank you. For whatever reason you did it. I needed it. Needed someone then." Mumbling into his shoulder, she wasn't sure he heard her until his grip tightened around her.

"And you know," he whispered into her hair, "the second time, I truly meant it. I wanted to. You are my family. And I…I couldn't let you die."

The tears started again, but for a different reason. "You're my family, too. Always."

"Forever."

"Yes." Squeezing him tightly once more, she then leaned back and wiped at her tears.

"You're a mess."

"At least it's dark."

He smiled a little and brushed the last of her tears away. "Things will be better tomorrow."

"I suppose you want to go back to camp now."

"We should."

She turned away, biting her lip. "I don't want to see him. Not yet."

He squeezed her hand. "You're my strong girl. You can do this."

Yes, she could. Maybe. "Can you go first? Let me know how things are there? I'll be right behind you."

Kei watched her carefully for a moment before nodding. Standing, he grabbed her hands and pulled her up, too. "I'll be with you."

With a nod she followed after him, until he stopped and grabbed her hand, pulling her up beside him. "Forever by your side," he whispered.

Kei always made her smile.

# Chapter 16:
# What Friends are for

Just before they reached the camp, Kei gave her hand a quick squeeze before leaving her to see how things were. It wasn't long before he let her know Prince had already settled down to sleep. Relief flooding her, she walked into camp.

Garen trotted up and bumped his head against her. She bent over and gave the giant wolf a hug.

Bo pulled her into his arms next. "Get some sleep, pup. Tomorrow will be better."

The tears stayed away, but so did her voice so she just nodded.

She washed up quickly before making her way over to her usual spot by the fire. Kei rested not far from Prince, the usual place for her between them. She didn't take it. Pausing, she glared at them both for a moment. Things had changed. She walked instead to Kei's other side and settled down next to him.

He rolled over, not really surprised. "Doing better?"

Nodding, she acknowledged his whisper and closed her eyes quickly as he took her hands in his. She wondered if Prince would be angry. Certainly he didn't expect her to continue curling up next to him every night. At least he was lying down already. It wasn't a problem to deal with tonight.

She was wrong.

He got up. He moved to her other side and settled down again.

She froze, eyes opening in shock. Kei seemed just as surprised. Her lips pressed together angrily when his hand slid over her waist. She picked it up and flung it back behind her. *Don't.*

*I thought you were not angry with me.*

*I'm not.*

*Then why–*

She rolled over quickly to face him. *Because you are either going to be home or dead very soon. I will need to get used to not having you here. Correct?*

He lowered his eyes, his face drawn and pale at her harsh words. *Yes.*

*Besides. I don't know why you bother. I'm fine.*

He looked up, a frown crossing his face. *You are not fine.*

*I am not a child!* Her mental scream carried. In her anger she hadn't bothered to control it. She wasn't touching Prince, and was therefore, using the pack's mind-speech. Garen whined. She wondered if they'd all heard everything. Not that it mattered really.

*Yes, Aro, you are,* he persisted.

Sitting up, planning on moving again, she didn't expect him to reach out and grab her. She gasped, choking on tears and scrambling to her feet and away from him. *Don't!*

Prince rose swiftly, reaching out for her again.

Suddenly Kei's arms wrapped around her, pulling her back against him, his face next to hers. "Shhh. I'm here." He looked to Prince. *That is enough.*

"But she does not–"

"No. You can't have it both ways, and you can't have everything."

"You do not understand. She needs me!"

Kei shook his head. "She can do without you. She has me. She has the rest of us. You hurt her. Did you think things would remain the same?"

158

# Broken Prince

"That is not–"

"Prince, stop." Bo stepped up next to Kei. "You aren't thinking. I believe I understand what's going on here." He smiled kindly down at Aro. "Consider your actions now and how they will make her feel. She isn't a child any more. She's a young woman."

Prince frowned and looked at her, really looked at her. She saw his eyes widen slightly but squashed down the faint hope rising in her chest. It didn't matter. Her being a child was only one of the many reasons he wouldn't ever love her. Moving her gaze to the ground, she pressed closer to Kei.

"Aro. Arowyn, please look at me," Prince said softly.

Taking a deep breath, she squared her shoulders and raised her chin. She wasn't going to cry anymore. She wouldn't.

"You are," he paused, searching for words. "You are dear to my heart. I do not wish to lose what we have."

His words ripped at her heart. Why did he have to be like this? Why did he have to be so…noble.

"You will understand, one day. I am truly sorry to have hurt you. I am."

She didn't know what to say. He watched her patiently, apparently waiting for her to say something. "Things won't be the same," she said quietly. "I'm sorry."

A muscle ticked in Prince's jaw before he gave her a brief, single nod. "Perhaps it is for the best."

She turned her head and looked up at Kei. "I'm tired."

Kei gave her another squeeze and then turned them and moved back to their place by the fire. She didn't look back.

Prince didn't try to join her again.

Morning brought painful silence. She avoided Prince, trying desperately to escape his pained and sorrowful looks.

Did he regret what he'd said to her? Part of her hoped so. The rest of her was just tired. Her dreams had been harsh and bloody. At least they faded from her memory quickly enough as the morning passed. She wished everything since she kissed Prince could be forgotten as easily.

The temperature had dropped in the night. Fog surrounded them, drifting through the trees on the slight breeze. It didn't appear too thick, so no one was concerned it would slow them down. It would clear up soon enough once the sun warmed the air.

Once they packed everything up, she grabbed her water skin and headed for the quiet of the trees. She moved at a brisk walk, fighting the urge to run. Running got her nowhere. Squeezing her hands into fists, she tried to stop her mind from running in horrified circles. She'd ruined everything. Her impulsiveness had certainly got the better of her this time. Now she had no idea what to do.

Garen padded up beside her. *Aro...*

*Don't.*

He snorted and turned his large head toward her for a moment before once again watching where he was going.

They walked silently for a while before she glanced over her shoulder. *Where's Kei?*

*Prince asked to speak with him.*

Her eyebrows went up. *Well, then.* She didn't know what to say to that.

*Prince does love you.*

Clenching her fists, she increased her speed. *I know. He's just not in love with me.*

*I know it hurts. But soon he'll be home. I wish you could forgive him.*

His words stopped her. "There's nothing to forgive," she said quietly. "It's not like it's his fault. I just..." She shook her head and rubbed her temples. "I did something stupid, and

160

I'm embarrassed and I don't know what to say. I changed everything and now I don't know what to do."

Garen's ears flipped back and forth as she spoke. When she finished he moved forward and pressed his huge furry head against her chest. Sniffling, she rubbed between his ears.

Taking a deep breath, she wiped tears from her eyes and raised her chin. "Let's go. I'll think of something. I just need a little time."

When they next stopped to rest Bo dragged her away before she had to worry about avoiding Prince.

Once far enough from the others to ensure privacy, Bo stopped and pulled her into a tight hug. She felt so tiny tucked against his broad chest and within his huge arms.

"What do you need, pup?"

Releasing a deep sigh, she pulled out of his arms. "For everyone to forget."

"You didn't do anything wrong."

She shook her head and frowned. "I made a fool of myself."

"You followed your heart. That's not a bad thing, Aro."

"It is when the other person doesn't love you back," she retorted bitterly.

Bo took both of her hands in his. "Aro, listen to me. You are a delightful, beautiful, intelligent woman. Any man will be lucky to have your love. The right one will come along. You're sixteen; you're not in any rush. One day, you'll make one lucky man a wonderful wife."

She shook her head and laughed. "Thanks."

His words were something her brother Paul would have said. It left a warm feeling in her heart. The loss of her brothers created a constant dull ache inside of her, but she had made new family. They were there for her just as much as her brothers would have been.

Bo smiled softly and ruffled her hair. "I had hoped it wouldn't come to this...between the two of you."

"You knew?"

He chuckled. "I think Prince was the only one who didn't." His smile turned wistful. "You look at him like Avery looked at you."

The thought of their dead friend made her breath catch. Before he died, he'd begged her not to love Prince. She'd never realized he loved her. The pain of losing him brought tears to her eyes and she brushed them away quickly. "I miss him," she whispered. "So much. All the time."

"I know, pup. I do, too."

Unspoken words filled the silence. They missed John as well. His death was too new to speak off. It still brought too much pain.

A breath shuddered out of her. She squeezed her eyes together tightly, trying to keep the tears away.

"Remember the ones we still have, Aro. Don't push Prince away. Remember you are friends. I'd hate to see you lose that."

She grimaced he'd brought the topic back around and looked away. "I don't know how to fix it."

"If you had time, I would say not to worry, and things would work themselves out. But he won't be with us much longer. Put it in the past, and start over. He wants to. I don't think you'll find it that hard. Do you want to be friends again?"

"Of course!"

"Then make it happen."

She looked over at him, taking in the seriousness of his face. Raising her chin slightly, she nodded. "I will."

"Good girl." He grinned. "We should head back then."

Her resolve melted. She shook her head and looked away. "You go back. I need a few moments."

Bo glanced around the trees. Though the sun had risen it remained cool and within the forest the fog remained. "We're keeping close to the fields. Don't go further in. It would be easy to get turned around in this mess."

"I'll be careful." She forced a smile and lightly punched his arm. "Stop worrying about me. I'm fine. I just need to think of what to say. I won't be too long." She paused a moment, thinking. "If you all want to continue on, I can meet up with you."

"We'll wait," Bo said firmly.

She watched him disappear into the fog and shadows. A deep breath sighed out of her and she turned on her heel to move further away. Not too far, she just needed a little more space.

A huge old tree eventually caught her attention and she settled down at the base of it. Pulling up her legs, she wrapped her arms around them and then rested her forehead on her knees.

The tears came without her even having to start thinking about everything.

Letting it all out, all of her pain and embarrassment and heartache, her tears ran in torrents and turned into wracking sobs.

One more good cry. That's all she needed and then no more. She'd find her strength again after this. It would hold her up and keep her going until everything was fine again.

Jen Wylie

# Chapter 17:
# Shadows in the Fog

Crying exhausted her. By the time her sobs finally petered out, a headache pounded behind her eyes.

"Rot," she muttered.

Unwrapping her arms, they dropped to her sides as she pushed back to lean her head against the old tree. The fog created an eerie silence amongst the trees. All she could hear was her rough breathing and occasional sniffle. She took a deep breath, and then another. She could do this. She could fix things with Prince.

Opening her eyes, she blinked back lingering tears. It seemed darker out. Looking up, she couldn't see the sky through the old tree's branches. Perhaps clouds had drifted over the sun. She hoped it wasn't going to rain.

Movement to her left caught her eye. Freezing in place, she slowly turned her head. Something dark moved through the fog, barely visible before disappearing again. It made no sound.

*Garen? Where are you?*

*With the others. What's wrong?*

*I don't know. I thought I saw something in the fog.*

Turning her head slowly, she watched the fog around her. Dark shapes continued to appear and then get swallowed again. She saw more than one and they seemed to be circling her. Her fingers moved toward her daggers.

A movement jerked her head to look straight in front of her. She blinked in surprise as a gasp escaped her.

*Were! There are Were!*

*Calm down. Where are you? How many are there?*

*I don't know. Not far from where Bo left me.*

The Were before her stood much taller than Garen, its shoulders broader. Unlike Garen's grey and white, it was mostly black. It stared at her a moment with strange blue and gold eyes. Slowly it began to move toward her.

She pushed back against the tree and broke eye contact, trying to watch either side to see if any of the others approached. They didn't. She caught glimpses of movement in the fog and nothing more.

Her gaze returned to the large Were. It stopped before her and lowered its head, watching her curiously. Suddenly it blurred and then a man crouched in its place.

She gaped at him, her eyes wide in shock.

Garen had never changed. She'd thought perhaps it was hard to do, or maybe when they did they ended up naked. No, this man shifted fully clothed.

His clothing didn't draw her attention. Her gaze remained riveted to his face. His eyes remained the strange blue shot with gold, his hair hung black and short and slightly wild. His features were handsome enough, though he looked older than she expected an immortal to be, perhaps in his early to mid-twenties. Maybe he was just really old. Or perhaps it was the scars.

Claw marks slashed one side of his face from cheek to jaw. Another shorter set marked the other side of his jaw and then continued down his neck to hide under his loose shirt. Unlike Bo's large scar, they were thinner and looked much older. She knew whatever had attacked him almost took his life. Immortals didn't scar, not unless they had no power to heal themselves.

His dark brows bunched together as he looked at her in concern. "Are you lost, little one?"

Tears welled in her eyes again. His voice…she'd never heard one so beautiful. Deep and sultry, soft, almost a purr.

"You should not be here," he continued.

She wanted him to keep talking, however his words finally made sense and she moved her gaze from his lips back to his eyes. "I know," she finally stammered. Her own voice sounded so coarse in her ears. She didn't want to speak again.

*Aro? What's happening?*

*They think I'm lost.*

Garen let out a mental sigh of relief. *Good.*

*Stay out of the woods!*

*We will. We're heading your way along the boundary.*

The Were stood and held out his hands. "Come."

She looked at his hands, up to his face, and then back at the hands. Letting go of her daggers wasn't something she wanted to do. His fingers moved, inviting her to take them.

Leaning forward, she slipped her hands into his and he pulled her up. Her hands looked dwarfed in his. She kept her eyes on them when he didn't let go.

"I will not harm you," he said quietly.

She looked up into his strange eyes again. Should she pretend to be a silly lost girl? Pushing away the fear creeping up her spine, she raised her eyebrows. "Do you swear?"

He chuckled. "On my honor."

She barely heard what he said. A smile curved her lips at the sound of his laugh. How could someone have such a voice?

*Aro?*

Garen's voice brought her mind back into focus. *So far all is good.*

The Were ran his thumbs reassuringly across the backs of her hands. His brow furrowed and she followed his gaze down to her scars. Glancing up again, she met his eyes. He let

167

go of one hand and raised it to brush the hair from her face. She jerked back, and tried to turn away, but from his low growl she knew he'd seen the scar on her forehead as well. His fingers feather danced over them, then slightly touched her cheek and by her lip. She must have scars there too. The lack of mirrors on their journey probably kept her from bursting into tears.

"What has happened to you?"

The sweetness of his voice didn't pull her in this time. Anger and embarrassment kept her focused on the trouble she was in. "Ship wreck. Slavers. Soldiers. Pick one."

His solemn face made her stand up straighter. She tried to pull her other hand away. He held it tightly and moved around her, leading her toward the boundary. She followed him willingly enough. Hopefully he'd get her there and then go away.

"You are not so lost, I do not think."

She didn't look at him, her eyes were too busy watching the fog around her, and the moving shadows of the other Were as they followed. His hand tightened around hers once again.

She glared up at him. "That hurts."

"I do not like to be played with, little one."

"I'm not little!"

His anger disappeared as he laughed out loud. He bent toward her. "Yes, you are."

The fog parted before them and she could see the fields beyond. They weren't far from the boundary.

*We're almost to the boundary.*

*We aren't far.*

She pulled toward it, but the Were stopped and pulled her back to his side.

"Why are you in our woods?"

She turned away, even though he didn't let go of her hand. "I was upset. I just needed to be alone for a little while."

"You are not alone?"

She grimaced but decided to stick with the truth. "Of course not. I'm with my family."

He nodded. "And where are they now?"

"Probably looking for me. They aren't in the forest," she added quickly.

He searched her face intently. She let him, staring up at him with nothing to hide. Well, other than the fact her family weren't all human. However, hopefully he'd never learn the truth of that.

"Let us go find them then."

Her eyes widened in shock. "No!"

*Aro? What's wrong?*

*The one Were wants to take me to you.*

*That...might not be a good idea.*

*I know that!*

The Were's eyes shifted to her forehead. "Did they do this to you?"

"Of course not! They're very protective. I don't want them to get worried and try to rescue me from you. That's all." She looked toward the boundary again. "Can I go?"

"Though that would be the most logical choice, part of me feels..." he hesitated.

She looked back up at him and waited while he regarded her thoughtfully. Her patience began to wear away. "I swear we are no threat to you. Or your forest. We are simply travelling the boundary. It is safest for us."

"Why is that?"

"It...because," she floundered for words. Stick with the truth. "There has been fighting. In the cities." She pointed north with her free hand. "We were in one, and it was attacked. We barely escaped, but the soldiers hunted us through the fields." She didn't have to fake the tears welling in her eyes again. "They killed John."

His face softened, as much as it could with all those scars, even though she knew he had no idea who John was.

169

"We have heard of that attack. Alar-En's pack has spoken of many humans trying to flee to the forests there."

An idea came to her. *Bo, ride up. Call for me.*

*On my way.*

"I'm sorry. That I broke the laws."

"Aro! Time to go! Where are you?"

She pulled against the Were's hand. "That's my brother."

He turned toward the sound and then without a word began walking toward the boundary, pulling her along with him. He stopped abruptly a few steps from the edge.

"Can I go now?" She took a step past him and looked north through the trees. Not far away a large tree had come down. Its leafy top fell outside the forest, blocking her view. It must have come down in the storm. The top leaves didn't seem to have started to wilt at all.

Bo rode around them, thankfully alone. "Aro?" He made a show of leaning over the horse's neck trying to peer into the trees.

"I'm coming!"

Bo's head jerked up and he smiled, riding toward her.

She pulled against the Were's grip. He ignored her, watching Bo as he approached. Turning and looking around, she saw Were pacing the forest behind them. Lots of Were. With a gulp she whirled back around.

*There are a lot of Were. Stay on the horse.*

Bo's smile faltered, though she supposed it could be because he saw the man holding her as well. He stopped the horse a good distance beyond the trees. "Aro?" His hand went to his sword, but didn't draw it.

With both hands she pulled, trying to free herself from the Were's grip. "Please. Let me go now."

He turned to look down at her and finally let go. His head snapped around suddenly. Before she could bolt to safety, his arm snaked around her waist and jerked her back against him.

She screeched and fought against him, stomping his foot and trying to elbow his kidneys.

"That is enough…Aro." His grip tightened around her and she gasped. He turned, moving her with him and she saw the other Were running north.

*Rot! You got to close! The Were are coming!*

"Stop! Stop them! Please, don't!"

Her captor looked down at her. She didn't pay attention to him. She sighed with relief as the other wolves followed his mental command and stopped.

"Where are the others?"

His beautiful voice was not pleased. She winced. "Past the fallen tree."

"What are you hiding, little one?"

She glared up at him. "I'm not. You just won't understand."

"Call them to come."

She pressed her lips into a thin angry line and glared up at him. "Fine." Turning, she cupped her hands around her mouth. "Boys! I need you!" *He knows you're there.*

None of them answered, but she knew they were coming. Bo pulled his sword slightly. She shook her head. She didn't want to fight. It wouldn't end well.

"You're the alpha aren't you," she said suddenly.

He looked down at her. "Yes."

Know your enemy. He'd be the one giving orders. *The man with me is their alpha. There are at least a dozen as wolves behind us.*

*Rot it all,* Kei muttered.

*Don't panic,* Garen added. *We can get out of this.*

Prince remained silent.

*I'm not panicking. I'm getting irritated.*

*That's actually worse, I think,* Bo said. From his horse, she watched him give her a warning look.

Forcing herself to calm down, she relaxed in the Were's hold.

She saw Prince ride around the trees. He didn't hurry. Her eyes narrowed as she searched for Kei and Garen.

Garen trotted forward from behind Prince and moved around the horse, coming to stop beside Bo. She didn't see Kei.

"A Were, and an Elf," the man muttered.

*Kei, what are you doing?*

*I don't think–*

*Get out here. He's angry with me already.*

*Very well.*

Kei burst out of the fallen tree, landing easily in a crouch before springing up again and jogging forward.

The grip around her waist tightened.

"I told you that you wouldn't understand," she muttered. Hearing movement behind her, she turned her head and saw the other Were creeping forward. Gritting her teeth, she glared at them for a moment.

*Rhee-En,* Garen whispered.

*Is it?* She heard Prince reply.

*Who is Rhee-En?* She looked up at the man holding her. Was he someone important?

Neither Garen or Prince answered her.

Her boys all stood before her now and tension tightened every muscle in her body.

"You are the ones found in the cave during the storm."

She couldn't help muttering a number of choice curses. Stopping mid-curse, she frowned. "Were you one of them? That attacked us?"

"No. This is not my land. We were on a chase."

"Where's your land?"

"You ask a lot of questions."

"It's a hazard of knowing me." Her boys all snorted and she glared over at them.

"My pack holds the next lands to the south."

"Great," she muttered. They were heading that way. Now they'd be forced to stay out of the forests. Certainly he'd have his wolves watching them.

"A sickly Elf, a Fey who is not wild, and a shiftless Were," the man, Rhee-En, mused.

"And us humans," she grumbled. She paused, her brows drawing together in confusion. What did shiftless Were mean?

He stepped them forward. "Do please feel free to explain."

Prince rode his horse forward a few steps and pulled off his silly, floppy hat.

The Were holding her sucked in a sharp breath. Did he recognize Prince?

He bowed his head slightly.

Apparently so.

"My…companions are assisting me home. We mean no disrespect being in your lands."

"Understood. Your journey has not been kind."

Prince frowned at the barb. "No. It has not. Time has become important. If you would return Aro, we will be on our way."

Rhee-En and Prince stared at each other as her heart beat furiously in her chest. Finally Rhee-En loosened his hold as he turned his attention to her. "Do you wish to go?"

She shook her head slightly, not understanding the absurd question. "Of course I do. I have to get Prince home."

He chuckled. "Prince? Is that what you call him?"

She grimaced, but nodded. Though she knew Prince's name, she wasn't about to admit it.

His brows drew together again. "You are the one the dragon saved."

She said nothing. He stared down at her. Her eyes narrowed slightly and she tilted her chin up, meeting his squarely. "He finds me interesting."

"You are human."

*I'm an interesting human.*

His eyes widened.

A satisfied smile curved her lips as she leaned forward. *My family include Were, Fey, human, and Elf. I love them all. I wish no harm to your forest or your people. Let me return to mine.*

He nodded, still in shock, and released her.

She took a step back and gave him a brief nod of thanks. Before he could come to his senses and change his mind she bolted toward her boys.

Kei reached her first and she flung herself into his arms, holding him tightly.

"Are you hurt?"

"No."

She pulled away and turned to face Rhee-En. Garen moved beside her, pushing himself against her and under her arm.

"My lands begin not far from here. You may travel and camp within the borderland woods if you wish." He gave another nod to Prince. "I wish you a safe journey." His gaze returned to her. "Keep an eye on your little one."

While she grumbled in protest, he turned and disappeared into the trees.

"I imagine that's not the last we've seen of him."

"No," Prince agreed. "Likely it is not."

She looked over at him and he smiled a soft, sad smile. Suddenly she grinned and gave him a sharp nod. His smile grew and reached his eyes.

They'd work everything out. She'd lost sight of what meant most to her when he'd broken her heart. Though she was still in love with Prince, she couldn't forget how much she loved him as a friend. Refusing to lose his friendship too would keep her going and help her make the right decisions, putting things in the past.

Jen Wylie

# Chapter 18:
# As Things Were

They continued swiftly on their way, keeping directly on the forest boundary. Everyone remained tense for some time, watching the foggy forest for Were and the fields for humans.

They stopped very briefly to eat at noon and headed out again quickly. Garen spotted humans now and then in the fields, forcing them to slip into the trees. The Were said nothing, but they didn't want to press their welcome.

Though Garen and Kei scouted and hunted, she stayed with the horses, not wanting to risk being the human caught in the forbidden woods.

She traded a few strained looks and smiles with Prince as the day continued before he finally sighed.

"Come here, child."

Inwardly she winced at once again being called a child, but she wanted so desperately to fix everything between them she forced herself not to snap at him.

When she approached his horse he stopped it and held out his hand. "Ride with me."

Her stomach churned but she nodded and allowed him to pull her up in front of him. His arms circled her to hold the reins and she leaned back against his chest, carefully making sure her thoughts remained well guarded.

They rode in silence, following Bo on his horse. Eventually she relaxed, the stiffness easing out of her muscles. A tired sigh escaped her and she closed her eyes, wishing she knew what to say.

"You do not have to say anything."

She couldn't help but laugh. Of course Prince would be watching for any stray thoughts she might have. He wanted to repair what they had too, didn't he?

*Of course, I do.*

"I wish you could forget it all," she whispered.

He smiled faintly. "We rarely forget...such things. Living so long, we treasure our memories."

"Humans forget things easily enough. Most things," she amended.

"Being remembered by others is very important to my people. Do humans not feel the same?"

She thought about it for a moment. "I guess we are. It's why a lot of us have children. Why royalty and nobles build monuments and I guess why a lot of people do the things they do."

"Our pasts make us who we are. We learn from them and–"

"I don't want a lecture on what happened," she said sharply. "I'd rather we didn't mention it again."

"Aro, I do not understand–"

She didn't wait to hear what he didn't understand. "It is embarrassing," she snapped quietly. "And it hurts. Leave it be. Please."

"Very well." They rode silently again until he shifted, put both reins in one hand, and wrapped his arm around her waist in a gentle hug. "I do not want you to be unhappy."

The quiet tenderness in his voice made her lips tremble. She fought back the torrent of emotions threatening her and pressed her arm over his.

*There are humans in the fields ahead,* Garen said.

# Broken Prince

Prince directed the horse to follow Bo quickly into the trees.

The distraction saved her from answering Prince's comment, which suited her just fine considering she didn't know what to say.

Their progress slowed as humans kept them to the woods and the terrain increasingly grew more rocky and steep.

From within the shadows of the trees Aro watched the fields of crops change to rocky pastureland. Old stumps littered the borderlands where the humans had cleared what had once been forest. She actually gasped in surprise when a miniature forest suddenly appeared. The trees were young yet, not much taller than her.

"I believe we have reached the lands of Westport," Prince commented. "The city has always done well, and is one of the more civilized few."

"Because of their Prince?"

"Partly. The southern cities have more land. If you remember the map I drew some time ago, the shoreline sticks out in the north, where Franua is, and then curves sharply inward. A bit north of here it slowly begins to curve west again. The forest border is a straight line north to south, which makes a difference in the amount of land the humans hold."

"Do they fight over it down here, too?"

"The fight over land is mostly in the mid to northern cities. They barely have enough land to provide food for the citizens. In the south, there are three cities fitting into the extended land area; Cliffdown, Westport, and Newhaven. They are all old, rich and well-defended. If they fight, it is rarely over land."

"One of them has an army massed," she reminded him.

"Yes, that would be New Haven, which is disturbing."

"Damon said it had moved north a bit. We should be able to get past them and get you home."

"We will see."

As they moved south the planted trees grew smaller until they came to an area of recently cut forest. From the woods, Aro watched humans working the churned earth. Some collected smaller pieces of wood, while others marked young trees that hadn't been damaged during the cut.

"Once the area is fully cleared they will replant. This is why the southern cities fair better. They plan for the future."

The afternoon continued and Aro remained riding with Prince while he taught her about how the southern cities managed the forests and their lands. It was something she hadn't learned much of in her tutoring. She found he made a good teacher and was surprised to find she actually missed learning.

"What is that?" A strange sound had begun echoing through the woods. It was familiar, yet she couldn't place it.

"The ravine must be not too far ahead. There is a quarry on the human side. You hear them cutting stone."

She had never seen a quarry. Or a ravine for that matter. The sounds grew louder and louder; the hammering of metal on stone by many hands.

Finally Bo stopped ahead of them and Prince pulled up beside him. Both Garen and Kei awaited them.

Aro leaned forward, her eyes widening in shock. The ground ended before them, dropping sharply. The ravine was wide. A dozen horses could ride abreast down it. She could see the stone on the other side, rising nearly straight up. Though layers of stone were visible and it likely wouldn't be too hard to climb, she had no idea how they would get the horses across.

"What do we do now?"

"You will make camp for the night."

They turned as one to see Rhee-En emerge from the trees.

Aro couldn't help but smile. She just loved the sound of his voice.

"There is a way across on the human side. However you would not make it without detection. There is another way down east of here, but the way up is even further east. You would not make it across before nightfall."

Aro glanced up at the sun. "We could camp down below. I don't want to waste time."

Rhee-En chuckled. "You do not want to be caught down there at night. The ravine is an old river bed. The river was diverted by an avalanche in the mountains more than a century ago. But it does still lead to the mountains and the Vor tend to use it as a way out."

"They have been quiet for decades," Prince said.

Rhee-En raised his eyebrows. "How long have you been gone?"

Prince stiffened behind her at the Were's condescending tone. She had no idea what they were talking about.

"They have been growing in strength the last five years. More and more are coming down into the forests." He jerked his head northward. "It was one of them we were chasing into Alar-En's lands." He gestured eastward. "There is a camp this way. Come, you can rest well tonight. We will keep watch."

They followed him, not having much of a choice in the matter.

"Are we in your land now?"

The Were looked over his shoulder at her and smiled. His tilted his head to the ravine. "The other side."

They arrived at an area by the ravine sheltered by rocks and a makeshift contraption of cut tree trunks and mud providing shelter from the elements. It wasn't large enough for the horses, but the skies had cleared up so rain wasn't a worry for the night.

"I will leave you to set up camp and return this evening." He looked to Prince. "There are things we should speak of, if you will permit."

Prince nodded. "Of course."

"My people will be patrolling. Do not be alarmed if you see them. If there is danger, we will let you know."

Aro slipped down off the horse and watched in amazement as Rhee-En walked away, only to suddenly shift into a wolf and bound into the trees.

Her eyes turned to Garen. He stared after the retreating Were for a long moment before giving himself a shake.

*I'm going hunting.*

He loped off in the other direction.

"He's never…" She fought for the word. "Shifted."

"No," Prince agreed. "He has not."

They exchanged looks.

"Do you know why?"

Prince shook his head. "I am not familiar with how Were magic works."

"The question is whether we should make an issue of it or not," Bo said.

Kei came up and took the reins of Prince's horse as the Elf slipped off. "Does it matter?"

Aro grinned suddenly. "It never does. We're family."

# Chapter 19:
# The Way Things Are

Garen returned just before dark. They'd already set up camp and gotten the fire going. Aro and Kei collected a good amount of deadfall from the surrounding forest while Bo watched the roasting rabbit and small bird Kei caught during the day.

Their food stores were depleted again and the more game they could find, the better. They'd barely have enough to get Prince home. No one said anything about what would happen after. For some reason it just wasn't a topic anyone wanted to talk about.

Aro tried not to think of it at all. The thought of continuing on without Prince left a despairing ache inside of her. She'd lost so many already. Even though he was only going home, he would still be gone.

Garen dropped a very large bird next to Kei. Aro raised her eyebrows. "Nice catch. We might actually have some meat left over tonight."

Kei picked the bird up by its long legs and headed away from camp to get it ready for cooking. Garen trotted after him, he liked some of the parts they wouldn't be eating.

The small bird and rabbit had finished so Aro removed them from the stick over the fire and split each into quarters. Everyone devoured their share. Aro saved Kei's portion and collected the bones for Garen. When they returned she set up the large bird on the spit while they ate.

Everyone sat in silence, almost full, and watched the rest of their meal cook.

"So, you know this Rhee-En?" Aro looked to Garen and then to Prince.

*All Alphas are known. There are fewer than twenty packs.*

Garen's answer was good enough, she looked to Prince.

"Alphas are the nobility of the Were," he explained. "They also, being immortal, usually hold their position for some time. The alphas are familiar to us."

"He seemed to know who you are."

Prince frowned.

She wondered what excuse for that he would come up. "Don't start with your secrets," she warned.

"I have been out of Rivenward before," he admitted. "We do have some contact with the Were, particularly those close to us. Rhee-En's land borders ours."

"So you've met him before," she pressed.

"Yes. Though it was some time ago."

"Can we trust him is the question," Bo said.

Garen snorted at the comment.

"Were are honorable. If he has given us permission to pass through his land then he will not go back on his word."

"Would the Elves know if he did something?"

Prince smiled slightly. "Yes. It is likely they know I am almost home."

Aro gasped at this unexpected information. "How would they know?"

He chuckled. "We have a Seer."

"Like the Fey?"

184

He smiled wryly. "She sees the future, yes. She is just not very good. Or she was not when I left. She was quite young, a child. Perhaps her talent and skill have improved."

Kei changed the subject, "Does Rhee-En know about us?"

*Unlikely,* Garen answered. *Unless he catches us mind speaking.*

Aro bit her lip. Whether they would get in trouble for forming a pack remained uncertain. "He won't read our thoughts?"

"Were are telepathic," Prince answered.

*We speak only. We do not read thoughts,* Garen continued. *Or invade minds. It is considered rude.*

Kei chuckled and Prince glared over at him. Bo's loud laughter erupted into the quiet night.

She took the moment to turn the conversation. "Garen, I have to ask you something."

His ears immediately dropped.

"Where do clothes go?"

He stared at her. *Clothes?*

She nodded quickly. "When he changed, he had clothes on! Where do they go?"

Clearly she'd caught him off guard with her question. It took him some time to reply. The boys finished their laughing, Prince muttering something under his breath.

*We have two forms, and one spirit. We shift our spirit from one to the other. The one not in use goes…somewhere else. Our bodies do not actually change.*

"Can you take anything?"

*There are rules. Clothing and weapons are usually fine. Sometimes things don't come back. Never are we to try to shift another living creature.* He paused. *Are you not going to ask?*

"It doesn't matter," Kei said softly.

"All of us are a little…different." Aro smiled. Garen continued to look like a sad puppy so she stood and moved to sit next to him. She wrapped her arms around his thick, furry neck and gave him a big hug. "We're a pack."

*Thank you.*

He slobbered a lick up the side of her face.

Jerking back with a squeal, she wiped at her cheek. "You did not just do that!"

Garen butted his head against hers and she hugged him again.

*I would rather tell you, than have you wonder. My story is not very interesting. Sometimes, the shift magic goes awry. When I was young, mine did so. I lost the connection to my human body and became trapped in this one.*

"Oh, Garen…"

*My pack could not help me, though they tried. Nothing could be done. They did not cast me out either, however a Were who cannot shift has little standing in a pack. After a time, I chose to leave and be on my own.*

"But you're with us now," Aro said firmly.

*Yes, though most of the time I do not understand you at all. You are certainly the strangest pack.* He turned his head toward the ravine. *Rhee-En comes.*

"Someone needs to turn the bird," Bo said.

Aro cursed and scrambled forward.

When Rhee-En approached their fire his sudden presence did not surprise them. She thought he looked a little disappointed.

Smiling in welcome, she gestured vaguely around the fire. "Please join us. Have you eaten?"

He nodded and glanced around the circle before choosing an open spot between Bo and Prince. "I have, thank you."

She grinned. "It's not quite ready yet anyway."

He chuckled and she had the sudden thought his voice would taste wonderful slathered over the roasted bird. Perhaps she was losing her mind.

"May we start with proper introductions? I am Rhee-En, alpha of the southernmost pack." He turned to Prince, a smile playing at his lips. "I believe they call you Prince."

"They do," Prince said sharply.

Rhee-En didn't press the issue, though clearly he knew Prince's real name.

"I am Bo, formerly of the Kingsport Palace Guard."

The Were's brows drew together. "Kingsport?"

"Across the sea," Kei answered quietly. He watched the Were carefully, his eyes very faintly glowing yellow.

"A Fey not caught in the fury. I can count on one hand the number of such I have seen in the last two centuries. Yet, you seem young and all of them were from before the fall."

Kei didn't answer, so Aro did before the silence became too unbearable. "Kei's parents were free of it, too."

"Who were your parents, young one?"

"Ketheris and Dalsia."

The Were again looked surprised. "I see. I did not know they had a son."

"You knew my parents?"

"Of course. My land surrounds Furia. Are they well?"

"Dead."

Rhee-En bowed his head formally. "I am sorry to hear that."

Kei looked away. Aro reached over and took his hand.

"And you are Aro, also from this…Kingsport?"

"Arowyn Mason, and yes."

"You mentioned a shipwreck before."

"I did. The Frans allied with our enemy the Gelanians and invaded. Kingsport fell and the Frans took many of my people as slaves, including all of us. Well, not Garen. The ship wrecked off the coast of Franua and we escaped."

He turned to Prince. "You have been in the west?"

Aro raised her eyebrows, from her short summary of events that was what he thought important?

Prince frowned. "Yes."

"How are things there?"

"The humans occupy the whole continent now, though are mainly gathered in great numbers along the coast and major waterways. Still, their numbers increase more rapidly than we had thought."

"They breed like mice," the Were muttered, shaking his head. "Even here, on the limited land we have allowed them, their numbers increase to the point they cannot feed themselves. In the north Cier-En is having trouble with them growing bold and trying to push into the forest. He says there could be war soon."

"This is not good news."

"They must not breach the boundary," Kei said softly, his eyes glowing brighter.

"Not to worry, there is no possibility of that. We are quite aware of the danger that would cause."

Aro struggled to follow the conversation. "What danger?"

Rhee-En raised a hand for her to wait and turned back to Prince. "That is not the worst of what I wanted to speak to you about." He paused, gathering his thoughts. "The Vor are rising again."

Prince nodded, his face more serious than she'd ever seen it. "You had mentioned that. How bad is it?"

"Growing worse each year. At first it was one or two. Now they are coming down in greater numbers and more often. It is worse here in the south, but is happening all up the Veil."

Bo interrupted. "What veil?"

"The Death's Veil. The mountain range."

"Do my people know?"

The Were shook his head. "I do not know. None have reached the wardwall. We have made sure of that."

"You have not sent word?"

"This happens from time to time, but it is getting worse these past few months. It is possible another wave is about to start. As you are heading home, I thought you could take word."

"Of course."

Aro took advantage of the momentary silence. "What are Vor?"

Rhee-En regarded her solemnly. "The Vor are dark creatures, monsters of your worst nightmares. We were created to fight them, humans were not. They would wipe out your cities in a day, and they would feed, and they would grow stronger."

"You talk like there is so much difference between us," she snapped.

"There is. You were not meant to be here."

She stared at him in shock. "What…" She didn't even know what to say.

"Humans," he clarified. "This world is a prison for the Vor. We, the Elves and Fey and Were, fought them on our home world and then were sent here in order to ensure they did not escape. This world was empty when we came."

"We…we didn't come from your world?"

"No. Though our makers certainly knew of your kind, thus the resemblance. Perhaps they even created you on some other world."

Bo laughed out loud. "Don't mind him, Aro. He is telling you tales."

Rhee-En growled. "I assure you I am not."

The entire idea, of other worlds, that humans were so different, was almost more than she could deal with. "How did we get here then?"

"I imagine the same way we did, through a Rift. The question we've not been able to answer is how that was possible. This world was supposed to have been blocked off. Your people arrived on the western continent. It was some time before we even knew they were there. Now, things are getting out of control."

She pressed her lips together and shook her head. "Maybe we were here first."

Rhee-En laughed. "No. You were not here. Our makers created this world. That is what they do." He glanced at the fire. "Humans do not understand we are protecting them. You are greedy creatures."

She couldn't really argue with that. A lot of humans were. If they weren't, she'd still be safe at home. She'd still have a home.

"I believe your dinner is burning."

Aro cursed and once again sprang forward to tend to their scorching dinner.

Rhee-En turned back to Prince. "The humans want the forests, and think to mine the Veil."

"That would not go well for them."

"No, it would not. Should they push the issue we will be sore pressed to continue our patrols if we have to fight them. If another wave of Vor is about to come, we will need the Elves. Out here."

Prince frowned and shook his head. "We guard from within Rivenward–"

"So you have in the past, yes. Even though our numbers are growing, we will not have enough warriors."

"Explain," Prince said sharply.

"Another reason we believe a wave is coming. Our birth rate has grown in the last twenty years and in the last five has more than doubled. We have even been seeing more Fey young. Yet that is part of the problem, we do not have them to fight alongside us as in the past. With their fall, we have lost half of our forces."

"The Fey will rise again."

Rhee-En turned to regard Kei. "Unfortunately, it is not likely. We know of your prophecy, young one, but it has been centuries and not come to pass. To find the arrow from..." His voice trailed off as his gaze shot to her. "Across the sea."

She raised her chin and met his gaze, though she couldn't keep the small, smug smile from twisting her lips.

"Surely not." Rhee-En swung to face Prince. "Is it her?"

The Elf shrugged. "I believe she is the arrow mentioned. What part she will play, I do not know."

"So this is why the dragon has taken interest. This could change everything." He stood abruptly. "I must go. Sleep well. In the morning we will guide you across the ravine."

Aro stared after him. Her mind remained a chaotic mess of thoughts. "Did that go well, or not?"

Bo snorted. "The question is whether he wants the Fey to rise or not. It sounded like he did. If so, we may have a new ally."

After checking the bird and finding it done, if a bit charred on one side, she pulled it off the fire to cool.

"About where we came from, was he just telling stories?"

"No, child," Prince said quietly. "Our histories say the same. He is much older than I. His father was one who came over."

"Wither me," she whispered, shaking her head. She had enough things to worry about. Monsters and Rifts and other worlds were too much for her.

"Put it from your mind, Aro," Prince offered. "It is of no concern to how we live. We are all here. We all struggle to survive. That is the way of it."

She tried to take his advice, but while attempting to sleep after they'd eaten, all she could think about was all of the differences which suddenly made sense. Humans were the only ones without magic and immortality. They were the only ones on the western continent. Her thoughts spiraled about, keeping her awake for some time until weariness finally had enough and pulled her down to sleep. Her last thought was wondering where, exactly, she fit in.

# Chapter 20:
# The Ravine

Distant howling and snarling echoing down the ravine woke Aro. The hard ground did nothing to help her get back to sleep once it stopped. The stars showed it to be early in the morning. The sun wouldn't rise for some time yet. Bo's snoring rumbled from across the fire. Beside her, Kei's even breaths proved he'd fallen back asleep as well. Sitting up quietly, she found Prince's curled up form.

He hadn't tried to sleep next to her that night, though she wasn't sure if it was because he finally understood how uncomfortable it made her, or if it had something to do with the watching Were.

More than likely the latter, she decided. He'd been different that night when Rhee-En had come. More…noble. She allowed a soft sigh to escape. The way he acted with them certainly wasn't how he interacted with the nobles at home.

Putting a little more wood on the fire gave her something to do. Once it burned low and soft, she moved beyond the ring of sleeping bodies and paced along the ravine edge.

Her head pounded with too many thoughts. Pacing and sorting them out helped to pass the time.

Humans being from another world? Not something she really needed to care about. It was history, nothing more.

Monsters attacking from the mountains? More worrisome. The little she knew didn't provide her enough information to decide on any course of action. They'd have to be careful on the rest of their journey. After that…well since she had no idea what they would be doing it wasn't something she needed to worry about now either. What she did need to know was how to fight them. She'd have to ask when everyone got up. Perhaps Garen or Prince knew.

As for Prince… Her steps faltered and she stopped. Though it hurt to admit it, she'd have to let him go. Both physically and with her heart. He wasn't hers and he never would be. He could not survive in her world. That much was obvious.

As for his…she would never know. He didn't love her, he would never ask her to go with him. She would only be a burden. One he didn't have time for, not with being a prince. After being gone so long surely he would be immensely busy. Not to mention anything he might need to do in regard to the monsters. War did not leave time for love.

"Did you swallow a bug?"

She jumped and blinked. She'd been staring right at Prince, but her thoughts had taken her so far away she hadn't noticed him wake and sit up.

"The look on your face," he continued when she didn't answer.

"Oh. No. I was just…thinking." She forced a polite smile, hoping he wasn't irritated she'd been standing there watching him sleep.

He tilted his head to look up at the stars. "The sun will rise soon. How long have you been awake?"

"For a while," she admitted ruefully. Crossing her arms over her chest, she stared down at him. "You should go back to sleep. You need it."

"You are not my mother, Arowyn."

She snorted.

He grimaced. "She would never do that, for one."

Somehow she managed to keep her sudden laughter quiet enough she didn't wake Bo or Kei.

He patted the ground beside him. "Come, sit with me."

Hesitation warred with the desire to be closer to him. Desire won, though her steps were slow and once seated she kept her distance, close, yet not touching him. Staring down at her fingers, she picked at her dirty nails. The silence was uncomfortable and uneasiness began to twist in her stomach.

"We should talk," he said finally, his voice quiet and strained.

"About what?"

"Whatever pleases you? I believe…it would help."

She bit her lip, wondering what they could talk about. Certainly not them, the nonexistent them. "Tell me about your home," she said suddenly. "What it's like there."

A light laugh spilled out of him and she looked up to see him smiling at her warmly.

"That I can do, with pleasure. However," He held out his hand. "I can show you much easier. If you will allow it."

She stared at his hand for a moment before slipping hers into it.

"Go into yourself, I will join you there."

She closed her eyes and pictured her inner spot. When she opened them again she stood on the barren land before her fortress.

Prince appeared a moment later and she forced a wavering smile. He walked up to stand beside her and turned her to face away from her towering walls.

*Now watch.* He spread his arms and the bleak landscape suddenly shimmered to be replaced by an image from his mind.

Her breath caught in her throat as her eyes widened at the beautiful scene of forests and lakes, rivers and meadows and in the distance the largest and most beautiful city she'd ever seen.

She barely noticed his arm slip over her shoulders as the scene changed from one beautiful view to another. With his other hand he pointed out special features; a waterfall, a massive tree, gardens. He took her into his city and showed her the beauty there. Towering buildings of fantastic architecture, monuments and fountains, and more gardens.

The people were even more startling in their beauty. They wore clothes she didn't even know how to describe, precious metals and jewels draped from necks and hair. She glanced over at him. What would he look like when he was healed and as he once had been? She thought him beautiful now, even pale and thin and dirty. Dark rings smeared beneath his sparkling blue eyes. He looked so tired. Was doing this a strain on him?

*Thank you,* she whispered. She noticed his arm around her then and heat crept into her face. Quickly, she lowered her head.

*Aro.* A finger lifted her chin. Gentle fingers brushed hair from her face and he smiled, looking into her eyes.

She stiffened, her breath catching in throat.

His eyes searched hers for a moment. She hoped he didn't see the pain still lingering in her heart. He sighed and looked away, yet tightened his arm around her, pulling her close to his side.

She didn't understand those strange looks, not at all. With a shaky breath she raised her chin and put an arm around his waist. Leaning against him, she stared out at the last image he'd shown her. Things were as they were. Perhaps, he gave her what he could. She would take that, and cherish it.

He gave her a brief squeeze and she looked up. Though staring out at the image, he was smiling.

# Broken Prince

She opened her eyes to the sound of quiet voices. The dim light of dawn turned the sky pale pink as the last stars faded away. Had she fallen asleep? Blinking rapidly to wake up, she suddenly stiffened. She'd somehow gotten close to Prince and fallen asleep against his chest.

Scrambling to her feet, she fought back embarrassment. It was no one's concern who she used for a pillow. She headed toward the trees to relieve herself.

Bo walked past, resting a hand on her shoulder. "Be careful, pup."

Her cheeks flamed but she nodded. "I am." She'd barely gone two steps before Kei caught her eye. He didn't say anything, but his tight jaw and drawn together brows spoke volumes. He wasn't happy with her.

She hurried into the shadows of the trees. "Wither me." She couldn't do anything right.

Returning to the fire, she sat down next to Kei as Bo handed out their portions of last night's leftovers. The cold meat sat heavily in her stomach. They only had four or five days left until they reached the gates to Rivenward. She could do this.

Kei reached out a hand, his greasy fingers twining into hers. *Will you leave me for him?*

Her eyes widened in surprise. *Kei...*

The pain on his face, in the tone of his mind voice, tore her heart apart. She squeezed his fingers. *Things haven't changed. You don't need to worry.*

He nodded and looked away, his look of pain turning to annoyance as he glared over at Prince.

Despite being surrounded by them, she didn't understand men at all.

Rhee-En arrived as they loaded the packs onto the horses. "Follow me. The way down is not far."

Prince and Bo mounted, the rest of them following on foot. They reached the trail down as the sun peeked through the mountains.

Aro stepped up to the ravine edge and peered down. "Is it safe?"

"For the most part," Rhee-En answered. "You will have to lead the horses and go slowly. Single file."

The narrow trail didn't look safe. The steep slope was littered with debris and rocks. At least she didn't have a problem with heights.

"We'll go first and clear the path as much as possible for the horses. Remember, don't rush." Before anyone could answer at least a dozen giant wolves bounded past them and began the descent. The clatter of falling rocks and branches quickly met their ears.

Aro peered over again, watching the Were swipe the debris off the trail as they made their way down. They didn't seem to have any worries.

Garen headed down the trail as Bo and Prince dismounted. Kei walked past her. "Me next." He flashed her a grin. "I'll catch you if you fall."

"I better not fall," she muttered.

Bo followed Kei, moving very slowly with his reluctant mount.

Aro turned and Prince motioned her to go next. "Do you want me to take the horse?"

"I am fine. Go on."

She frowned. He seemed paler than he had the day before. Maybe he just hadn't gotten enough sleep. Heading down the slope she kept looking back to check on him. He seemed to be doing well enough, watching his step, with one hand on the rock for balance.

They all made it down safely and waited while Bo checked the horses' hooves for stones. The Were circled restlessly around them until they started on their way again.

198

They set a fast pace and Aro wondered if they worried about more monsters attacking them in the ravine. She wished they weren't moving so quickly, she still needed to ask someone how to fight them.

A large black wolf fell in beside her. *You run well for a human.*

*I run with a Fey.*

Rhee-En's deep laughter echoed in her mind. Though still beautiful, she found it wasn't quite as distracting as it had been. Maybe she was getting used to his lovely voice.

*The route up is not far. But come ahead with me. I wish to show you something.*

She increased her pace, passing Kei and Garen. When they finally stopped ahead of the others her breath came in quick gasps. She needed to run more. Her nose wrinkled at the sudden rotten smell. "What is that?"

*One of the Vor. Not too large. But troublesome enough.*

Stepping forward, she found the carcass in the shadows. What it had looked like while living she had no idea. "Do they smell like that alive?"

*No. They have very little scent. Which makes them more dangerous.* Rhee-En sat back on his haunches. *Vor is a general term for a large number of creatures. They have little in common, except for being dark in nature and appearance, and want for destruction and death. Some have the minds of animals, others are more intelligent. Some work together, others do not.*

"How do you kill them?"

*The usual ways; vital organs, cut off heads. Luckily none carry poisons. The problem has always been in their numbers. They tend to come in groups of various species. The ones to watch out for are the Vor-ai.*

"What are they?"

*I doubt you will ever see one. They are the minds behind the continued attacks, the most intelligent of them all.*

199

*Also the most deadly, at least for us. They can take incorporeal form. Do you know what that means?*

She shook her head.

*Turn into...something like a fog. They kill in that form, but we cannot harm them. We can only kill them when they are solid. The Fey could bind them. Only the Elves can destroy them.*

"Why won't I see one? Not that I want to," she added quickly.

*They only come out of the mountains for the major assaults. We call those waves, when thousands come down. It does not happen often. They throw everything at us, we destroy most of them, they go back into hiding to gather their ranks again.*

The thought turned her stomach and she swallowed quickly. "And you think one of these waves is coming? Why? What do they want?"

*There has not been a wave since before the Queens fell. We are long due for one. As for what they want, the Elves guard the Rift that brought us here. It could not be closed. They want to go home.*

Aro nodded in understanding. She wanted to go home, too.

*Let us go, the ravine is not a safe place.*

She followed him back to the others. *Why did you show me that? Why tell me everything?*

His head cocked to one side. *In case you are the one.*

She was really getting tired of that prophecy.


The Were noticeably relaxed once they'd made it up the other side of the ravine. Perhaps because of the dangers below or maybe they were just happy to be home. They'd finally entered Rhee-En's pack lands.

The alpha shifted once they'd all reached the top.

"Thank you for guiding us," she said formally.

"I wish you safe travels," he replied. He looked to Prince. "May your journey be swift. Travel southwest and you will reach the river before nightfall. Stay the course and you should find it near the easiest crossing."

"Thank you, again, for everything." She smiled, looking at the surrounding Were as well.

He walked up to her, stopping close. "You travel with interesting companions. Stay safe, little one. Perhaps we will meet again one day."

"I would like that," she said politely.

Regarding her steadily for a moment, the sudden boom of his mind voice startled her. *Hear me all, the human Arowyn is welcome in my lands.*

She blinked in shock, but quickly gathered her wits. "And Bo," she said quietly, tilting her head in his direction where he waited on the horse.

"Yes, of course." *Let that be, the humans, Bo and Aro.* He laughed out loud. "Bo and Aro."

She grimaced, but a smile overcame it. "We've heard that before, you know."

"I imagine so."

"Why did you do that?"

He gestured to Kei. "You travel with a Fey. Perhaps one day he will wish to visit Furia. Even in ruins, it is beautiful. You should see it, if you can."

"I will try."

He reached out and cupped her cheek in his hand. She froze, surprised by his action. His thumb traced a path along her cheek and across her lips. "You are an intriguing young woman. It is a shame you are mortal."

Sound erupted behind her. Both Kei and Garen growled and she heard two swords slide from their sheaths.

*Easy, boys.*

The Were played a dangerous game. She wondered what he thought to accomplish. Though his motions indicated an interest in her, his face had not been tender or loving, merely thoughtful.

Her eyebrows rose as she waited for the Were's reaction to her overprotective friends.

He looked over her shoulder and bared his teeth. A low growl of warning rumbled from his chest.

She laughed.

Startled, he dropped his hand to stare at her in surprise. *You should fear me. You do know this?*

*Apparently I'm not like most women.*

A smile twitched at his lips. *Apparently.* "We return to the pack now," he said out loud.

She nodded and stepped back, wanting to avoid any further incidents. His actions and words surprised her and she wasn't quite sure what to make of them. All she did know, was her boys had not been happy. She almost feared to turn around in case she had done something wrong.

Watching the wolves fade into the trees gave her some time. Turning your back on a pack was not only bad manners, but not a smart thing to do either. Though they had been nothing but helpful to them, she wasn't sure how much she could trust them.

Once the last wolf ran out of sight she spun on her heel. "Ready to head out?"

Prince frowned down at her. "Arowyn."

"I didn't do anything!"

His frown deepened. "I dislike his interest in you."

"Believe me, so do I."

*She does not act submissive to the alpha,* Garen commented.

Heads turned to regard him in surprise.

She hadn't thought about how the Were worked within their packs.

*Arowyn is our alpha female, but he does not know this. To him she is merely a mortal human. Even so, most humans fear the Were. He is impressed by her bravery and strength.*

"There's nothing to worry over," she insisted.

"Very well," Prince snapped. He turned his horse and headed into the trees.

She fought back the urge to throw something at his back and followed.

"Be careful," Kei whispered, falling into step beside her.

"Always."

Jen Wylie

# Chapter 21:
# A Different Kind of Fighting

They reached the river Rhee-En mentioned before dark. Garen located the crossing and they stood on the shore debating whether to cross now or in the morning.

The river was wide and fairly fast moving. The crossing showed shallow waters a good distance out, but they were uncertain if it remained that way the entire distance across.

"If I'm going to get wet," Bo said. "I'd rather do so now. We can dry off at the fire all night."

"Would it be safer? Over there," Aro asked. Talk of the Vor, and the fact they'd been encountered recently made her nervous.

Prince frowned. "Vor prefer not to cross water. However, they could have found a way across, or others could have come down from the mountains on the other side of the river."

Aro looked up at him and sighed. "We might as well go now then. Like Bo said, I'd rather not be wet all day tomorrow either."

Aro mounted behind Prince, and Kei behind Bo. The river deepened in the middle, and despite hopes of staying dry, boots and pants did indeed get wet. Garen swam across easily enough and met them on the other side.

A bit further downstream they found a favorable spot for a camp and managed to have everything set up and dinner started before darkness fell.

After a meager meal that didn't do much to relieve her hunger, Aro stared into the flickering flames of the fire. Her thoughts rambled, bouncing from the Vor, to other worlds, to the fact Prince would be home soon.

If they remained on schedule they would reach the gates of Rivenward in three or four more days. They had almost made it. Prince seemed strong enough to be able to complete the journey. As promised, they would get him home safe. Part of her knew she should be happy about it, the rest of her wished they had more time. Though the journey had taken months, almost a year if she counted in the many months they'd wintered in the city up north, it didn't seem like that long. How had time gone by so fast?

Bo ruffled her hair as he walked by. "You should get some sleep, pup."

She nodded, though worried she'd not be able to get any at all with the way her thoughts ran around in her head. Tomorrow would come soon enough.

Kei settled down next to her. She rolled over, watching Prince where he'd found a spot not far from her. Would he notice if she stayed up all night and watched him sleep?

He turned his head as if he'd heard her thoughts and a small, sad smile crossed his lips for a moment. "Sleep well, Arowyn."

"You, too," she whispered. Rolling over, she concentrated on listening to the sounds of the night around them. Night animals skittered around. Something chittered. The fire popped and crackled. Bo started snoring.

Sleep came and went and she tossed and turned. The feeling of being watched woke her more than once. She didn't roll over to see if it was Prince.

# Broken Prince

Light rain made for a damp start to the morning. At least in the distance they could see blue skies. Travelling in such weather put her in a foul mood. She stumbled along next to the horses picking their way carefully through the wet underbrush.

Kei and Garen came and went, grumbling in her mind about the wet and rain and how it interfered with scent trails.

She slipped on a patch of wet leaves and cursed under her breath.

Prince pulled his horse to a stop. "Do you want to ride?"

Wiping soaked hair from her forehead, she grimaced and then nodded. He pulled her up in front and settled himself again.

"Thanks," she murmured. The warmth of him at her back distracted her quickly. Heat flushed her cheeks and she let out a slow, quiet breath. Since they touched she had to remember to keep her thoughts carefully guarded. Things remained mostly good between them. She didn't want to ruin the friendship with stray thoughts of how much she still loved him.

They rode in silence, which suited her fine. The dismal rain continued through the morning until the wind began to pick up. It quickly blew the clouds away and sunshine wrapped them in warmth. Between it and the wind she thought they might actually dry out by noon.

The horse spooked suddenly to the left. Her balance shifted and she scrambled forward, trying to grab onto the mane. Before she could, the horse reared, shrieking out an ear-piercing scream. Only Prince's arms to either side of her kept her in place. Her body slammed back against his as he struggled to hold on to the reins. The horse crashed back to the ground. Prince's chin banged off the back of her head and she cried out at the sudden unexpected pain.

The horse swung and twisted and then bucked, sending them both flying from the saddle. The sudden impact with the nearby tree sent pain lancing through her shoulder. It was quickly forgotten as she dropped and hit the ground.

Landing on her side sent new waves of pain through her body. With a groan she tipped over onto her stomach and pushed herself up on her elbows. "Rotting horse…" Her fingers dug into the dirt as she struggled to push past the pain.

Her head snapped up, her mind suddenly focusing in on the sounds of chaos in front of her.

Bo struggled to keep control of his horse. He fought one-handed with the reins, spinning the panicked animal in fast, tight circles. He held his sword in his other hand and cursed loudly as they spun, his head turning every which way.

He was surrounded.

Her mouth dropped open at she stared at their attackers. Their long claws and small stature immediately identified them as Fey. Wearing ragged leather and furs, even from a distance she could see how filthy they were. Four of them gracefully circled Bo and the horse, easily keeping out of reach of both hooves and sword.

"Wither me!" She scrambled up to her knees and spun around in the dirt, searching for Prince. "Rot it!"

He'd hit a tree as well and had fallen into a limp heap at the base of it. Flinging herself forward to reach his side, she then shook his shoulders. "Wake up!"

His eyes fluttered, but he remained unconscious. "Rot!" She smacked his cheeks, but he didn't stir. *Kei!*

*We're coming!*

Standing quickly, she drew her daggers and stood over Prince, turning to keep an eye on the Fey. She counted four of them and debated whether she should leave Prince's side to help Bo or not. Were there more?

She'd fought with Kei before, but that had just been training. Worry knotted her stomach. Could she fight wild Fey? As they circled, she could clearly see all of them were in full fury with their glowing red eyes.

Garen burst from the trees, knocking a dark haired Fey to the ground. Their battle quickly became one of claws and fangs and snarls. Kei appeared next to another, eyes red and claws striking.

A pale haired female darted at the horse. Bo finally lost his seat as it panicked, rearing and bucking. Once free of its rider it bolted into the trees.

*Prince! Wake up!*

She spared one last glance for him before rushing forward. Strategies and training flashed through her mind as she crossed the distance between them. Approaching the two Fey closing in on Bo, she muttered curses under her breath…

And sheathed her blades.

Gritting her teeth, and hoping she hadn't lost her mind, she flung herself at the closest Fey, bringing them both down to the ground. Twisting and rolling to keep away from the deadly claws, she finally managed to get above the growling Fey. She slammed her flat palm onto his chest and before he could react…pulled.

"Let it go!"

The Fey stared at her in shock. She didn't give him a choice. With all the force she could muster she ripped his fury from him, pulling and pulling until she fell back with a gasp once his eyes had returned to a normal, not glowing, gold.

The Fey gaped at her and began to shake. His claws and fangs retracted. Before she could say anything else he sprang to his feet and ran.

His power thrummed through her. His fury danced along her nerves, burning and pushing for violence. Stumbling to her feet, she spun around and saw Bo closest to her.

The Fey's power made her feel invincible. She repeated the same tactic, springing onto the back of the female Fey engaged with him. She also ran as soon as her fury disappeared.

"Aro, what are you doing?"

She shook her head, trying to control her erratic, heavy breathing. She'd never taken so much before. Unlike Kei's fury, theirs was much wilder. Of course, for all she knew they'd been trapped in their fury for five hundred years.

"See to Prince. He's hurt." She couldn't see Garen and the dark haired Fey. *Garen, where are you?*

*On a merry chase.*

She ran toward Kei, ignoring Bo's comments and curses behind her.

Kei noticed her approach...and her glowing red eyes. *No more!*

*Can you make them stop? Do you want to kill them?*

His frustrated growl rumbled through her mind as he evaded the other Fey. It didn't escape her notice he wasn't attacking. He faced another woman, this one with a dark mess of tangled and matted shoulder length hair.

Aro's brow drew down in confusion and she frowned. The woman didn't seem to be trying to kill him either. She kept trying to sneak quick glances behind her, but Kei prevented her each time, keeping her occupied with his feints.

*Hold her for me. It doesn't take long.*

*I don't—*

*Hold her!*

The next time the woman became distracted Kei lunged forward. They scuffled and the woman screeched as he finally managed to get her into a position where she couldn't use her claws against him.

Aro sprang forward, pressing her hand on the woman's chest and pulling the fury into her. The Fey tensed, and then held still, her eyes widening as the color shifted from red to

210

orange. As they turned yellow tears appeared and she slumped back against Kei. He continued to hold her, and Aro pulled her gaze from the woman's face to meet his.

Still in his fury, his red eyes blazed angrily at her. His lip curled up slightly, showing fang, and low growl met her ears.

Kei wasn't happy with her, at all. Pressing her lips tightly together, she looked back at the woman. Her eyes no longer glowed. Aro pulled away the last of her fury and power and stepped back.

Kei released his hold and the Fey dropped to the ground. "What have...how did you..." She raised her hands and stared at her fingers. Suddenly her head snapped up and she whirled around where she sat, searching amongst the trees. "Meena! Aron!" Before they could react she flung herself away, finding her feet and disappearing into the shadows of the forest.

Aro turned, searching to see if any of them had returned.

The forest remained silent.

Jen Wylie

# Chapter 22:
# Power of the Fey

The power of three Fey coursed through her.

Fire. She burned from the inside out. Her vision blurred and she stumbled as the trees swayed around her.

*I've lost him.*

She had to think a moment before she understood the Fey Garen had been chasing had eluded him. Blinking again, she shook her head, trying to clear it. She needed to get rid of the power, like she'd always done with Kei. Let it go...

"Aro!"

The urgency in Bo's call shocked her back into focus. A hand grasped her arm and she looked up at Kei. His fury had gone and he looked worried more than angry.

"Prince."

"Rot!" How could she have forgotten he'd been injured? How bad was he, to have Bo call for her so sharply? She raced through the trees, Kei catching her arm and righting her balance when she stumbled more than once.

Finally she found them and slid to the ground where Bo knelt, Prince on his side in his arms. Before she could open her mouth, Bo tilted his unconscious body, revealing the Elf's back.

Through the dark red of blood she saw the slashing wounds crossing his back from shoulder to hip. Claw marks.

"What? When? How?"

213

Bo shook his head. "I don't know. But they're deep and he's lost a lot of blood. He won't wake."

"Rot!" She leaned forward, lowering her head to look at Prince's face. Had she ever seen him so pale? His lips were tinged blue. Fury overcame her. She shouldn't have tried to save the Fey. They'd killed her Prince. They–

"No!" Sitting back, she pressed her fists to her temples and squeezed her eyes closed. Now wasn't the time for hysterics. Prince needed her. Pushing through the rage roaring within her, she struggled to think…

"The horses," she said quickly. "We need the supplies. Go," she snapped. Kei stood, and she held out her arms to take Prince from Bo.

He snorted at her commanding tone, but slipped Prince onto her lap.

"Hurry! Get Garen to look, too!"

She pulled Prince close to her, wrapping her arms around him and pressing her face against his. "Don't die!"

How long would it take to find the horses? She let out a snarl of frustration. She couldn't think! If only the rotting Fey power wasn't roaring through her!

A gasp nearly choked her. Leaning back, she gently brushed the hair from his face. "You're not going to be happy with me," she whispered.

Dipping her head down, she pressed a kiss to his forehead.

It took only a moment to settle him against her. Her hands pressed over as much of the seeping wounds on his back as they could.

Inhaling a deep breath, she then let it out slowly, pushing the wild power within her down her arms and through her hands. Resistance was brief. The power flowed sluggishly at first and then her rage at the wasting time pushed it through faster and faster.

# Broken Prince

*Heal, my prince. Heal quickly. I won't let you die. I won't!*

He didn't answer, and she feared the power wouldn't work. Perhaps she'd been too late.

His body jerked suddenly, and then again. She leaned over him, holding him more tightly, and continued to push the power and fury into him.

The scream that ripped from his lips startled her. She flinched back, releasing him as his back arched against her hands. He slid from her lap to the ground, curling in on himself.

Power and fury remained within her. She hadn't given it all to him, and wondered if she should continue. Reaching out, she stopped when he flinched away from her touch.

"Do. Not. Touch. Me."

Pain from his words brought anger instead of tears. He lived, because of her. She should have learned by now not to expect any thanks.

Sound behind her interrupted her mental rant. She swung around.

The missing Fey froze, eyes blazing as he regarded her a moment. Baring his fangs, he snarled and then bolted away through the trees.

The fury within her reared up, demanding she follow. Pressure lanced through her chest, pulling her to get up and run. Before she could think about it, she did, racing through the trees after him.

For a moment she worried for Prince, but if he was well enough to snap at her, he should be fine. Then all her thoughts focused on the Fey she chased. When she caught him… she wasn't sure what she would do.

Everything became clearer, her hearing sharpened, and strength soared through every part of her. If she hadn't been focused on her quarry she might have given all of that more thought. Instead she pushed the thoughts aside and ran. Her feet pounded across the forest floor as she weaved through the trees. Silence was not a priority. Catching the Fey stole all of her attention.

Soon she caught sight of him again and pressed herself even harder. He wasn't breathing hard, yet neither was she. Glancing over his shoulder, he snarled at her and veered to the right. She followed, carefully tracking his movements as he tried to lose her.

He feinted to the left. With a burst of energy she flung herself forward to the right. Not noticing she hadn't taken the bait, he ran into her path and she hit him hard in the back, sending them both tumbling to the ground.

Twisting and rolling, she avoided his claws, finally coming to her knees beside him and smacking her hands down on his chest. The strange action took him by surprise and that brief moment was all she needed to steady herself and begin to pull his wild power and fury into her.

He didn't fight her, but she didn't slow down or trust him. Prepared to dodge or fling herself away at any sign of aggression, she kept her eyes locked on his until the red faded down through the colors and the light finally died.

The Fey stared up at her in shock, his eyes the normal golden color of his kind.

She pushed back from him. "You're free now. Go." His fury bombarded her senses. Dizziness blurred her vision as his power surged through her. "Go! Go, go!"

The Fey scrambled to his feet and fled into the trees.

She turned onto her hands and knees, fighting the rising wave of nausea. Too much power. Too much fury. Though she'd given much from the first three to Prince, she hadn't given it all. This one, he had been strong, maybe too strong for her. Her skin itched and burned. The urge to rend and kill and destroy pushed to overwhelm her. Yet wrapped around the fury came the need, the yearning, to have a focus for it. Was that what the queen did? Provide that control and focus?

"Arowyn!"

She started at Prince's unexpected cry. He sounded… furious.

"Rot it all…" Struggling to her feet, she found her own tracks and broke into a run. Not quite the wild dash she'd just had, but fast enough.

She'd given Prince a good dose of power…and fury. She hadn't known how to separate the two when giving it to him. In her haste to follow the other Fey, she'd forgotten to drain the fury part out of him.

She'd known he'd be furious with her for giving him Fey power. Having actual fury within him as well…she didn't know what he'd do.

"Arowyn!"

By the time she neared where she'd left him he'd called her name so many times she lost count. His insistence didn't help her own fury. She needed to disperse it, and the Fey power, as well. Prince called again and she stopped abruptly. He'd moved. She turned east, slowing her speed to listen for him. Finally she spotted him and slowed to watch him.

Like some wild thing he crashed through the underbrush ahead of her, not even bothering to try to go around the thicket in his path.

His hair framed his face in a dark tangled mess, tatters of ripped cloth hung from the back of his bloody, ruined shirt. The way he twisted and turned, he seemed to at least have used the power she'd given him to heal.

Moving forward warily, she used the time to try to calm herself so she could get rid of the fury within her. The raging emotions were distracting, and she would rather talk to Prince without having unnatural anger fueling her words.

"Arowyn!"

"I'm here," she forced out quietly.

Spinning to face her, his eyes narrowed. Suddenly he charged toward her and she scrambled backward, not expecting such a reaction.

"What have you done?"

Banging her back up against a tree, she winced at his roar. She didn't try to escape, she needed to touch him and drain the fury. She needed to deal with the consequences of her actions.

However, the look of violence on his face, and that he didn't slow as he approached, changed her mind and she ducked to the side.

"Let me explain!"

He spun and sprang at her again. "No! You gave me Fey power. Fey!"

"You were dying!"

"I am quite aware of that," he snarled. "You should have let me go."

She shook her vehemently as she evaded him. "You know I can't do that."

"First you use Were magic to bind me into a pack and now this? Do you know what you've done?"

"It will fade. If you'll just stop I can take the fury away."

He froze in mid-step. "You have done this before. With Kei. How…" He shook his head.

"I don't know how, just that I can do it. It's fine–"

"You foolish girl!"

A growl of frustration rumbled out of him and she took a step back at the sudden rise in anger. His words made her own fury spring forth again and she gritted her teeth against it.

It distracted her enough she only had time to raise her hands as he darted forward. Grasping her wrists, his momentum carried them back until she hit another tree.

"Foolish, foolish child! You have no idea the powers you are playing with."

"I'm not playing," she snapped. Raising her chin she glared up at him. "I needed him. Like I need you. I do what I have to do."

His head bowed down, closing the distance between them. "Says the little human girl. You understand nothing of our ways or of magic. Always the child–"

"I am not a child!"

His glowing red eyes stared heatedly into hers. "No," he finally said his voice soft and husky. "You are not, are you?"

Her brow furrowed at the sudden change, but she didn't have a chance to reply. His head dipped down and his lips pressed to hers, forceful and demanding.

Surprise froze her for a moment. He was kissing her? After everything he'd said? The fury within her rose in a frenzy, a whipping mass of red. She kissed him back, pushing against him, trying to push him away. Trying to get closer.

He shifted, pinning her hands above her head against the tree and then he pulled back. His blue eyes hid behind the faint red glow of the fury.

"I should not be doing this."

She gasped for breath, her gaze dropping to the angry line of his mouth. "I don't care."

"You should. Nothing will come of this. This is…nothing."

His words cut through her like a knife. Pushing against him, she tried to break free of his hold. "You rotting–"

Lips covered hers, silencing her. As his tongue traced across her lips she twisted, trying to break free but kissing him back at the same time because she simply couldn't stop. Finally she found leverage. Jerking her arms down, she pushed her knee into the side of his leg and tried to escape to the side.

His foot shot out, tripping her, but he didn't let go of her wrists and she pulled him down with her. Hitting the ground hard, she twisted and turned and kicked, trying to get away. Too easily he overpowered her. When had he gotten so strong?

She tried to scream in frustration but then his lips were on hers once more, his tongue pressing for entry. Parting her lips, new sensations sent tendrils of heat through her body. She finally understood why people kissed like this. Melting beneath him, he finally released her hands and she wrapped her arms around his neck.

He kissed her until her brain felt like it had melted and when he finally pulled back she fought to find her breath.

Red eyes once more glared down into hers. "Do you understand yet, Aro?"

She shook her head, having no idea what he was talking about, not even wanting to try to understand. Her fingers tangled in his hair and she pulled, trying to bring him back down to her.

"It matters not what I may or may not feel for you. This will never be."

She frowned, pulling her hands from his hair and bringing them down to rest on his shoulders. "Will you stop with all of that?"

"No." He kissed her again, a soft press. "Do you wish to come home with me?"

She blinked up at him in confusion. "But, you said…"

"Yes, you would be my pet. I would buy you a beautiful collar and you could kneel at my feet in court. Would you like that?"

Her fury rose so swiftly she felt like her skin was on fire. The flames burned through her, a roaring furnace of anger at his betrayal.

"And when the Elves learn of your special mind gifts, they will enjoy playing so many games with you. Likely they would destroy your mind. Perhaps for the best, as life at court, even for pets, is neither easy or safe."

She barely managed to mute the cry of denial that tore up her throat. Her fingers clawed into his shoulders and she pushed, throwing up her hip as she rolled him off of her.

A startled oath rumbled out of him as he hit the ground. Following her momentum she rolled on top of him and then flung herself to the side.

"Why are you doing this to me?"

He caught her ankle and jerked her back to him. Her fury flowed around her, whipping her anger as she fought with him in the dirt until he finally pinned her beneath him once more.

Pressing his body down against hers, he caught her wrists and pinned them next to her head. "I can not seem to stop." He kissed her. "Despite knowing better, I am attracted to you. Lust, desire, is a powerful thing it seems." He kissed her again and then trailed kisses along her jaw and down her neck as he spoke. "This power you have given me, this fury, is not helping. I am so angry with you, for so many reasons. Yet the worst, is the anger toward myself for wanting you so much." His lips left her neck as she froze and he raised his head to gaze down at her.

She stared up at him, his words shocking her more than he could possibly know. They hurt her, more than she expected.

He wanted her.

He wanted her and right now. In this moment, she had him.

Thoughts of fighting him fled and she raised her head to tentatively kiss him before dropping back to the ground and waiting. She had to try.

Their red eyes burned into each other for a long moment. A slight smile curved his lips and then they descended to hers once more.

Surrendering to him, she pushed a scattering of thoughts and doubts aside and simply…felt. The weight of his body over hers. The pleasure his touch and kiss sent through every part of her. The warmth and pressure of his lips on hers, the feel of his tongue searching her mouth and warring with her own. It wasn't as she'd imagined it would be. Fueled by their fury, it was rough and wild, but it sent her senses reeling and her heart raced so quickly she feared it would suddenly stop altogether.

She could feel the power within him, within her. Their fury mixed and twinned around them both, pulling them closer. She didn't understand why it wasn't pushing her to attack and fight. It seemed to want him closer, to be pulling them together.

A hand slid down her side and she shivered against him. Cool fingers slipped under the edge of her shirt and hit her burning skin. Gasping against his mouth, she arched her back and moaned as his hand slid up along her side, caressed her ribs and–

He was simply gone, torn from her. Starring up at the canopy of the trees she gasped in shock before pushing up on her elbows.

She saw the last thing she expected.

Kei had him by the back of the neck, but only for a moment. Prince twisted away and snarled, swinging at the Fey. As she scrambled to her feet, Garen sprang forward, snapping at Prince. Bo caught him by surprise from behind, catching his arms and holding him immobile.

"What are you doing!" Kei's eyes glowed red and he lunged toward Prince.

"No!"

Everyone turned toward her and she jerked back under their angry stares. Her fury rose once more and she crossed her arms in annoyance.

"What have you done, Aro?" Bo grimaced as Prince struggled against him.

Her brain struggled for an acceptable answer. "Saved his life. Again."

Prince threw back his head and laughed. "And I merely repaid her for it," he said bitterly.

She sucked in a startled breath. His words suddenly came back to her, all of them. Striding forward, she slammed her palm on his chest and ripped the fury from him.

His eyes quickly returned to normal. By the time she was done, he sagged back against Bo.

Stepping closer, she tried to reign in her sudden anger. "You do not play games with me," she whispered furiously. "Ever."

Raising his head, his beautiful blue eyes laughed into hers. "Learn not to be played with then, little one."

"You rotting bastard." She pushed him in the chest. "If you don't love me, then do not ever kiss me again. Understand?"

"Oh, I do," he snapped. "And you never give me Fey power again. Understand?"

She growled in response. Kei grabbed her arm, pulling her back when she moved to spring at Prince.

"Aro?"

"Leave me alone." Fighting to contain the overwhelming anger and disgust she felt for herself, she turned her back on them all and fled into the trees.

Jen Wylie

# Chapter 23:
# Letting Go

Her whole body trembled in anger as she walked. It felt as though some violent, living thing tried to burst free from within her. Clenching her fists and teeth, she focused on staying in control.

Eventually she stopped, dropping to her knees. Each breath came frantic and quick. Her heart beat just as fast, almost a roar in her ears.

Prince's words repeated themselves over and over in her head. He didn't love her. She'd only ever be a pet. A pet! She couldn't control the anger she felt toward him. Or toward herself for allowing things to come to this. She should have let things be. She knew how he felt, or thought she did. Now she had confusion on top of the anger. Now everything they'd had was ruined.

She couldn't relax, couldn't let the power and the fury go like she had in the past.

It overwhelmed her, consumed her from the inside. She rocked back and forth, trying and failing to calm down and let the power go. She wanted to scream, to roar out her fury so it echoed from one end of the forest to the other. She didn't. She'd be trained well enough on the importance of being quiet in unknown territory.

Leaves crackled behind her and she stopped her rocking. The light step told her it was Kei. He stopped behind her and crouched down.

"Leave," she whispered, her voice hoarse as if she truly had been screaming.

A hand touched her shoulder and she jerked it off.

"Relax. Let it go," he said quietly.

"I can't!" She spun on him then, raising her hands to hit or push him away.

He caught her wrists. She fought against him, but knew she wouldn't win. He was faster than her, stronger than her. He was Fey. She wasn't.

He jerked her forward, catching her by surprise. A moment later his arms were around her, holding her close, her head tucked under his chin.

She tilted her head back but could only see his neck. "I want to rip your throat out," she whispered. Her words shocked her, so too did the fact she meant what she said. The additional fury from Prince certainly made a difference.

"I know."

She lowered her head and clenched her teeth together. He understood. Of course he did. He was Fey. She wasn't, but Fey power currently ran through her.

He held her, tightly yet gently, pressing his cheek against her hair.

"I asked you not to do this," he finally said.

"I didn't take yours, did I?"

"We don't know what it's doing to you. You know that. But you did it again. Four times." His arms tightened around her. "Why?"

"They reminded me of you. When you were caught in the fury. Would you have had us kill them? I know it's not their fault. I wanted to help them."

He sighed against her hair. "You have to stop."

"I…I don't think I'm supposed to." She paused, trying to gather her thoughts. "When I saw them, the urge to help them came on so strong. When the last one ran, I had to follow. Something inside pushed me to do it. I think I'm supposed to do this, Kei. I might not be your Queen, but I think I'm supposed to help your people."

"Aro…" A low growl of frustration rumbled from his chest. "You are more important to me."

She closed her eyes and took a deep breath, and realized her breathing and heart had calmed while Kei held her. The fury still boiled within her and before it took control again she quickly concentrated on letting it go.

As it seeped away her body relaxed against Kei. She hadn't realized she'd been so rigid against him.

"Better?"

She nodded and shifted in his arms so she could look up at him.

He frowned, his gaze flicking back and forth between her eyes.

"What is it? Are they still red?"

"No. There are flecks of gold in them."

Her eyebrows went up. "No there isn't. They're brown."

"There is now."

Her tongue flicked over her teeth as her hands went to her ears. Everything else seemed normal at least. "Brown was boring anyway," she muttered. "We should go back."

They stood silently and headed back.

"There's blood on your hand."

Kei looked down, shrugged, and then wiped it on the back of his pants.

Her eyes narrowed. She was quite certain it hadn't been there before she'd run off. "What did you do?"

"He deserved it."

Her feet planted themselves in the ground. "Kei!"

He stopped and turned to face her, crossing his arms over his chest. "I didn't kill him," he muttered.

She gaped at him, not sure what to say.

"He disrespected you. Doing that to you," he snapped, his voice rising in anger. "You aren't some whore! You're a lady."

"What...but..." She shook her head in confusion.

"I know," he continued more quietly. "The fury didn't help. But he's an Elf. He should not have treated you like that."

"I'm not a lady. I never was."

His eyes brightened in renewed anger. "You are! You're our lady. My lady. You don't see yourself like we do. Your strength. Your loyalty and honesty and beauty. You don't need a title to be a lady, Aro."

She shook her head. He didn't understand. "He didn't make me. It's fine."

"No. It's not. Did you want it to be like that? That isn't courting."

"I wanted him! I want him and I can't have him!" She took a deep breath, realizing her voice was getting quite loud. "For a moment he wanted me. He was mine."

Sorrow crashed down on his face and he took a step toward her, hands outstretched pleadingly. "Don't let him do this to you."

Biting her lip, she shook her head and looked away. "You don't understand," she whispered.

"No. I don't. You deserve to be treated better than this."

"What am I supposed to do?" She pleaded with him.

He bridged the distance between them and wrapped his arms around her. "Let him go."

Somehow, closing her eyes against the tears actually kept them away. Maybe she'd cried enough over Prince already. Kei was right. She had to let him go. A few more days and he'd be gone. Maybe it was enough time for her to salvage their friendship. Anything else…it would never happen. Not now. Not in this time and place. Not ever.

Jen Wylie

# Chapter 24:
# Back for More

She avoided looking at Prince as she joined the others. Bo and Garen had found the horses like she'd asked, so they were able to set out immediately.

For a time, she kept to herself and the others let her be. Space and the shadows of the trees hid how she kept bringing her fingers to her lips. They were tender to the touch and a little swollen. He'd kissed her and said such terrible things and kissed her some more. Trying to understand only made her head ache.

At the sound of a horse drawing close she jerked her fingers away. Glancing up, she saw with relief it was Bo and not Prince.

"How are you doing, pup?"

The concerned look on his face made her force a small smile. "Good enough. I've been better. I've also been worse." She shrugged and looked away, pretending to watch her footing.

"You worried us. When we returned with the horses you were both gone. We called, but you never answered."

"I didn't hear you." She frowned. "I don't know why."

"Be careful, pup. I don't know what you did with the Fey. But I know the others are worried. I am, too." He raised a hand as she opened her mouth to protest. "But, I also recall the prophecy. You don't believe in it, but perhaps there is some

231

truth to it. You took their fury. Perhaps this is what you are meant to do and if so, then that is the way of it. There are some things you can't fight and some things you shouldn't. Healing the Fey is a noble cause and I support you in that."

Blinking up at him in disbelief, she finally shook her head, not sure what to say. "Thank you," she eventually managed.

"Now as for you and Prince…" Bo let out a loud sigh. "I'm sorry, if we overreacted."

Her head jerked up and she looked back at him in surprise. His words made her think, and after a moment she smiled softly. "It's what my brothers would have done, I think."

He chuckled. "Yes, they would have. Or perhaps something even worse. We know you can take care of yourself, Aro. It's just hard sometimes. We want to protect you."

"I know." Thinking of her brothers made her chest suddenly ache. "After we get Prince home…do you think…" She stumbled over what to say. "Maybe we could try to find out what happened?"

He nodded thoughtfully. "I don't know if any word will have reached over here, but we can ask around."

"Do you…do you want to go home?"

Looking off into the distance he shook his head slightly. "I don't know if there is even a home to go back to."

"True," she said quietly.

"We'll figure everything out, no worries."

Straightening her shoulders, she nodded sharply. "Yes, we will. Together."

"Of course," he agreed.

She didn't avoid Prince for the rest of the day, but she didn't seek him out either. He kept to himself, following behind them all on his horse and not speaking a word to anyone.

A few times she thought of speaking to him through the pack bond, but she couldn't think of what to say. The idea of apologizing irritated her. This time, she hadn't done anything wrong. He'd kissed *her* after all. She refused to apologize for saving his life.

Most of the day she kept herself occupied thinking of scenarios. What he might say, how she would reply. However she didn't understand how men thought. Even worse, he was royalty and an Elf. Who knew what might be going through his arrogant skull.

As the afternoon wore on she kept playing what had happened over and over in her mind. Yet already the details, the exact feelings, were beginning to fade. She stopped suddenly, as something finally occurred to her. Blinking rapidly in surprise, a smile slowly formed on her lips and then she darted through the woods.

Approaching Prince warily, she watched him closely before trotting up to walk next to his horse. For a few moments she said nothing, but kept shooting glances at his face. The side facing her showed a swollen lip and a black eye. She winced. Kei must have hit him more than once. His face remained a stony mask and her confidence began to fade.

"H-how is your back," she finally stuttered out.

"Well enough," he answered stiffly, not looking at her. She chewed her lower lip, trying to pick out her words. "You just keep coming back for more."

Her head jerked up at his scathing words. "What?"

"Like a puppy that has been kicked. You just keep coming back, hoping the next time you will get some affection instead."

Lips trembling, she turned her attention back to the ground and struggled to remain calm and not say something that would make things worse. "I…I…"

"I...I...," he mocked. "Go away, Arowyn. I do not want to deal with you right now."

Her feet planted themselves to the ground. Staring at them, she clenched her fists and sucked in a number of deep breaths as his horse walked on. Finally she raised her head. "I just wanted to thank you," she called out. "I realized, you had me pinned beneath you. You...you touched me."

The horse stopped.

"But I wasn't afraid. I wasn't scared at all. I didn't even think about them and what they did to me." She raised her chin, even though he hadn't turned around. "I wasn't scared. So... maybe there is some hope for me. One day I'll find someone who does want me and I'll be able to be with them. Now I know that, so...thank you."

His head turned slightly but she didn't wait to hear what horrible words would come from his mouth this time. Her escape worked, the only thing she heard was him call her name.

By the time they made camp exhaustion weighed heavily over her whole body. Dinner wasn't very good, she being too tired to put much effort into it. Ignoring Prince, she gave faint smiles to the others when they fussed over her.

Before settling down to bed she shouldn't have been surprised when she turned and bounced off of Prince's chest. Taking a startled step back, she frowned up at him. "Sorry, I didn't see you there."

Clearing his throat, he looked off to the side. "I would like to speak with you a moment." Her lips pressed into an angry line as she raised her eyebrows. "If you would walk with me?" He gestured to his left, off into the trees.

She laughed and shook her head. "No. I don't want to hear any more of your rotting comments on how everything is my fault. You can go and shove–"

"Arowyn, please." Clamping her lips closed on what else she'd like to say, she shook her head again and crossed her arms. "Please," he said again.

"Fine," she snapped. "If you start, I'm gone."

He nodded and held out his hand. She ignored it and stomped past him. After a while she stopped in a slightly open area where at least some moonlight shone down and spun to face him.

Uncertainly crossed his face for a moment before it disappeared and he frowned.

"Well? I'm tired. What do you want to say?"

"You seem to have a strange affinity for magic."

She raised her eyebrows, trying to decide if she should be offended or not.

"It concerns me, that you took the Fey's power and fury."

"Bo thinks that is what the prophecy meant. How I'd help them."

"You arc human, Arowyn."

"I am?"

He frowned and shook his head in annoyance. "Just, please be careful. You were…a bit out of control."

"So were you," she muttered.

"Yes, and on to that…"

She winced.

"I would like to ask," he stressed, "that you not do such a thing again. I am almost home, having magic of Were or Fey on me will not go unnoticed and would prove…troublesome."

"Then don't almost die anymore."

"You do not understand the implications–"

"No," she snapped loudly. "You don't seem to understand I prefer you being furious with me, or never speaking to me again, to being dead."

His entire body jerked in surprise.

"Rot," she muttered in exasperation. "Have you ever actually been *in* love, Prince? Because you don't seem to understand my feelings for you, or why I act the way I do."

With a grimace he looked away. "I have...not," he said quietly.

Her shock actually kept her silent.

He shifted uncomfortable. "I love my family, though I know that is not what you mean. Other women...I have desired some, but there has never been one I would even consider spending forever with." He raised his eyes to hers. "Do you see the difference between us? You do not have to consider forever, your lives are so short. We do, and forever is a very long time. It can take Elves centuries to find a mate, some never do."

She cleared her throat, but couldn't meet his eyes. "Well, I hope you find yours one day."

"You have distracted me," he said after a moment of awkward silence. "Please, no more magic. I do not want it."

Anger bubbled up inside of her. He didn't seem to understand. "Magic is magic! Stupid elf, have you thought how this could make you stronger?"

"Once I am home, I will be strong enough. I do not need your help. I do not want it." Throwing up her hands, she turned away in frustration. "I am not finished, please." She turned back, pressing her lips together to keep from snapping at him.

"I would," he hesitated a moment, his brows drawing together. "I apologize, for all that I said earlier. You are not deserving of it. I was...confused. And angry. The fury, I believe, reacted strangely within me." He looked off to the side. "I have never felt such intense emotion before."

"Are you going to apologize for kissing me now?"

His head snapped around to look at her, yet he didn't say a word.

"I don't want you to. So don't."

With a sigh, he shook his head. "Arowyn, child–"

She held up a hand, silencing him. "Do not, ever, call me a child again." Before he could respond, she turned angrily on her heel and headed back to camp.

Kei settled down next to her as they readied for sleep. Prince kept his distance. Upon his return he'd sat and stared vacantly into the fire, ignoring everyone.

She turned to face Kei and raised her hand. Taking it in his own, his golden eyes searched hers. Closing her eyes, she gave his hand a squeeze.

*I'm fine,* she told him.

*Are you sure?*

*Yes. He doesn't even know what love is.*

*I'm sorry.* His hand squeezed hers again.

*Don't be. I'm done.*

She had trouble falling asleep. Despite her desire to let everything go, she couldn't stop thinking about Prince. As she tossed and turned and spent forever staring up through tree branches she finally squeezed her eyes closed and concentrated. Once, she'd locked her love for Prince away, trying to hide it from him, from everyone, from herself. She did so again, cutting it away and forcing into the deepest part of her fortress. It hurt, oh, how it hurt. She locked the pain away as well.

Finally she was able to sleep. Her dreams were full of blood and death instead of him.

Everything had returned to normal.

Jen Wylie

# Chapter 25:
# Back and Forth

Prince looked like he hadn't slept at all and stumbled about the camp as they packed up. She helped and smiled and treated him exactly like she did the others.

Throughout the day she returned to her old routine of running with Kei, who didn't say a word about her change in behavior. She laughed and joked with him and when they would occasionally circle back to the others she did the same with Bo and Prince.

Prince, on the other hand, watched her warily at first, and then seemed to wilt under her happiness.

For the first time in weeks she felt free, like a great weight had lifted from her shoulders…and her heart. It gave her hope she would get over him, knowing she'd be able to survive without him when he left.

She and Kei found a spot to camp for the night and she ran back to guide the others while he began work on the fire pit.

When she found them she stopped and waited for Bo and then walked beside him as he rode, pointing out the direction to go.

They talked for a moment of the campsite and then he paused and looked down at her. "What did you say to Prince?"

She frowned. "Nothing. We came to an understanding."

"I don't think he understands," Bo muttered.

She raised her eyebrows, but then looked away and shrugged.

"He seems very...conflicted," Bo continued.

"I don't know about what. He made things very clear. I didn't say anything that should confuse him."

"He's been watching you and–"

"I don't care, Bo," she said wearily. "I'm done. I'm not playing his games anymore and I'm not going to pretend I'm his little child to coddle and take care of. I'm not a child. I'll be his friend. I've been acting like his friend. That's all he's getting."

Bo let out a deep sigh and rubbed at his scar. "You're right. Forget I said anything."

She nodded and brought up the topic of what they'd have for dinner. His words bounced around in her head though and she cursed under her breath.

Once dinner plans were settled she stopped and waited for Prince to catch up.

"The camp's not far," she told him. He nodded, but didn't reply. Letting out an irritated breath, she continued, "It's by another small stream. So we can all get cleaned up a bit."

Walking beside his horse silently, she lowered her head and scowled. Why did he have to make things so difficult?

"I have been thinking," he said.

"That can't be good." She eased the harsh words by looking up at him and smiling. Her smile faltered at the look on his face.

Sunlight shone down on his dark hair. His head bowed, he stared at his fingers as he fiddled with the reins. Dark brows drew together as he held his lower lip between his teeth, clearly uncertain.

She turned her attention back to the woods and gave him time to sort out what he wanted to say. Part of her wanted to run. Whenever he spoke, it never ended well. He didn't speak for a long time, so she sucked in a breath and smiled. "Garen says another two days and we'll reach the wardwall, then maybe a day to get to the gates of Rivenward." He nodded absently, still lost in his own thoughts. "Don't lose sight of Bo," she said finally and started jogging ahead.

"Aro, wait!" She stopped and let him catch up again. "I think," he said slowly, keeping his eyes on the reins. "I need you, more than I thought." He turned his gaze up to the sky. "I thought you needed me, but you take care of me as much as I take care of you."

"Glad you noticed," she said wryly. "That's what friends do," she added.

With a sigh he lowered his head and closed his eyes. "I think you have always done more for me than I thought. What you do with your magic, I think you have kept me alive. You have been with me almost since the slavers took my amulet. When I think back, I should have died long ago, before you even started giving me the power of Were and Fey."

She shook her head in confusion. "I don't–"

"It is disturbing, I know. I do not understand it. Or you."

"That makes two of us."

He smiled weakly. "You are the only woman I have ever met who made me think so much."

She laughed. "That doesn't say much for you."

He smiled softly but it died quickly. "I find myself so often confused when it comes to you." He pulled the horse to a stop, and she stopped as well. "You bind me to a pack and you fill me with Fey power. You are changing the very essence of who I am, and now I find I do not care. You have changed who I am, what I believe in." He shook his head as she stared up at him in shock. "That first simple kiss, such an innocent thing, destroyed me. It tore apart the walls I had built, the rules I have lived by, that had been bred into me. It sent my thoughts down paths they should never have gone. Would never have, if not for you.

"I should have ignored it, made nothing of it. Yet I could not. Something within me will not let the memory go."

Her heart stuttered in her chest as her mouth worked, trying to find words. Instead she reached out and stroked his horse's neck. "What are you saying," she asked quietly, forcing her words to come out evenly.

With a shake of his head, he sighed. "I wish I knew."

His words sent the spark of hope rising within her back into the darkness. "I wish you did, too." Giving the horse a pat, she set her shoulders and raised her chin to look up at him. He wasn't playing games this time, she could easily see that from the tortured look on his face as his eyes searched hers. For what, she had no idea. "Let's get to camp. I'm hungry."

Glancing away, he smiled sadly and nodded.

Men. She would never, ever, understand them.

Aro put the few small game animals Garen and Kei had caught turning the day on the fire while the boys unloaded and finished setting up camp. It never took them long. They didn't have much.

Once the animals were roasting she started digging through the packs, grinning in triumph when she finally found what she was looking for.

Still smiling, she walked over to where Prince sat and crouched down next to him.

He looked up at her, his head tilting sideways curiously at her smile.

"Take off your shirt," she demanded.

A rare wry smile crossed his lips before he did as she asked. "A little forward this evening, are we?"

She snorted and moved behind him. "I wanted to check your back…" Her words trailed off as she stared at his skin.

He turned his head slightly, trying to look at her. "I think it is healing well, yes?"

She nodded, her fingers reaching out to trace a pink line of new skin. "It's…wither me. You healed so fast." Her fingers continued to trail across his warm skin. She cleared her throat and jerked her hand back. "There are a few areas with scabs still. Most of it is fully healed though." She laughed suddenly, her eyes tracing across his back. "You have scars, but you don't."

His brow furrowed. "I should not. Not from this."

"Yes, but…" She couldn't stop her fingers from reaching out again, tracing a claw mark down across his back. "It's healed over the old scars, so you can still see the claw marks."

"Ah, I see."

She leaned back, her brows drawing together. "It wasn't a Fey." Spreading her fingers, she rested her hand against his back. "Turn a bit, so the others can see."

He did, craning his head trying to look himself.

"Did you see what attacked you?"

"No."

Kei walked over and only looked briefly before he shook his head. "Not Fey," he agreed as he went back to the horses.

*It isn't Were either, before you ask.*

Prince tensed under her hand and she removed it quickly. No one offered what it could have been. The only other answer being their new enemy, the Vor.

The silence quickly became uncomfortable. She shifted and then stood, holding out her hand. "Go get cleaned up in the stream." She held up her other hand. "I found the needle and thread. I'll mend your shirt."

His eyes searched hers until she looked away. He stood and placed his shirt in her hand. "Thank you," he said quietly.

She watched him leave, her heart pounding in her chest. "Rot it all," she whispered. Closing her eyes tightly, she pushed her feelings back into her fortress, adding extra locks and a chain.

She turned and scowled at the boys when she found them all staring at her. Finding a spot near the fire so she could keep an eye on dinner, she sat and put all of her concentration into sewing the tears with small neat stitches. It was a little chore. Something a friend would do.

"You two…" Bo started.

"Be quiet," she snapped.

He chuckled.

Kei plopped down next to her, making her poke her finger. She swatted him, sucked her finger for a moment, and then decided more blood stains on the shirt wouldn't be noticed anyway and went back to sewing.

"Turn the meat for me," she asked absently.

Kei did and she flashed him a grin.

"It's good to see you smile again," he said softly.

She shrugged. "It feels better, too." She grinned again. "Not as much work."

"Everything will get sorted out."

"I know. One way or the other."

She sewed as quickly as she could, but still wasn't done by the time Prince returned. It was a challenge to keep her eyes averted from his half naked dripping form. "I'm not done yet, sorry."

"Your turn. It can wait."

With a brief nod, she fled for the stream, happy the suns descent added more shadows in the trees. The water was shallow, but she still stripped and scrubbed herself and her clothes.

# Broken Prince

Once finished, she wrung her clothes out as much as she could before putting them back on. Sitting around the fire next to Prince in her underclothes didn't seem like a good idea. While walking back to the fire she struggled to finger comb the knots from her hair. At least the dirt was out of it.

Muted voices made her pause, but she couldn't make out who was talking. Drawing nearer, she saw the boys all sitting around Prince, seeming to be in deep discussion.

Kei turned and smiled but they stopped whatever they were talking about.

Checking the meat, she cast a glance over at Prince. Once again, he seemed lost in thought.

Finding the meat done, she handed it out and then sat next to Kei. *What were you talking about?*

*You.*

She grimaced over at him. *Anything good?*

*I believe Prince is the most confused Elf in history.*

*Wonderful.*

*I find it amusing,* he admitted.

She laughed out loud, choking on a piece of meat. The others looked over at her but she just shook her head and regained control of her mirth.

Her smile died as a beautiful voice entered her head.

*Keep watch tonight. Vor have been sighted.*

"What is it?"

She cleared her throat and answered Kei. "Rhee-En. He said to keep watch tonight. Vor have been sighted."

"Ask him how far west of the mountains," Prince said.

*How close are they?*

*Close enough. We are tracking two groups now. Call me if you come across any.*

*We will. Thank you.*

Aro rubbed at her forehead, her appetite gone.

"Well?"

245

"They're close. Rhee-En said they are tracking two groups of them. We're to call him if we see any."

"If we see any, calling him will be the last thing on our minds."

Handing the rest of her meat to Kei, she wrapped her arms around her legs and stared into the fire. They were almost there. Why did there have to be monsters?

Aro drew last watch. She grumbled at her bad luck. She didn't know how she could possibly sleep.

She curled into a ball by the fire, Kei sitting close on one side. Someone sat on the other side of her and she turned, frowning to see it was Prince.

He glanced down at her and gave her a small smile. "Go to sleep. They will not make it this far east."

Biting her lip, she managed a nod and turned over again. For once, she wouldn't argue on having him close.

The sound of whetstone on metal as Prince sharpened his sword lulled her to sleep.

# Chapter 26:
# Time

Bo woke her up for her turn at watch. It actually surprised her that he didn't pretend to forget just to let her sleep.

Pacing the edge of camp, she rubbed at her gritty eyes. Though she'd fallen asleep quickly, she hadn't slept well. The night had been clear and quiet, until the growls and snarls of wolves in the distance carried to them. She wished she knew how far away they'd been.

Keeping busy, she checked the low fire and then sat and cleaned her daggers. She always kept them sharpened, but took the time to go over each one carefully.

She quickly ran out of things to do and found herself staring blankly into the flickering flames of the fire. Blinking rapidly, she looked around the camp, wondering how much time had passed.

With a start, her eyes locked onto Prince. His blue eyes stared steadily into hers. A shiver ran up her spine and she held her breath at the intensity in his gaze. How could he affect her so strongly? He had some strange hold over her heart, constantly stealing it from her just when she thought she'd managed to get it back and lock it away. She knew he would never be hers, but her heart didn't seem to understand how things worked.

He blinked and she tore her gaze away, turning back to the fire. The flames reminded her of the feelings rushing through her; hot, wild, intense, burning. If she didn't control them, she would get hurt. Closing her eyes, she took a breath to steady herself.

She heard Prince move and glanced over to see he'd sat up, arms around his raised knees. He watched her still, his head tilted slightly to one side as if trying to figure her out. Perhaps he felt just as confused as she did. Her lips twitched at the thought. Would serve him right.

*What are you thinking, Aro?*

His voice startled her. *I...nothing really.* She ran her fingers through her hair nervously, or tried to. They got stuck in her tangles. She grimaced in irritation.

*Do you still have your comb?*

*I think so.*

*Go and get it.*

She hesitated a moment, but then got up and dug through her pack. Finding it buried in the bottom, her fingers clutched it tightly as she walked back, her steps growing slower as she approached.

Prince spread his legs and patted the ground between them. "Sit."

She did, trying not to sit too stiffly. He held her hair, starting to comb at the bottom. He'd done her hair before, but that seemed like so long ago. He worked silently and she began to relax, keeping her eyes on the fire and trying not to notice how close he was, his hands in her hair, the way his arms would occasionally brush against her.

All too soon he stopped. "Finished."

She turned and smiled softly, not meeting his eyes. "Thanks." Carefully, she glanced up at him. "Do you want me to do yours?"

He didn't speak, just nodded. She scrambled up and moved to kneel behind him. His hair flowed softly between her fingers. It hardly even needed combing. "Your hair is so nice," she murmured.

He chuckled. "It is just hair."

"Well, it doesn't get tied up in knots like mine."

"You have beautiful hair."

Smiling a little, she didn't bother arguing. She didn't want to fight with him. Instead she enjoyed the quiet pleasure of being near him and doing something so…domestic. Pulling the comb through one last time, she reluctantly sat back. "Done."

He turned around to face her, his back to the fire. "Thank you." Tilting his head, he looked into her eyes and smiled. "This is better."

Her brows drew together in confusion. "Better?"

"You have been acting strange."

She sighed and looked down at the comb in her hand.

"Talk to me, Aro. Please."

"I just…I've been trying to keep our friendship. I don't want to lose that. I don't want to fight with you. I don't want you to be angry with me when you go. To have your last memories of me being like that."

When he didn't say anything she glanced up. "You have to talk, too," she whispered.

"I dislike our fighting as well." His lips twisted into a grimace. "It has been difficult for me to understand your feelings." He took a deep breath, and she held hers, waiting to finally hear what he had been thinking, how he felt. "Before I left Rivenward, the seer spoke to me, and told me what she saw. She spoke of me finding a child that I would love with all of my heart. I know that is you. What she said came to pass."

"What else did she say?"

"Not much that made any sense," he said ruefully. "A lot of babbling about choices and how often she saw the possibility of my death."

"That is…worrisome."

"I didn't think much of it. She was a child, barely come into her powers. She didn't know how to speak of what she saw."

Aro paused, gathering her thoughts and wondering if she should speak them at all. "How do you know she didn't mean you would fall in love with me? Not just love me as a child?"

He blinked at her in surprise. "I…I…"

Shaking her head, she forced an apologetic smile. She had to just…stop. She couldn't force him to love her. "I'm sorry. Forget I said that." Straightening, she forced a brighter smile. "We're friends. We love each other in our own ways. That's enough."

"What I feel for you…" He paused, struggling for words, and then reached out and rested his hand over hers. "I care for you as if you were my own child."

Pain lanced through her, but she nodded. "I know."

"But…children grow up. You have grown up. I…I am conflicted about that. I…" He shook his head, at a loss for words. "I think of you sometimes," he whispered, not looking at her. "And it is…" He shook his head again and pulled his hand away from hers. "I am sorry. When it comes to you, there are times I cannot make sense of my thoughts."

"I understand," she said, even though she didn't. She just didn't want to talk about it anymore.

"We do not fall in love easily, Arowyn. For us, it is something that occurs over a very long time."

Clearing her throat, she wrinkled her nose and looked up through the branches at the fading stars. It didn't escape her notice they didn't have a very long time. She didn't. She was human, not an immortal. "So, did the seer girl say anything about fighting the Vor?"

His sad smile returned, letting her know he was quite aware she changed the subject. "No. But that does not mean we will not. Aro–"

"Time to get everyone up, I think." Jumping to her feet, she turned, tucking her hair behind her ears when it fell into her face. How long had it been since she'd brushed her hair?

"If the one she loves will return it, then she will give him time. If he does not, then time will go on."

Aro jerked around, hand going to the dagger at her side. "Kei?"

He stood by the fire, staring down into the flames. She couldn't tell if they glowed a faint yellow or if it was just the reflection of the fire in them.

"Kei?"

Prince stood and stepped up next to her. "Kei," he said sharply.

The Fey started. His brow furrowed as he looked up at them.

She rushed around the fire, panic stealing her breath away. "What's wrong? Why did you say that?"

"Say what?"

"You said… I don't know. Something about time." She looked over at Prince. "Did you hear?"

From his intense stare she assumed so, but he didn't answer.

Kei shook his head in confusion. "I don't…" He looked down at her, his eyes wide and panicked. "I don't know." He glanced over at Prince. *Talk later.*

Biting her lip, she looked down and took his hand, giving it a quick squeeze. "Let's get Bo up. We should get moving."

Prince remained silent for a moment, his gaze still riveted on Kei. Finally he turned, heading for the packs. *He spoke prophecy, Arowyn.*

*I know. But where did he hear it?*

*His grandmother was a seer. He may be as well.*

She bit her lip. The way things tended to go, it shouldn't surprise her Kei might be a seer. But it did, and it worried her too.

"Ride with me."

Aro shook her head as Prince mounted. "Not now." She glanced over at Kei. "Later."

His gaze followed hers and he nodded. "Very well. But we must stick close together today."

As he and Bo rode toward the treeline she chased after Kei as he darted into the trees.

*Stay close,* Garen said, following the horses.

*We'll be back soon.*

It wasn't hard to catch up with Kei, but he didn't stop when she did reach him. She followed, matching his pace, trying to stay as close to him as possible. Finally she reached out and grabbed his arm, pulling him to a stop.

His hair stood up wildly as always, but it was the wildness in his eyes that made her pull him close and wrap him in her arms. "Talk to me."

Fingers gripped her tightly as his head pressed into her neck. A shudder ran through him and then he pulled back.

Her arms held him fast, not letting him go far. "Kei, I'm here."

With a sigh he gave in, relaxing in her arms and touching his forehead to hers for a moment. "What's happening to me?"

"I don't know," she whispered. "But I'm here. Tell me what's wrong."

"I have strange thoughts in my head. Now I'm speaking them. They don't make sense."

Worry knotted her stomach. She forced herself to stay calm and not let her feelings show. "For how long?"

He shook his head. "I don't know. A little while."

Feeling him begin to tense up again, she raised her hands to cup his face. "We'll figure it out. Together."

Closing his eyes, he nodded. "Together."

"So…is it just words? Do you see anything?"

"Just words. Why?"

"Prince said it sounded like prophecy. But seers, they see things, right? I think," she said slowly. "What you're saying is what was in your mother's book."

He shook his head, hair falling into his face. "But I don't remember ever reading it."

"Could you just not remember?"

"I don't know." His lips pressed together in frustration. "Maybe."

She lowered her hands, taking one of his in her own. "So, let's walk and think." For a while they walked silently, heading back toward the others. "The book was important," she finally said.

"Yes. Mother never let me even touch it."

"Damon wants it. Is there some magic she could have used to hide it? In you?"

Kei stopped abruptly. "Bindings."

When he didn't elaborate she tugged on his hand impatiently.

"It's our magic. Bindings. I only know a few." He ran his fingers through his hair. "She could have."

"Perhaps she wanted you to remember when you were older."

"Or the magic is fading."

They regarded each other, mulling the ideas over. They made more sense than him suddenly becoming a seer.

"So?" She knocked shoulders with him. "At least you aren't a seer."

He smiled, relief flooding his face. "True."

"Let's go back."

He didn't move, pulling her back when she stepped away. "Thank you," he said softly.

"Always by your side," she reminded him.

His arms wrapped around her, holding her tightly for a long moment. "You always make me sane."

She laughed and squeezed him back. "Glad I'm good for something."

# Chapter 27:
# Monsters

They stopped late in the afternoon to break for food, having to travel into the forest to find water for the horses. Aro ate quickly and then paced nervously. They hadn't traveled far into the trees, but a sense of unease kept her worried and impatient to get back to the forest's edge.

Garen's low growl brought her up short.

*Fey are near.*

Turning slowly, her eyes searched within the shadows of the trees. Finally she just turned to the others. Of course everyone else but Bo knew where they were, though whether they used their better sight, hearing or smell, she didn't know. She found it irritating and took a breath to push back the unexpected pain of being different, of not being good enough.

Once she knew where to look, she found them easily enough, tentative shadows just beyond where they'd stopped. Moving forward, she ignored the warnings in her mind from the boys. When Kei appeared silently at her side she ignored the angry look he gave her and kept walking.

*This isn't a good idea.*

*They aren't attacking. They must want something.*

Stopping a short distance from them, her eyebrows rose. *There are four of them. The same four?*

*Yes.*

*You could have said so.*

255

Kei's lips twitched at the irritation in her mind voice.

Two of the shadows broke away, moving forward hesitantly. As they stepped into the light she couldn't help a small smile. Their eyes were golden. Not glowing. Not red.

It appeared they had tried to clean up. They'd bathed, and the woman's long dark hair no longer hung in a matted mess. The man's hair was dark as well. Short, but long enough to curl a bit around his small ears which curved up into delicate points. Their height and stature, even their features to some extent, reminded her of Kei.

The silence grew awkward as they all continued to examine the other. Kei's hand moved to rest gently at the small of her back, a quiet show of strength and support.

The Fey's eyes followed the movement and then turned to her.

"You are bonded?"

The surprise in his voice stole hers away. She glanced at Kei. *How did he know?*

"Yes," Kei answered. *All Fey can sense a binding.*

"Mated?"

"No."

The woman nodded slightly. "She is not Fey." Her head cocked to the side slightly and she sniffed. "Yet she has a faint scent of us." The Fey's eyebrows rose as she looked to Kei again.

Heat rose to her cheeks at what the woman implied. To have someone's scent all over them... "I am Arowyn. This is Kei."

"I am Lissana, my mate Cano." She turned slightly and gestured into the trees. "Our son, Aron, and his mate, Meena."

Cano shifted restlessly. "We would thank you, for what you did. You are...there is a prophecy. That we would be healed." He glanced to Kei and then back to Aro. "That is you?"

Aro nodded and smiled faintly. "So it seems."

They both smiled, relief easing their stances. "We had hoped…" Cano began.

"We are sorry. For before," Lissana said softly. She glanced at her mate. "We have another son. If we can find him, will you help him? Will you free all of us?"

It struck her then, the enormity of what the prophecy actually meant. What it asked of her. She had no idea how many Fey were left, but she did know how dangerous the endeavor would be. Not only dealing with the wild Fey, but in fighting to not get lost in it herself. "I…" She looked up at Kei and the intense pleading his eyes stole her words away. "I will try," she said finally. "I have something else I need to finish first."

Cano reached out a hand and Kei immediately grabbed him by the wrist.

Lissana stepped forward, her hand resting on her mate's arm. "We would never harm her. Never."

Kei dropped his hand, but his face remained hard.

The two Fey raised both of their hands slowly. Each laced their fingers together, making a fist, and set it against their heart. "On our honor, so do we swear," they said in unison.

Aro blinked at them, having no idea what they were doing. However, Kei relaxed next to her and gave them a sharp nod.

"You should not stay long. The Vor are about. They have split and are moving fast." Cano looked past them to the others. "They will be attracted to the magic of your group."

Aro nodded. "Thank you."

The pair paused for a moment, Lissana smiled slightly and Cano ducked his head, and then they slipped back into the trees.

She stared after them, emotions conflicting within her. "Aro?"

Shrugging off thoughts of prophecy and Vor, she turned and gave Kei a grin. "I'm fine. That was just…strange."

His golden eyes searched hers for a long moment but he didn't say anything. For once, she felt thankful he rarely did.

They walked back to the others. They'd gotten very little out of the packs, and everything had been loaded back onto the horses already. Bo and Prince stood next to the small pool of water, letting the horses have one last drink before they headed out again.

Leaves rustled in the wind and Aro paused, her muscles tensing.

The birds had gone quiet. Her head snapped around, hands going to her daggers as something crashed through the woods. The rustling grew louder.

There was no wind.

The horses ears flicked forward and they both raised their heads. Rearing suddenly, they scrambled wildly back from the pool. Bo and Prince fought to keep a hold of the reins.

"Run!"

Aro whirled around to see Cano sprinting through the trees.

"Run!"

The horses panicked further at the screaming Fey rushing toward them. A rein snapped and Bo's horse spun and bolted. Prince struggled with his, and then gave up and danced away as the horse reared again, deadly hooves kicking at his face.

Aro spun, eyes searching the forest, the pounding of the fleeing horse for a moment drowning out the strange rustling sounds. Dark shadows flowed toward them, the rustling became louder. Her eyes widened at the strange creatures scuttling toward them. Drawing her daggers as she turned around and around, her breath caught in her throat. They were everywhere.

# Broken Prince

What they were, she had no idea. The bodies hung low to the ground, shiny and black. Skinny legs jutted out from the sides. The sound she'd heard was a mix of them moving through the fallen brush and the legs brushing together. They reminded her of crabs, but much larger than any she'd ever seen. The smallest had bodies the size of her head, the largest were twice that. Her eyes shifted to their strange tails. They curved up from their backs and hung over the top of their bodies, ending in a long lethal spike.

"What are they?"

"Vor," Cano said quietly.

She turned to him, surprised he remained. The panic had left him now. He stood stiffly, poised to strike, eyes darting back and forth. "Where is your family?"

He started and stared at her for a moment. "Not far."

She paused a moment. "Do they need you?"

He glanced away, which was answer enough.

"Go to them."

"No, you must be protected."

"Go," she snapped angrily. "Fight with your family. I will fight with mine."

His eyes went over her shoulder, and then he nodded. "Fight well, Arowyn. We will return if we can."

As she nodded his eyes slipped immediately into a glowing red. Fangs grew from his mouth, claws shot out from his fingers. Then he was gone, sprinting back the way he'd come, dancing through the strange creatures, crushing some, slashing through the tails of others.

She and the boys were circled now. For some reason the creatures paused, only their tails moving, darting forward and back as if itching to attack and impale them.

"Stay close," Bo said behind her.

She looked over her shoulder. He and Prince had their swords out. Garen stood next to him, his fur bristling, ready to fight. Kei stepped to her side, eyes red and claws clacking together.

"No running now, I guess," she said quietly.

"We would not make it far," Prince replied.

She knew what he didn't say, that it was he and Bo who wouldn't. They were the slowest, had the least stamina.

"We need to steal less skittish horses next time," she muttered.

Bo snorted and she grinned over at him.

They were family, they would fight together. Her eyes went out to the enemy before them.

Perhaps they would die together, too.

*Rhee-En, the Vor are here.*

# Chapter 28:
# The Little Things

When her eyes met Prince's, her amusement vanished. Though not as haggard as he'd once looked, his paleness and dark, tired eyes worried her. Her mouth opened, and then clamped shut as he suddenly strode forward.

Stopping abruptly before her, his hand rose to cup her cheek. She stared up into his eyes, not understanding what he was doing. Something dark and burning replaced the tiredness, making her stomach clench. She couldn't help leaning into his hand a little, but stopped short of closing her eyes and sighing.

She locked her eyes on his, even though she knew he would see the love she felt for him.

A moment seemed like an eternity, yet neither said a word.

Bo cleared his throat and she jerked as Prince dropped his hand. His eyes remained on hers, searching them for something.

"Stay safe, child."

With just a few words, he ruined everything.

Anger welled up inside of her. Grinding her teeth in frustration, she stepped back and turned away from him. "Don't call me that."

Kei glanced at her, his red eyes flashing in fury, and pressed his lips together tightly when he saw her face. He whirled around to face Prince.

"I'll be glad when you're home. Then you'll stop hurting her."

"I would never hurt her," Prince said fiercely.

Kei shook his head. "You can't make up your mind. It's not that hard," he said bitterly. "You love her or you don't."

"Things are not so simple."

"Aren't they?"

Heat rushed to her face. This wasn't happening. Not here, not now. Such a distraction before battle could kill someone.

Straightening her shoulders, she raised her chin. "Protect Prince," she said flatly.

"Aro," he said sharply.

She refused to look at him. "That was the deal. We'd get you home. Now isn't the time to argue."

"You are such a–"

"Here they come," she interrupted.

The creatures began to scuttle closer, darting forward and back. Suddenly they moved, a dark mass pressing to overwhelm them.

She stomped and kicked at them, surprised at how easily she could knock them away. The spikes were another matter. Despite twisting away, one sliced down her calf. At least it hadn't impaled her leg.

*Run, we will deal with them.*

Aro snorted at Rhee-En's delayed response and sliced at a tail. *A bit late for that.*

*Why are you in the forest? I warned you–*

*We're near the border,* she snapped at the Were. Dodging another spike, she spun and sliced. She really needed to get a sword. The daggers were much too short for this sort of opponent.

*What do you face?*

*They look like crabs, with spikey tails.*

*How many?*

262

She didn't answer for a moment. *Enough,* she thought finally.

*What else?*

*What do you mean what else? This is quite enough.*

*They rarely run alone.*

The words sent a chill down her spine. *Nothing else.* She remembered the other Fey then. *There are four Fey fighting near us.*

*With you?*

*Against the Vor, yes.*

*Are they wild?*

*Not anymore.*

Rhee-En paused. *We will speak of that later. Where are you?*

She snorted. *I don't know.*

*We will find you.*

She didn't reply to that. They would or they wouldn't, she was too busy to worry about it.

Bodies crunched under her feet and she stumbled into Kei.

"Spread out," he growled.

She nodded and took a moment to glance at the boys. Bo and Prince stood back to back. With their swords, they were able to keep up with the creatures pressing against them. Kei was right though, they all stood too close together.

*Garen, Kei, we'll circle out farther.* The thought had barely left her head and the two broke away, tearing into the seething mass of black.

A smile tugged at her lips as she followed. It proved easier to fight as she spun and darted through the creatures. Not standing still, she moved too fast for them to strike her. Garen tore through them, claws slashing through tails and body, teeth ripping off tails as he ran by.

Bo cursed loudly, but she couldn't spare a moment to look. *You good?*

*I'll live.*

Springing forward, she pushed harder. Soon she became lost in the dance. The sounds of the boys' snarls and growls and curses faded away. Spikes slashed her legs. Blood dripped down, pooling in her boots. She fought on until her heart laboured in her chest and her arms grew heavy with fatigue.

A clawed hand caught her as she stumbled. Righting herself, she blinked to clear the blur in her eyes. Kei remained beside her.

*Take.*

She shook her head and stumbled again.

A flurry of claws appeared before her. Kei cleared the few in front of them and then he whirled to face her. His clawed hand carefully, but forcefully, grabbed her chin. His red eyes met hers. "Take."

Understanding jolted through her and without thinking she pulled. Power and fury flooded into her, spreading strength and energy through every limb.

Before his eyes could change he jerked away from her. "Good."

Renewed, she pressed forward to fight again, but paused as her eyes roamed the forest.

Broken black bodies scattered the forest floor as far as she could see. She hadn't realized they'd all been moving. Staying in one spot left too many carcasses, bad footing to fight on.

Garen sprang past her, teeth tearing into one of the few remaining creatures.

Her eyes sought Bo and Prince and her breath caught as she saw Bo down and shirtless, Prince wrapping his leg with cloth.

She ran over to him and crouched by his side, resting a hand on his bare shoulder. "How bad is it?"

He grinned up at her. "Just a scratch, pup."

Prince jerked on a knot and Bo sucked in a sharp breath. "It went straight through. We need to get it cleaned." He stood and jerked his chin behind them. "The pool is not far."

Aro helped Bo stand and pulled his arm over her shoulder.

"I'm fine," he grumbled.

She snorted as she started them walking and he limped. "Just a scratch? I have scratches and I'm not limping."

"A deep scratch then," he amended.

They reached the pool and started cleaning up as best they could. Garen stuck his snout in the water and swished it around, snorting when he finally pulled it out.

*They taste horrid.*

Aro chuckled and sat, debating how to go about dealing with the multiple slices on her legs. Some were deep and she was fairly certain she had a few chunks of flesh missing in a couple of spots. With the horses and their packs gone, she wasn't sure how to tend them. Unlike Bo, she rather wanted to keep her shirt on.

Kei paced around them, claws clicking.

"Can you not stand still," Prince snapped.

She looked over at him, eyebrows raised. "He's keeping watch, there might be more."

He turned to scowl at her and then froze. His gaze shot back to Kei. "Why would you give her more? What are you thinking?"

A groan escaped her. Though Kei had given her very little of his power and fury, there must have been enough for her eyes to take on the familiar magical glow. Probably not red, but even the mild yellow would alert Prince to what they'd done. Human's eyes didn't glow with an inner light.

"I was tired. He didn't give me much."

Prince whirled on her. "That matters not! Magic is not something to be taken lightly. I understand it is how you will help the Fey, but this was not necessary."

Anger pulsed through her. Springing to her feet, she resisted the urge to tie his mouth shut. "Don't tell me what to do."

"You never listen anyway."

"Why should I? Because you care about me like I'm your child," she mocked. "You're not my rotting father!"

"This temper of yours!" He raised his hands to his head like he wanted to pull out his hair, snarling in frustration. "And you cuss like a soldier!"

She stared at him incredulously. "What exactly do you think I am?"

Bo slapped his palms loudly on his thighs and leaned forward. "And that, is enough of that," he said sharply.

Aro pressed her lips together tightly. Frustration made her grind her teeth together. She wasn't done. She wasn't near being done, with all the things she wanted to say.

*While you've been fighting, something comes.*

She looked over at Garen and let out a deep breath, trying to calm the anger inside of her. Prince just made her so furious!

Garen turned south and she followed his gaze. For a moment, she saw nothing, but then she heard it. Something cracked. Looking higher, she saw a tree sway and then fall. A chill ran down her spin. What could possibly knock down a tree? The ones in the forest were not small, rising high into the air with trunks thicker than she could wrap her arms around.

"Rot," she muttered, eyes locked in the direction of whatever approached. Her thoughts whirled. Should they stay and fight or try to run?

Her legs began to ache and she glanced over at Bo. Running wasn't an option. Leaving him behind wasn't. Yet the creature didn't seem to be moving too quickly, perhaps they could get away. Unless it wasn't the only thing out there.

Her fight with Prince forgotten, she looked to him. "Thoughts? Fight or try to move as quickly as we can?"

Prince also looked to Bo.

The man in question snorted. "I can move, but I'll hold you back. I imagine the horses are long gone?"

*Yes,* Garen answered. *They are not near.*

"I worry there is more out there. Or whatever comes can move faster than it has been. How intelligent are these Vor?"

"It depends on the type. These," Prince kicked at a carcass. "Not very."

"It reminds me of the battle of Tennen, though." At Bo's blank look she continued. "First wave was thousands of barely trained men, but the numbers took their toll and weakened their opponent for the stronger, but smaller, force to come. It's a simple but easy tactic."

"Where did you learn that?" Prince stared at her as if she had grown an extra head.

"I'm quite certain I've told you I had tutors," she said, rather offended.

"I assumed it was in history, or–"

"More womanly things," she interrupted harshly.

Bo drew his sword and tested his leg. "We'll fight. The Vor," he added roughly, shooting a look at her, Kei and Prince. "Not each other."

Pushing the anger down showed her what she struggled to hide. Fear. She didn't want her boys to get hurt. Losing them…

Forcing a small, embarrassed smile, she nodded to Bo and then turned to face the approaching enemy.

Losing them wasn't an option.

Jen Wylie

# Chapter 29:
# Fighting for Family

When it finally broke through the trees, quite literally, she could only stare for a long moment. She hadn't thought it would be so huge.

The large Vor looked so strange she didn't even know what to make of it. Shades of dark grey and black, it towered above her. The head sat on a long thin neck, large dark eyes filled much of the face, the nose being mere slits. Of course, it had a massive jaw and mouth full of teeth. The barrel chest continued to a short body. Wide back haunches led to thick legs and long tail. The front legs however, were thinner and longer with three claws on each finger, two short and a longer middle claw.

Her eyes flicked over the beast, picking out the dangers immediately. The middle claw and the tail. She'd have to watch the reach of the neck. The mouth she definitely wanted to avoid.

Her own mouth became dry. She clenched her daggers tightly, trying to control her suddenly shaking hands.

"We need to retreat," Prince said. She looked over at him, her eyes wide. "We cannot fight that."

*Kei and I will try to lure it away. Go,* Garen said.

Her eyes moved to Bo. He trembled, not from fear she thought, but exhaustion and pain. Likely blood loss, too.

A new fear tightened her chest as she turned back to the creature.

Catching sight of them, it paused, tilting its head to regard them with frightening shrewdness. Shifting its weight, it turned, its back end crashing and knocking down another tree. Lurching back and forth, more trees came down.

Her heart sped up in her chest. It was making room to fight. "Wither me."

A gasp slipped from her lips as it drew ever closer. The beast had numerous wounds; the end of its tale even appeared to be missing. Had the other Fey been fighting it? Or the Were? A lump formed in her stomach, wondering what had happened to them.

"Aro, we need to go. Now!"

Not paying attention to the boys, she nodded, eyes still locked on the monster towering in front of them. "Go."

Her fingers relaxed on her weapons. Raising her chin, she pushed away the fear. Fear could kill you. She might die, but she would do so protecting her family.

This time she wouldn't be afraid. This time, she'd save them.

"Take care of Bo."

The boys' startled curses faded behind her as she ran to face the beast.

It saw her coming, but she knew it would. She hoped her size and speed would work in her favor. Her charge wasn't reckless. Each speeding step she planned. As the beast turned she adjusted her course.

Kei appeared suddenly at her side. Her eyes flicked to him only long enough to see the fury on his face. He didn't say anything, not even with his mind voice. A quick glance to her other side showed Garen had also joined her. He didn't remain silent.

*Reckless! We will talk later of this, but now, now we are with you.*

She didn't reply. Not only because it would distract her, and she didn't know what to say, but the beast now loomed above her. Aro dove under the swinging head and passed a reaching claw, ducking under the arm to slice at the soft spot there before continuing on. Her blades moved quickly as she ran, drawing blood where she could. Most of the outer hide proved tough and her small daggers did little damage. She switched tactics, spinning to ram a dagger into the flesh up to the hilt, pulling out and turning to strike with the other.

Now and then, she caught sight of Garen and Kei. Like her they ran in to attack and out again. The beast did not slow. Thick dark green blood oozed from a multitude of wounds, but it wasn't enough.

Her heart beat a quick steady rhythm in her chest. Frustration replaced her fear. Would the rotting thing never fall? Watching its movements, she ran in again, hoping to cause more damage to soft spots on its underside. She avoided teeth and claw and thrust both daggers in low on its chest. Instead of pulling out, she threw herself to the side, trying to tear wider wounds.

Her balance gave as one of the daggers popped free and she scrambled to keep her feet. A jerk freed the other blade and then she dropped and rolled as teeth snapped where her head had just been. Claws swiped for her next and she rolled again, only to scramble backward further as the other set of claws tried for her as well.

The beast raised its head and flung itself to the left. Finding her feet once more, she saw Prince stabbing into the beast's side.

Her breath left her lungs in a loud whoosh. Turning in a panic, she found Bo near the safer rear of the beast, cutting into his flank.

"Stupid, stupid boys." Her words had little anger in them. After all, she did understand. She wouldn't have left them either.

271

Taking a deep breath she ignored her tiring limbs and sprung back into battle. Eventually the beast would die. She hoped.

*Arowyn, how goes the battle?*

Rhee-En's voice made her curse out loud. She swung at an arm as it passed over her head before answering. *Little things are dealt with.*

*Impressive. All are well?*

*Still alive. Fighting the big one now.* She struck the beast again and grunted when it suddenly moved, its side striking her and almost knocking her to her knees.

*The... which is it?*

Finding her balance, she ran along its side, looking for another weak spot. *I don't know! It's rotting huge and won't die.*

*Can you–*

She'd forgotten about the tail. Closer to the beast's rear she flung herself to the ground as it whipped toward her. *Not a good time, Rhee-En.*

Springing to her feet once more, she caught sight of Bo, still standing and fighting away. She put her worry of him from her mind and backed away, wanting to get out of the reach of its tail.

*We will be there shortly.*

Garen darted past her and flung himself onto the beast's side, teeth and claws sinking in.

Her eyes caught a delicate looking spot and she dashed toward the front again. The creature spun, moving faster than she thought possible.

Its head whipped around and she realized it wasn't her, but Garen it had concentrated on. At least originally. It immediately caught sight of her and its head snapped forward, huge mouth open wide and snapping teeth. Dodging away from the body the teeth barely missed her.

Its swiping, clawed hand caught her by surprise. The air exploded from her lungs as it hit her side and sent her off her feet and flying. She struck the ground hard and rolled before her body stopped against a tree.

Pain lanced through her body and her foggy mind tried to decide which had hurt more, the blow from the creature or hitting the ground.

Gritting her teeth, she took a long deep breath through her nose and blinked rapidly, trying to clear the fog away. She'd ended up on her stomach, one arm awkwardly pinned beneath her chest.

Cautiously, she lifted her head, hoping she'd been thrown far enough away the beast couldn't reach her in her current vulnerable position. Relief washed through her to see she wasn't anywhere near the fight. With a muttered curse she pulled her pinned arm free. Her free hand still held a dagger, but the other she'd dropped at some point.

"Rot." Her brothers would have given her so much trouble for having lost a weapon.

Pain throbbed throughout her body. Shifting up onto her forearms, a sharp breath hissed through her lips as fire lanced around her left side. Bowing her head, her arms trembled as she tried to force the pain down and not fall flat on her face. Her fingers curled around her remaining weapon tightly, it's presence a comfort, and a reminder she needed to get up.

*Aro!*

Her head jerked up at Kei's voice. *I'm fine. Just need to catch my breath.*

He didn't reply, but she could see him attacking the beast with renewed fury.

His worry prompted her to get moving. She didn't want to distract the boys. Clenching her jaw tightly, she pushed up to her knees and then lurched to her feet. Her vision swam and she swayed, stumbling back a step before finding her footing again. Pain spiked through her legs and tore through the side of her stomach. Heat flushed her face, sweat beading on her forehead. Forcing her eyes open, she blinked rapidly, trying to focus. Clenching her dagger tightly, she took a step forward, her other hand going to her side where she must have pulled something. Maybe she'd landed on a rock.

She stopped. The weapon fell to the forest floor.

Staring straight ahead, for a moment she refused to look down. Yet she could feel the warm blood flowing, *flowing*, over her hand. Through the tear in her shirt she hadn't known she'd gotten, she could feel her skin. Not her skin, something smooth and silky and as warm as her blood. She pressed her hand harder, feeling the silky parts move inward.

She didn't want to look, but she couldn't help herself. Her head tilted down and her eyes locked on the blood covering her shirt from the front around to her left side. A rip as long as her forearm started at her belly, the fabric hanging loose. Her hand now shaking, she slowly tipped it away from her body.

Blood pooled against her fingers as she stared at the wound. It cut just to the left of her belly button and slashed across to her side where it then curved upward to end at her ribs. The gash was deep and open, giving her a clear view of what she'd never wanted to see, her insides.

Pressing her lips tightly together did little to muffle her whimper of panic. With both hands she pushed, trying to slow the bleeding. Her legs trembled as her vision blurred and she stumbled backward and to the side, weaving like a drunk as she fought to stay upright.

"Kei," she gasped out, the word barely a whisper.

Her legs finally gave out and she dropped to her knees. The forest spun around her as she gasped in panicked breaths. One moment she sat upright, the next she stared at the continuing fight with her cheek pressed against dirt and leaves. She blinked rapidly, seeing double, then realized the Were had arrived, and it wasn't multiples of Garen she watched attack the beast. Certainly it would fall now.

Everything began to dim and she let darkness pull her away.

Her boys would be safe now.

The quiet darkness surrounding her shattered. Pain returned with a vengeance, burning and pulsing and slicing deep within.

With a strangled scream her eyes shot open and she flung herself upright. Or tried to. Strong hands held her down, pushing her flat onto her back again.

"Stay still, pup."

She blinked up at Bo. His face faded in and out of view. It took her a moment to realize her head rested on his lap. The pressure on her shoulders came from his large hands holding her in place.

Tears slid from the corners of her eyes as she fought to stay still. It was impossible. Her body squirmed, trying to evade the constant pain.

A roar startled her and she gasped. Blinking her eyes clear, she turned her head and saw the Were and Kei still fought the giant Vor. No, not Kei...the other Fey. Her lips trembled as emotion crashed through her. They'd come back.

A burst of pain and discomfort in her stomach made her back arch. A snarl of half scream, half curses erupted from her dry mouth.

"Hush! Calm down, child!"

With a last curse she tried. Her breath came in quick irregular gasps. Her heart thudded wildly in her ears. Lifting her head slightly, she saw Prince kneeling beside her. Blood covered his arms up to his elbows. His fingers disappeared into her wound.

With a gag she struggled again. "What…"

"He's trying to see if you're cut inside. Stay still."

"I'm going to be sick," she whispered.

One of Bo's hands left her shoulder to gently stroke her forehead. "Slow, even breaths."

In. Out. In. Her entire body trembled with her effort. "I can't." Her voice squeaked and cracked. She squeezed her eyes closed as tightly as she could. "Wither me, make it stop."

She couldn't keep her mind from dwelling on the knowledge the pressure in her stomach was Prince. Inside of her. It was just so… wrong. A shudder wracked her from head to toe.

Pain spiked again and her back arched. Hands on her hips pushed her down. Her breathing quickened even further as fear and panic overwhelmed her.

"Kei!" Her scream echoed through the trees.

The hands on her hips moved. "I'm here. I'm here."

Prince muttered under his breath and new pain brought tears to her eyes.

"I hate you, I hate you," she gasped out.

His hands stilled for a moment before continuing.

"She doesn't mean that," Bo said softly.

"I know." Prince's voice cracked.

She writhed in pain underneath him. Her teeth ground together as she tried to hold in another scream.

"I think she is well inside," Prince said, his voice strangely even. "But the bleeding is bad. She has lost so very much blood."

The ground shook beneath her. Prince removed his hands. She opened her eyes and hazily watched him strip off his shirt and press it against her side.

"What do we do?"

"I do not know. We have nothing to tend her."

The howl of wolves drowned out what anyone said next. She wondered what it meant. Had one of the Were died? Was she dying?

Despite the pain, her eyes fluttered closed.

Pain flared across her cheek and she snapped them open again.

Prince bent over her, his face too close. "You must stay awake."

Blinking slowly, she tried to focus. His face faded in and out. Voices murmured around but she could no longer make out what they said.

*Arowyn, can you hear me?*

*Rhee-en?*

*Yes. The Vor is dead.*

*Good.*

*You are gravely hurt. The prince has asked for our aid. I will...*

His voice faded away. She ignored another sting on her cheek, the shaking of her shoulders, and let the darkness come again.

Jen Wylie

# Chapter 30:
# Rot it all

Quiet voices teased her into consciousness. She couldn't make out what anyone actually said, or even who spoke. As her mind slowly rose from a deep sleep her other senses assaulted her.

Skin itched, feeling tight and hot. Her hair hurt. Limbs felt strange, both numb and heavy. She didn't have the energy to try to move, so didn't even bother with an attempt. At least her heart beat slow and normal within her chest, her breaths came shallow but even. Her nose twitched at the overpowering smells around her. The air seemed thick with sweat and herbs and scents she couldn't identify with her half-asleep mind.

"Give her more."

The voices stopped. A door creaked open and then thumped closed. Heat pulsed through her body. Pain pounded through her skull and behind her eyes.

A foul taste coated her tongue. She choked and swallowed. If only she wasn't so hot. Twisting on the bed, she tried to escape the heat, to find a cool breeze, anything. Something cold and wet covered her forehead and she sighed. The coolness moved over her face and neck and she relaxed, her mind drifting off again.

Voices once again roused her. The terrible heat had disappeared, but the horrible taste in her mouth remained. Her tongue stuck to her teeth, the roof of her mouth. She tried to make spit, to lick her dry and cracked lips. Her body felt odd and heavy. She didn't worry too much that she had no strength to move. Certainly it was normal after being so sick.

Cracking her eyes open, she relaxed at the weak light meeting them. Blinking slowly, her eyes struggled to focus. Finally they cleared and she took in her surroundings. The room was small, the walls made of logs. A closed wood door centered the wall across from her. She was indeed in a bed. A bed! A light sheet covered her. A thicker wool blanket sat folded past her feet. A lantern hung by the door. Turning her head slowly, she saw another on the table beside her. If there were windows, she couldn't see them in the dim light and they were certainly shuttered. Unless it was night. She realized she had no idea when it was.

"Arowyn," Prince said softly.

She started when he stepped forward out of the shadows. Lantern light flickered over his drawn face. He did, however, look clean. A brown cloak hung over his shoulders, under it a new dark shirt.

"Water," she managed to croak out.

"Of course." He poured some from a jug on the table into a small wooden cup. Leaning over her, he lifted her head gently and held it to her lips. "Slowly now."

Once finished he carefully withdrew and pulled a chair closer to the bed, taking a seat.

She worked her tongue around her mouth and licked her lips, trying to get the foul taste out and remove all traces of dryness. Trying to sit up brought no response from her body. Everything felt numb and heavy, as if her body had fallen asleep and not woken up yet. "I feel strange. I can't...I can't move."

"It is a side effect of your medicine. It will fade."

His answer made sense, so she let her worry fade away. "Where am I?"

"Rhee-En brought you to a small Were settlement."

She nodded, but her brows drew together. Were had settlements? She'd never really thought of how they lived. "How long?"

His head lowered slightly so she couldn't see his face. "A…few days."

He was lying, but she didn't know why. Nor did she care. Other more important worries distracted her. "Was anyone else hurt?"

His hand slipped into hers where it rested on top of the sheet at her side. "No. Nothing that has not healed already. Other than Bo's leg, but it is doing well."

"Just me. Being troublesome," she said weakly, trying to force a smile.

His gaze locked on their hands and he nodded slightly.

Unease filled her and her smile faded. "I'm still alive. So the Were helped, right?" His hand squeezed hers tightly for a moment, but he didn't answer. "Prince," she whispered, fear making her voice waver. "Tell me what's happened? Where is everyone?"

"It is almost dawn. They are sleeping. Rhee-En has gone for them." His thumb moved back and forth, gently caressing the back of her hand. "Your injury was severe," he started slowly, his voice low. "You lost so much blood." His eyes flicked over to meet hers. "The Were tended your wound, yet you did not wake. You then fell into a fever. They gave you every treatment they could think of to fight the fever, to keep the pain away, to try to heal you."

"I'm awake now, so it worked?"

He lowered his eyes and slowly shook his head. "You would not wake. There is medicine rarely used it is so dangerous, called allorum. We gave it to you tonight. It broke the fever, but…" His quiet words trailed off.

"But?"

Lips pressed together tightly, he pulled his hand from hers. She watched as he carefully pulled back the sheet.

Thankfully she saw she wore a short cloth top, but her eyes locked on the thick wad of bandaging at her side. Her stomach around it looked bloated and bruised. His fingers shaking, he pulled the bandaging back.

Bile choked her as the stench of rot wafted up around them. Closing her eyes against the putrid mess of rotting skin and puss, she struggled not to vomit. "Enough," she gasped out. "I see."

The bandage gently rested against her skin again. Eyes still closed, she struggled for calm as Prince pulled the sheet back up. Rot was usually fatal, unless in a limb and it was removed. Gut rot? She had no chance to survive.

She wished she'd died fighting. Regrets of everything she hadn't done and wouldn't ever be able to do, settled heavily into her mind. She hadn't even managed to get Prince home.

"How long do I have?"

When he didn't answer she opened her eyes again. He sat forward in the chair, elbows on his thighs and head in his hands.

"The allorum has bought us only a little time. We can't give you more."

She nodded, even though he wasn't looking at her. "So… I can say goodbye to you all," she whispered.

The door slammed open, startling her. Kei bounded into the room and around the bed. She smiled at his wild hair and the faint yellow glow to his eyes. His face lit up when he saw her awake and he bent over her, pressing a kiss to her forehead.

"I missed you."

"Me, too," she said, her voice choking with emotion.

Bo pushed Kei further to the side and took her hand. "How you feeling, pup?"

"I've been better."

# Broken Prince

Garen nosed between Kei and Bo and she smiled as he rested his head on her chest. *We have worried for you.*

*I know, I'm sorry.* She wished she had the strength to raise her hand to stroke his soft fur. When she tried she got only a trembling limb for her efforts.

"Arowyn."

She looked up as Rhee-En entered, closing the door behind him. "Thank you," she said. "For helping."

His head bowed and he sighed deeply. "I regret we cannot help you more."

"I know, it's… I understand." She fumbled for words and gave up. Weariness stole away all attempts of thinking.

Rhee-En held out a small clay bottle. "The allorum."

Prince turned away. "No."

"Give it to her and she will pass in her sleep."

"I said no!"

"She will not heal. You know this." The Were set the bottle on the table. "If you do not, she will die in agony." Prince stared at the wall, saying nothing. "I did not think you so cruel."

Aro trembled and Kei took her hand, holding it tightly.

"She's right here!"

"It's fine, Kei. Prince told me."

"I am not cruel." Prince stood, his mouth a straight angry line. "I just cannot let her go."

She blinked in surprise.

Rhee-En scowled. "It is there, when you change your mind." He turned to her and bowed slightly before turning on his heel and leaving the room.

The silence went on and on as no one could think of what to say next.

Aware she had so little time left, Aro smiled, wanting to make it as easy on her boys as she could. "You'll all be fine. I know you will."

Garen whined, Bo cursed, and Prince returned his face to his hands.

Kei bowed his head over hers. *Don't leave me.*

*I don't know how to stay.* His tears dripped onto her cheek. Lips trembling, she tried to stay calm. She didn't want to cry in front of them. She didn't want them to remember her that way. "I'm sorry I'm not immortal like you. I don't have magic to heal myself."

Prince's head shot up and he stared at her intently for a moment before his gaze moved to the Fey still hovering over her. "Kei, would you bind to her again?"

Aro's breath caught in her throat. Her eyes locked with Kei's. The third binding. Mating.

Kei opened his mouth and then shut it again as he stared at her. Prince didn't know they'd bound together twice already. Her head spun, she didn't know what to think.

"I don't know," he whispered, straightening. Shaking fingers ran through his hair. "It's not like the others. It's not—"

"Others? *Others?*" Prince's voice rose as he sprang to his feet. His hand slammed down on the table. "What *others?*" His gaze turned on her, burning and angry.

"Two," Kei answered for her. "Friendship. Family. The third…" his voice trailed off weakly.

"Mating. I know," Prince snapped. Knuckles pressed against his temples. His nostrils flared as he fought to control his anger.

She didn't understand why he was so angry. Because she hadn't told him?

"Would it save her?"

Kei looked at her again. "I don't know. It is…much stronger magic, but…I don't know if she would survive it. The binding is…not like the others."

"No," she whispered hoarsely. "No."

"Arowyn, now is not—"

# Broken Prince

"I said no." She closed her eyes against the tortured looks on their faces. "I won't do that to him."

Hands clasped hers. She didn't have to open her eyes to know it was Kei. "I don't want to lose you."

Shaking her head, she squeezed her eyes closed more tightly. "No," she repeated. "I am mortal. I will die anyway. I won't…I won't put you through losing a mate."

*Arowyn, please.*

*No, Kei.*

*I love you, already. We would grow to love each other as mates. I know we could.*

She sighed, and opened her eyes. "I know. That's not why." The panic in his eyes nearly destroyed her. "I love you, but I can't give you forever." She closed her eyes again. "Just let me go."

Kei's fingers squeezed hers tightly. Lips pressed against her forehead. A sob choked him. Then he was gone, the door banging loudly behind him.

His soul wrenching roar echoed into the small room. She flinched. Pain streaked through her body. Not all it stemmed from her wounds. The anguish in Kei's scream tore at her very soul.

Tears burned behind her eyelids. She refused to open them, to let Prince see. He'd use it against her. Her sorrow wouldn't go away. Clenching her teeth, she tried to stop the trembling, to keep from breaking down into soul wracking sobs.

"Is the pain coming back?"

Prince's voice sounded so hollow and quiet she had to clench her fists. "I just…need a moment. Can you go? Please."

"Arowyn. Look at me."

She didn't want to, but the pleading in his voice gave her no choice. Her eyelids flickered open and she met his steady gaze.

His fingers brushed hair from her forehead. "Always so troublesome," he murmured.

"I heard Rhee-En," she said gently into the silence. "I want to take it. Let me say goodbye, and let me go."

Dark hair hid his face as he bowed his head. His shoulders slumped and he raised a shaking hand to his face.

"I'm sorry," she whispered. "You can't heal me. I can't heal myself."

Prince raised his head and stared at her for a long moment, his expression frighteningly blank. Without saying a word, he turned and left.

Closing her eyes again, she let a few tears trickle out. At least he hadn't slammed the door.

How did she always manage to ruin everything? Death loomed over her, yet she'd managed to run off the two men who meant most to her.

"Don't cry, pup," Bo said softly, taking her hand now.

Garen pressed his wet nose against her cheek and then sat.

"I just…" A sob stuck in her throat.

"We're here." His hand squeezed hers. "We're always here."

Somehow she managed to squeeze his hand back.

# Chapter 31:
# Life and Death

"Your leg is doing better?" She sniffled and took a slow breath. Pushing away thoughts of what she wouldn't have and what she would lose, helped calm her tears. If she concentrated on her boys, she could get through this. They mattered the most.

"Yes, it is." He shifted awkwardly.

Her chest tightened and more tears threatened. The foul air pressed down around her and she wrinkled her nose. "Is there a window?"

Nodding slightly, he released her hand and moved toward the head of the bed. "Prince closed it. The light hurt your eyes with your fever. We had some rain in the night as well." He removed a short wood bar and then pulled open the shutters. Fresh, crisp air immediately flowed into the room, bringing in the cleansing scent of rain. Little extra light came in and she remembered Prince saying it had almost been a dawn when she woke up.

Bo turned, pulling a small wooden chair by the wall close to the bed. Sitting, he took her hand once more and gave it a quick squeeze.

She relaxed against her pillow, still amazed she had one, and a bed! The softness beneath her, the memories of home it invoked, brought her strange comfort and peace. "Have the Were been treating you well?"

"They have. It's nice here. Quiet."

She smiled softly. "Tell me."

Bo spoke of the small settlement, describing the few buildings, the families living there. "The children follow me and Kei around when we're out. They've not seen a human or Fey before. They're quite…cute."

"The Elf doesn't amuse them?"

"The Elf has lost his mind," Bo said flatly. "Everyone is thankful he has no magic right now." At her confused look the irritation on his face faded away and he sighed. "He wants you healed, but everything they've tried has failed. And they have tried everything, Aro. Everything."

Lips quivering, she looked away, trying to ignore the rising pain those words caused.

"Perhaps being a prince, he's just not used to not getting his way. He's quite a temper we've not seen before, I'll say that much."

"He'll be fine," she whispered, trying to convince herself. "I suppose they aren't used to death. Not like we are."

"True." Bo regarded her silently for a moment. "Or he loves you more than you think," he said softly.

"I know he does." It was hard to speak. "Just not…" She didn't finish. Being reminded Prince wasn't in love with her hurt too much. She wished Bo would stop bringing it up.

Relief suddenly calmed her pain. At least Prince truly hadn't fallen in love with her. Not like she loved him. She'd seen what losing someone you loved could do with Kei's reaction, and he only loved her like a sister. The pain she still felt for her own family's loss reminded her Kei would hurt for some time. At least Prince wouldn't have to deal with her death to such an extent.

It struck her then how selfish and stupid she had been, how blind. She refused to bind with Kei because she was mortal, yet she'd expected Prince to love her. At least he didn't. She wouldn't hurt him.

"He'll be fine," she said again.

Bo grimaced and Garen whined again. "He's calling for us now." She raised her eyebrows questioningly. "For some reason he's trying to find Kei and he's not answering. He wants us to help."

She tried to raise her hand to shoo them out and failed. "Go. I'll rest."

He hesitated a moment and then winced.

Garen snorted, his ears flicking back in annoyance. *He's persistent.*

Giving her hand a squeeze, Bo stood. "We won't be long. Don't..."

"I'll stay awake," she promised, forcing a small smile. Watching him leave, her smile turned genuine. Bo reminded her so much of her brothers. Often quiet, always there when she needed them, there even when she didn't know she did. Yet still he had his boisterous side, his quick jokes and loud laughter. Bo made her smile.

Garen looked back at her a moment before going out the door and Bo closed it behind him. She wished she'd gotten to know him better. He'd really bonded with Bo, and she felt so happy for that, especially since he'd lost his closest friend John. Garen had remained quiet and distant with her though. She wasn't sure if it was because he thought her his alpha or for some other reason. They'd only had a few weeks together. Regret pulled at her heart again. Time was something she'd run out of.

The future was something she'd tried very hard not to think about during the last year. Getting Prince home had been all that mattered. Afterward...she hadn't wanted to think about a time without him. She'd lost so many of her boys, her brothers, Kendric, Avery, John. Prince wasn't dying, but she'd never see him again. To her, it was much the same thing.

She watched the increasing light play long the wall in front of her for a while. At least it didn't hurt her head. Her body remained heavy and numb. Though she could move her head from side to side, she couldn't lift it. Concentrating, she worked with her fingers and toes until they wiggled. She even managed to gain more control to turn her wrists and ankles. Stopping there, she didn't try for more. The numbness kept the pain away. She had no idea how long the allorum would work and didn't want her efforts to bring the fever and pain back more quickly.

The door creaked open and she smiled.

A woman walked in, closing the door behind her with a push of her foot. Turning, she then froze and stared, her eyes quickly darting around the room.

"Good morning," Aro said softly.

The woman paused, adjusting the jug and pile of cloth in her hands. "Good morning, Arowyn." Moving once more, she set everything on the table and then cast her a sidelong look. "This is the first time I've come and you've been alone."

Aro turned her head to regard the woman. Obviously a Were, the woman's height and toned body still surprised her. Short brown hair framed a pretty face and deep brown eyes watched her carefully.

"Are you thirsty?" Aro nodded and the woman poured fresh water from the new jug. She paused a moment, regarding the clay bottle on the table. "They gave you allorum."

Aro nodded again, and then concentrated on not making a mess as the woman raised her head slightly and tipped the cup to her lips.

"Rhee-En wants to give me more," she said, once settled again.

The woman let out a deep, sad sigh. "It would be the most peaceful way."

"That's what he said." Aro looked away. Talking of her upcoming death seemed too strange. "Prince doesn't want to," she said into the growing silence.

# Broken Prince

"Prince? Ah, Prince Shael. Yes, he has been quite…adamant you will recover."

Aro smiled at the way the woman said his name. She'd heard it so few times. The Were pronounced it Shay-Elle, though prince had said it to her more softly, with less emphasis on the El.

The woman busied herself with changing the sheets. Given the muscles on the woman's arms, she wasn't surprised how easily she shifted her around to get to the bottom one.

"May I ask you a question?"

"Of course."

"Why are the Were helping me?"

The woman raised her eyebrows. "Why wouldn't we?"

"I'm human," Aro stated.

"Not a normal one though," she said with a smile. She shrugged. "We help for many reasons. The prince asked it of us. Nor would be turn down someone in need, even if you are mortal." She paused for a moment, adjusting the pillow. "Our Alpha is quite taken with you. A human girl who mind speaks like an Elf, runs with Fey and Were, and has gained the attention of a Dragos. I heard also, how you fought the Vor." She flashed a feral grin. "You have a fighter's heart.""

Heat rose to her cheeks. She'd never really thought about how different she'd become.

The woman chuckled as she shook out a new sheet. "Despite your illness, you are a pretty little thing. It doesn't surprise me the men jump over themselves to help you. It seems men are men, no matter what race they are."

"It's not like that," Aro protested.

The woman tucked the sheet around her. "Isn't it?"

Her mouth opened and closed as words escaped her. "They're my family," she finally muttered.

"More water?"

"Yes, please." Happy the topic had dropped, she managed to drink another half a glass.

"I would offer broth, and change your bandage as well, but Prince Shael is out harassing everyone in full force again, so I imagine he has some new idea. I will wait for now."

"Thank you, for everything."

She nodded and gathered up the dirty sheets. Heading for the door, she paused before leaving. "I do hope they can save you."

As the door closed Aro whispered, "Me, too."

After the woman left, she heard muted voices outside the door. With a curse under her breath, she realized she'd never asked the woman's name. Paul would swat her upside the head for such bad manners.

The voices stopped and the door opened. Relieved not to be alone again, another smile appeared on her face. For being so close to death, she certainly smiled a lot. The thought brought forth a weak laugh.

Prince raised his eyebrows. "You are in good spirits, considering."

His words sobered her immediately and she frowned at him in annoyance. "Be nice to the dying girl."

Slamming the door closed, he strode toward her, his eyes flashing in anger. "Do not say such things!"

"I'll say what I want," she snapped. "You need to be more polite. Everyone is talking about you being an arrogant, demanding–"

"Enough, Arowyn," he said softly, raising his hand as the anger drained out of him. "I am sorry." Pulling the chair back to the side of the bed, he sat. "This is...difficult for me."

Her own anger died and she looked away from the despair on his face. "I know. I'm sorry, too." The following silence weighed heavily on her. "Prince, can you promise me something?"

"Of course," he answered quickly.

"Try not to forget me."

A long silence met her words as he struggled to stay composed, his eyes closing for a moment, fingers rising to his lips. Finally he straightened and his eyes met hers again. "You are rather unforgettable, my Arowyn." He leaned forward and smiled down at her softly. "But I am going to save you this time, and then we will be even."

"You have this annoying ability to say the perfect thing and then ruin it by still talking."

A smile twisted his lips. "Do I now?"

"Yes," she grumbled. "You do. Quite often, in fact." She changed the subject. "Did you find Kei?"

"Yes," he answered finally." He paused, as if about to say more, but changed his mind. "I have sent them all out, and some of the Were as well, to find the Fey you healed."

She stared at him dumbfounded. "Why?"

"Your comment earlier gave me an idea. I am hoping they will agree to give you their power again. Along with Kei's, I hope it will be enough to heal you."

"But I don't know how to heal. I never have before when I had power in me."

"I will teach you, while they search."

"Is it that easy to learn?"

"You have incentive, do you not?"

She scowled at him. "I'm human. I'm sure you haven't forgotten that," she said bitterly.

"No, I have not." He stared at her for a long moment, his blue eyes tired and sad. "We are running out of options, however. You are special. You do things you should not be able to. I am hopeful this will work." He gently picked up her hand and held it in both of his. "Now we must begin. We do not have much time."

"Prince, I don't–"

"Please." His eyes searched hers. "Please, Arowyn. Do this for me. I will beg you if I must."

Tears burned her eyes and she fought to keep her suddenly quivering lips still. Her prince did not beg. That he would say such a thing…

"I will try," she finally managed to whisper.

"Thank you," he said solemnly. "Now, enter your mind. I will join you there."

When she opened her eyes a relieved smile lit her face to find she stood on her own and, in her mind at least, seemed well and whole.

Her fortress remained tall and strong. Turning, she took in the still barren landscape and dark sky. She tilted her head up, her eyebrows rising in surprise. The rolling clouds had disappeared and though still dark, the sky wasn't near as dismal as it used to be. She didn't understand why they would change now when she was so close to death. Perhaps because she finally understood so many things.

Looking to the side she saw Prince staring at her, a faint smile of relief upon his face.

*Everything seems to be fine. The walls are holding.*

*Yes, though if you came under attack I do not think they would hold for long.*

*True,* she agreed with a grimace. *But at least I won't have to rebuild them. I worried being sick would destroy everything.* Letting out a deep breath, she tucked a stray lock of hair behind her ear. *So, what do I do? Teach me.*

A rare grin appeared for a moment before he turned serious once more. *The ability to heal is born within us. As we grow, we learn to use it instinctively.*

She frowned. *So you don't know how to teach me?*

*Not from the experience of learning myself, no. Yet I am certain I can guide you. You simply must become aware of your body.* He stepped forward and cupped the side of her head with his hand. *You have learned to become aware of your mind, which is a rare thing amongst mortals. It is not much different from that.*

His nearness, the touch of his hand, distracted her. She pushed thoughts of him aside and tried to figure out what he was talking about. *What do I do?*

*Your mind is within your body already, simply step out from here. Not to the outside world, but further within.* He dropped his hand. *Close your eyes and push. I will be with you.*

She did as he asked, but nothing happened. Trying again, she cursed in frustration. *Nothing is happening!*

*Try harder. Imagine yourself moving through a wall, from your mind into your body. It is not a thick wall, not hard to pass through. You can do it. Glide through. Push.*

His litany of instruction lulled her into a calm state. Her breath slowed, her body relaxed. She spread herself out, searching for the wall he spoke of. Finally, after what seemed like forever, she hit something. Her eyes snapped open and she smiled. *I think I found the wall!*

A relieved breath sighed out of him and he rubbed at his forehead. *Well, that is progress. Now try to get through it. Hurry, Arowyn. We do not have much time. Kei has found the Fey, they are all returning now.*

How long had passed? She had no idea. Hope fluttered within her chest. Perhaps she would survive. Closing her eyes once more, she quickly found the wall and tried to push through again and again…and failed. *It's not working!*

*Again.*

Her attempts continued. Prince believed in her. Though weariness began to descend on her from all of her efforts, she kept trying.

*You can do this, Aro.*

Eyes still closed, she shook her head in defeat. *I'm tired. I can't–*

*Again.*

Jen Wylie

# Chapter 32:
# Inside Out

*Bo and Garen have returned. They want you to know they are here.*

Aro opened her eyes and struggled to focus on Prince. Trying to break down the wall stole all of her strength away. Weariness dragged her down and her shoulders slumped as she shook her head in defeat. She'd failed. She couldn't do it.

Prince took her face in his hands. *Do not give up. You can do this.*

*I can't get through,* she cried.

*Yes, you can.* His hands gripped her face tightly. *You are one of the strongest women I know. Everything you have been through and you still stand tall and fight. You keep going. Do not give up now,* he said fiercely. *Never give up!*

His words lifted her heart and she smiled wryly that he'd finally called her a woman. Not that it mattered really. Yet, his belief in her meant something. It gave her something to hold onto.

Pulling from his grasp, she flung herself at the wall again and again. How strong could it possibly be? Certainly it would break eventually? Stepping back, she spun toward it, intending to give it a swift side-kick.

Instead, she spun right through.

The shock froze her for a moment, and then panic set in. Her body had disappeared, sound, sight, everything vanished. *Prince!*

*I am here. Well done, Arowyn.*

She couldn't breathe, couldn't feel. *What do I do?*

*For now, orient yourself. Feel where you are. Sense your body. Kei and the other Fey have arrived. I am still with you, but I must speak with them.*

*Don't leave me here!*

His faint laughter echoed around her...in her? The relief in it chased away much of her panic.

*I am always with you.*

Comforting words. Words she wished she could read more into. Instead, she did as asked and tried to sort out where she had ended up. Normal sight had gone, yet a strange wash of color surrounded her.

Everything felt inside-out and upside-down. After a few moments, she began to make sense of the colors around her. She could feel her blood pumping through veins and saw them as multitudes of thin strings of light around her.

Discomfort tugged at her. Something felt wrong...hot.

*Power is coming to you now.*

*I feel wrong.*

He took a moment to respond. *The allorum is wearing off. Your fever is returning. We must act quickly. Move toward your wound.*

Move? She didn't know how to move, or which direction to go. Frustration pulsed through her. She felt her heart rate speed up. How much time did she have?

Picking a string of colors, she focused on them and pictured herself moving closer. Actually moving startled her for a moment and then a sense of relief and pride washed through her.

*The other way.*

*Of course,* she muttered back to Prince and then made herself turn and head in the opposite direction.

The colors washed out for a moment as power suddenly coursed through her like a lightning strike. It hummed around her. The fury erupted from it, red flames blazing in every direction. She didn't know what to do. *Prince!*

*Ignore it for now. We will contain and guide it soon enough.*

The strange colors around her continued to catch her attention and threatened to distract her. She followed veins and arteries, slipped down her throat and past heaving lungs.

*Almost there.*

The heat within intensified. Ahead, the normal rainbows of colors changed to sickly greens and black. Drawing closer the simple feeling of wrongness overcame her.

*Very well done. Pause here. Now imagine gathering the power to you. Collect it and send it forth to the wound. Direct it to heal, to make things as they once were.*

*You expect too much from me,* she grumbled. Everything he told her turned out to be easier said than done.

*And yet you always manage to accomplish what I ask. You can do this.*

Doing as instructed, she called the power to her, surprised when it actually came, if somewhat sluggishly. With a great shove, she pushed it toward the sickness within… and screamed.

Eyes snapping open, she heaved up in bed. Had the pain not been so excruciating, she would have wondered about now being able to move.

Her boys surrounded her, and now held her down. Bo had her feet, while Kei and Prince each held a shoulder and arm. The pain lessened for a moment and she didn't fight them as they pushed her back down.

"You didn't mention to go slowly," Kei snapped angrily, his eyes glowing red. "That healing quickly hurts?"

"No," Prince admitted. "But we do not have time..."

Kei growled his frustration.

"You should have made time," Rhee-En snarled.

His voice shocked her and she turned her head to find him next to Kei. She hadn't expected him to be there.

Listening to them argue, she panted past the pain and overwhelming heat flooding her body. The four Fey stood near the end of the bed, watching her with wide, glowing eyes.

"Thank you," she choked out. "For coming."

Cano nodded to her, his hand snaking around his mate's waist and pulling her closer. "Of course. We will aid you as we can."

"Who is next?" Prince looked over his shoulder at the Fey.

"I will," Aron said quietly, the glow in his eyes rising to red as he stepped closer. He hesitantly touched her leg.

Her breath hissed out at the surge of power and fury. "Prince, I'm not inside!"

"Try from here. You understand how it works now. You have seen the wound."

Squeezing her eyes closed, she fought to control her erratic breathing so she could concentrate.

Prince squeezed her shoulder. "We are here. The Fey will keep the power coming. You just have to keep pushing it at your wound and healing. You can do this."

Kei slipped a hand into hers, the other remaining on her shoulder. "It will hurt. Hold tight."

Somehow she managed to gather more power like Prince had shown her. Pushing it once more, she couldn't prevent another scream of pain. She'd never felt such agony. Voices faded around her as it rolled over her, attacking from every side. No matter how much she screamed or thrashed about she couldn't get away from it.

"Too much is escaping," Rhee-En said.

"I am amazed she has the control she does. It will have to do."

"Her eyes are glowing."

"They do that," Kei answered quietly.

The pain faded again and she stopped fighting, collapsing back onto the bed. Her heart thundered in her chest, her breaths came in frantic, pain filled gasps. "Wither me," she whispered.

Prince stroked her forehead, pushing hair from her face. "Well done. It is almost over. Stay strong, little one."

The fury within roiled, urging her to get up and fight. Her eyes darted about the room. Lissana reached forward, sending her power. Garen paced along the wall. Rhee-En stood slightly back, watching her with wide, fascinated eyes. Did he think her some kind of monster?

Power and more fury surged through her and she gritted her teeth. Lissana had given her much more than the younger Fey had.

"Again," Prince commanded.

She didn't want the pain. How much more could she take? Her entire body trembled already.

Gathering the power, she shoved it down. Pain blinded her, white pulsing lights filling her vision. A searing pressure bore down at her side. Arching her back, her heels scrambled to dig into the bed as she screamed.

Kei's hand tightened around hers but it didn't help. The agony would destroy her.

Fury swelled and broke as she fought the hands holding her down. Their strength overpowered her. The pain lessened slightly, but not enough. She needed her hands free to rip herself apart and relieve the still growing pressure.

"Help me," she gasped, writhing on the bed and staring up at the broken faces of her boys. Tears streaked down Kei's face. Prince had paled, his face hard and set as he fought his emotions. "I'm tearing…apart…I want…" She screamed again.

Prince cursed and scrambled to remove the sheet now twisted around her. "Kei, hold her." Cano reached for her, but Prince held up a hand. "Wait!"

He tore the bandaging from her side and cursed again. "The wound has closed. I need a knife!"

Kei shifted over her, taking her wrists in his hands and holding them to her chest, pinning her down.

A knife… Squeezing her eyes closed, she shook her head frantically. A choked gasp rattled from her as Prince cut into her side. Warmth followed, sliding down her side and then something cool, wiping, wiping along her wound and side over and over again. The scent of rot overpowered her. Someone gagged. The door creaked open, letting in more fresh air.

"Now, Cano."

"No!" She wailed and fought against Kei. "P-please, no!" More fury exploded through her but she couldn't overpower the weight of him on her chest.

"Fight, Arowyn. Heal yourself."

She wanted to rip Prince's throat out. He didn't understand. The pain controlled everything, now a living thing destroying her from the inside.

"How long can she withstand this? A human heart is not meant for such stress."

Rhee-En's words caused a shudder to run through her. Would she die in agony then?

*Aro, please,* Kei begged her. *Don't leave us. Keep trying.*

*Kei…* A sob shook her. Sweat ran down her face and stung her eyes. It soaked the sheet under her. The new power overflowed within her and she struggled to control it. Finally she managed to grasp some of it and forced it to move, to heal.

Pain…pain…pain…

"Kei!"

"I'm here."

Her eyes fluttered open as he put more weight on her, trying to control her frantic flailing. She would never escape the pain. Her breath hitched into short, desperate gasps. The fight left her, her body going still except for a constant, jerking tremble.

"Once more," Prince said quietly. "Kei."

Tears flooded her eyes. She couldn't do it again, she just couldn't.

Kei released her wrists, his hands slipping up to cup her cheeks. "Look at me."

Blinking rapidly, she cleared the tears and met his flaming red eyes. Certainly her own matched his now. His face lowered and he pressed a kiss to her forehead.

"You can do this," he told her firmly, his eyes holding hers once more.

Fury swirled within her, wanting something to fight. She pushed it away. She wouldn't fight Kei. Nodding to him slightly, she waited for his power.

It came swiftly, the power and fury crashing through her.

*I love you,* he whispered fiercely through her mind, his eyes still locked on hers.

She shuddered, not from his words, but the power raging within. His power was so much stronger than the other Fey.

*Heal, Aro. Finish it. Stay with me.*

His mind voice vibrated with such power she couldn't refuse his command. Power gathered once more, a massive swirling ball. With a last, final burst of strength, she pushed.

Despite Kei's weight across her chest, her back flung into an arch of agony. Every limb trembled. She couldn't even breathe. His fingers tightened further around her face, his now

303

golden eyes never leaving hers. Her scream strangled into a gasp as the pain suddenly spiked and then abruptly vanished. Wilting, exhausted, her eyes fluttered closed. The sound of her raging heart pounded loudly in the sudden silence of the room.

Wet, coolness swiped along her side once more.

"It is done," Prince whispered. His hand rested briefly over her closed skin, trembling slightly. "You did it, child."

Her eyes snapped open, blazing in red fury.

# Chapter 33:
# Fury of Five

"How could you do that to me!" Kei barely stopped her as she tried to fling herself off the bed. His hands caught her shoulders as he twisted and shoved, pushing her back onto the bed.

She spit curses, snarling and fighting beneath him. The fury of the Fey reared up within her, demanding battle, death.

"Arowyn," Prince began, his voice slightly strangled.

"Out!" Kei struggled to hold her down as she fought furiously against him. His head turned slightly and he jerked it toward the open door. "I can handle this. Out!"

A screech of frustration and anger sprang out of her, drowning out whatever the others said. They left though, and quickly, the door banging closed behind them.

"Let me go!"

"Easy, Aro," Kei whispered, his voice frighteningly calm.

With a surge of strength, she bucked and pushed, throwing him off of her. As he stumbled back against the wall she sprang to her feet on the bed and crouched, one hand out to steady her on the soft surface.

Kei raised his hands defensively. "You have the fury of five Fey in you."

"I know," she snapped. She did know. She knew this wasn't her, but she couldn't control it. The knowledge further fed the fury within her.

The desire to fight trembled through her. She shifted, ready to spring even though she knew it wasn't Kei she wanted to fight. Her enemy was the Vor, yet there were none here.

Kei gestured to her. "Come."

With such an invitation she couldn't resist. Her muscles bunched and then propelled her forward, off the bed and onto him. Her wild launch sent his back crashing into the wall.

The breath whooshed out of him and he…chuckled.

The strange reaction froze her for a moment as her eyes shot to his face in confusion.

He took advantage of her surprise to wrap his arms around her, pinning her upper arms and holding her tightly to his chest. A hand cupped the back of her head, pushing it down into the curve of his neck.

His strength amazed her, yet she fought against it, kicking and twisting, striking him as she could with the limited use of her hands.

"My vicious one," he murmured into her hair.

She lifted her head, and found herself face to face with him. His nose brushed hers, but she could only stare at the lips a mere breath away from her own. Their ragged breathes mingled. For a moment they both became perfectly still.

Her eyes flicked up to his and she sucked in a sharp breath to find them no longer golden, but glowing faintly yellow.

A low, sultry growl rumbled from his chest.

Red eyes narrowing, she growled in return.

His growing fury swirled with hers, pulling her tighter to him, joining them together. Something else abruptly pulled at her. For a moment she sensed it and understood the forces wrapping tighter and tighter around them. Their bindings.

With a heart wrenching cry she turned her head away, struggling against his hold. When her head nearly collided with his, he once again pressed it to his shoulder.

Fighting harder produced only a few growls now and then from him. He continued to hold her, firmly, as if he'd never let her go. She found it hard to breath, both from his tight embrace and her face being pressed into his neck.

Slowly, the fight bled out of her. The fury retreated, giving her back control.

Trembling against him, she relaxed into his arms, letting out a tired and relieved sigh. How did he have the power to calm her madness? She didn't know, didn't care really. Perhaps it was their bindings. Perhaps it was just him.

Turning his head slightly, he pressed a kiss to her hair and relaxed his hold. His hands stroked down her hair and back.

"Let it go."

Keeping her eyes closed, she concentrated on being calm, on being safe. She didn't need to fight. The fury could go. Slowly, the red and black swirls of furious flame dissipated within her.

"We need to work on that," she said quietly. "I can't keep losing control of it."

He nodded against her hair. "I know. We will. Together."

"Together," she whispered back. A breath shuddered out of her. "What was...I felt..." Her voice trailed off. She didn't know how to describe the strange feelings or the even stranger magical pulls she'd just experienced.

He took a moment to reply. "Us."

She didn't understand, but didn't have the energy to question him further.

His hold on her shifted. "Come, you should rest now."

Leaning back, she looked up at his tired face. "Thank you, Kei."

His sudden smile brightened the entire room. "You're still with me. Thank *you*."

The door opened and she turned, smiling to see it full of her boys. Seeing her no longer in a fury, they piled into the room. It wasn't until Bo held out an oversized shirt she realized she stood around in her underclothes. Slipping it on quickly, she paused only a moment to look at the scar on her side. The part curving up by her ribs was fairly thin. However the strip from her side to almost her belly button was thick and mangled. It reminded her of Prince's back. No, it looked worse.

A small smile tugged at her lips. Her first battle scar from the Vor. She realized then she truly did plan to help the Fey, to heal and fight alongside them.

Weariness built as she hugged everyone and they all spoke excitedly about her being healed. Kei quickly changed the sheet on the bed again as she got passed around.

"Aro needs to rest," he finally said.

Before she could do anything, Prince stepped forward and scooped her up into his arms. She squeaked in alarm, her eyes wide as she looked up at him. "I can walk."

"Yes, you can. But I want to carry you."

She didn't know what to say to that. Instead she returned goodbyes to the others as they left once again. From the few irritated looks at Prince, she thought he must have mind spoke to them. Sometimes she forgot she didn't always hear every conversation going on around her.

Prince set her down gently, spread a sheet over her, and tucked her in.

"You should get some sleep, too."

Pulling a chair over, he shrugged one shoulder. "I will."

"Thank you," she said after a moment of awkward silence.

He winced and wouldn't look at her. "I am sorry, that it caused you such pain."

"But I'm alive."

"I would have taken your pain for you, if I could have."

"I know," she answered truthfully. "Right now, I'm just trying to forget it." She grinned. "Us mortals have a wonderfully bad memory for some things, like pain."

"I hope you do," he answered quietly, still refusing to look at her face.

She bit her lower lip, uncertainty rising within her. Had she done something wrong? Maybe she'd said something bad she didn't remember?

He stood suddenly, startling her. "Get some rest."

Before she could answer, he strode to the door and left.

Confused and hurt, she stared at the door, wondering what she'd done.

A thump on the windowsill above her startled her again. Tilting her head back, she saw Kei perched on the sill.

"What are you doing?"

"Waiting for him to leave." He sprang down to the side, landing beside the bed. "I thought you might have trouble sleeping." He made shooing motions at her. "Move over."

"Then why did you leave," she grumbled, turning on her side and wiggling as close to the edge of the bed as she could.

"Prince wanted to talk to you." He climbed in and curled up to face her. The bed was small and his knees pressed against hers. Taking her hands in his, he gave them a tight squeeze.

"He didn't say much. He wouldn't even look at me."

Kei sighed. "Don't worry, Aro. You didn't do anything. You almost dying broke him apart. He thinks too much."

Sadness made her breath catch and she lowered her eyes. She never wanted to hurt any of them.

Kei leaned his head forward and thumped his forehead against hers. "Guess what."

She raised her eyes to look at him, a smile turning her lips at his playful mood. It was hard to be upset when he acted so very happy.

"Our eyes match now."

She blinked rapidly. "They do?" Maybe that was why Prince looked so upset.

He nodded and grinned again, clearly pleased.

"I didn't grow claws or teeth did I? Are my ears pointy?"

He laughed and grinned again. "Not yet."

"Kei!"

"Sleep now," Kei said softly, yet a smile still lighting his face. "I'll watch over you."

With a huff she closed her eyes. Even as she drifted quickly to sleep, a smile still softly rested on her face.


"How are you feeling, pup?"

When she'd awoke Kei had gone, but Bo and Garen were back. Sitting up, she yawned into the back of her hand. "Not awake. Stiff. Hungry."

Bo chuckled. "That's a good sign."

"Where is everyone?"

"Kei is speaking with Rhee-En about everything that happened."

She raised her eyebrows. "That should be interesting. Kei being so talkative."

Bo's loud laugh filled the room. "True. The other Fey are helping the Were prepare dinner. Apparently it will be ready soon. Prince and Kei got into a fight on whether to wake you up or not."

"He's still in a mood?"

"Seems so." He shrugged. "He's gone for a walk to 'think'. Whatever that means."

"No idea," she admitted.

The door opened and the Were woman who'd tended her before came in. "Arowyn! Good, you are awake." She smiled as she approached, setting something on the chair as she passed. "Lie down a moment. I just want to give you a final check over."

Aro did as asked, watching as the woman examined her scar.

"Fascinating. You will need to watch the muscles. Do some stretching exercises a few times a day. You've been through a traumatic ordeal. Try not to exert yourself for a while."

Aro grinned. "I'll try."

"Come. Let's get you to the bath house before the food is ready. I've some new clothes set aside for you. I'll have them sent over."

Sitting up, she smiled again. "Thank you." The thought of a bath made her giddy. "I'm sorry, but I don't remember your name."

"Cassia," she answered with another smile. "Here." She turned and picked up what she'd left on the chair, giving it a shake. "It's cool out this evening. This is for you."

Slipping off the bed, Aro eyed the beautiful heavy cloak. It reminded her of the one Prince had worn. "For me?"

"Yes, now come. You're wasting bathing time."

Slipping the cloak on quickly, Aro flashed a grin at Bo, who shook his head and chuckled. A bounce affected her step as she followed Cassia from the room. Bath time!

After scrubbing herself almost raw, making good use of a variety of soaps, and then just soaking in the large tub of warm water, Aro felt like an entirely new person.

Jen Wylie

Her new clothes consisted of dark leather pants and a dark cloth shirt. They actually fit. That she matched her boys didn't bother her. Having new clean clothes meant more to them than the Were could possibly know.

Dinner consisted of a deer roasted over a pit in the center of the small settlement, bread with cheese, and baked corn. They ate until they couldn't fit another morsel in.

Sitting around the fire afterward, she couldn't keep a smile off her face. *Clean and fed and safe. What more could a person ask for?*

Her smiled slipped for a moment as she noticed Prince had gone off again. She wished she knew what was wrong. Rhee-En walked up and crouched by her side.

"I am pleased to see you so well."

"Thank you, for everything. I can't thank you enough."

He smiled, the firelight dancing across his scarred face making him appear vicious. "I hope you will visit us again in the future. I assume you wish to continue your journey."

She blinked at him in surprise. "Yes, we would."

"Kei had mentioned so. One of your horses did not survive. I am not sure if they told you that yet. We can lend you another. Tomorrow we will get everything organized, if that suits you."

"Yes, of course. Thank you."

With a nod he stood and moved on to talk to someone else.

She turned to where Kei sat beside her, raising her eyebrows. "He's rather...efficient."

"He is," Kei agreed. Holding out his hand, he jerked his head toward the buildings. "You've lots to do tomorrow. Time to sleep."

She let him help her up, Bo and Garen following behind them. Turning slightly as they walked, she tried to catch sight of Prince.

312

For a moment she thought she saw a hooded form standing in the shadows watching her, but she couldn't be sure.

Now that she'd recovered, she would share one of the larger buildings with the boys instead of remaining in the sick house. Rhee-En's reaction to her insistence of this during dinner had been amusing. However, she'd been quite adamant.

They quickly got settled into the rows of small beds. Aro didn't know whether to be pleased she got a bed again, or put out there was no room to curl up with anyone. Once she sank into the softness of her bed, she quickly decided another night or two would be quite fine with her.

Jen Wylie

# Chapter 34:
# Once More into the Woods

Cassia found her first thing in the morning and drew her away to teach her a number of stretches. The exercise helped ease some of the stiffness she'd woken up with. The Were correctly diagnosed the stomach muscles on her side needed work. Though they didn't pain her, her flexibility had decreased considerably.

After washing up, Bo led her to the settlement's center to eat more than she should have for breakfast. The rest of the morning she spent going through all the packs with Bo and Kei. Though the one horse hadn't survived, the Were had been able to retrieve their things. They sorted, cleaned gear, and repacked.

Bo went to talk to Rhee-En about a few supplies they needed while Kei gave her a short tour of the settlement. By the time they reached the center again, cold meat and other dishes were being set out for lunch.

Prince hadn't appeared yet and she didn't remember seeing him that morning either. She hoped someone fed him. Watching the few children run about the tables and play gave her an excuse to keep looking around while she waited to eat.

When the sun totally disappeared everyone looked up and froze.

Aro stared, eyes wide, at the massive dragon flying over them. "Rot," she muttered as it finally passed by and the trees hid it from view.

If the dragon was Damon, Rhee-En wasn't going to be happy with her. If it wasn't him, they were all in even more trouble.

Getting slowly to her feet, she turned and started walking slowly out of the settlement. Running would have been better, but she didn't want to panic the Were or frighten the children. Currently they were yelling and bouncing about how they'd just seen a real live dragon.

Garen darted ahead as Bo and Kei fell into step on either side of her.

Her heart sped up within her chest as she quickened her step, eyes darting around the small buildings and trees.

Kei glanced over at her. "Is it Damon?"

"I don't know. I'd assume so." She shook her head with a frown. "What is he doing here?"

"Prince tried to reach him," Bo stated. "When nothing else worked. He never received a response as far as I know."

"Rot," she muttered. They'd almost passed the last houses of the settlement and she let out a deep breath of relief. Now as long as the Were kept away, they should be safe.

Garen dashed out of the trees ahead of them. *It is Damon.*

They continued walking until Aro saw someone ahead of them. She stopped, trying to decide what to do. "You all stay here," she said finally, turning to look at each of them. "I mean it. He has a temper and I don't want him to hurt you. Keep your thoughts as guarded as you can."

Garen thumped his rear onto the ground to sit but didn't look happy. Bo muttered under his breath and crossed his arms.

"Kei?" She gave him a stern look.

"Fine. But if you need us…"

"I know you have my back. No worries."

The boys now taken care of, she raised her chin and marched forward. She wasn't afraid of him. He'd proven he wanted her alive. That didn't mean he wouldn't hurt her though. However he appeared to appreciate her strength more than anything else.

He walked a few steps to meet her, but she stopped a short distance from him, not wanting to be in reach. "Damon," she said, giving him a polite nod.

"Arowyn." He regarded her thoughtfully. "I had heard you were…unwell. I am pleased to see that is not true."

"I've recovered, thank you."

"I see."

They stared at each in silence for a moment. She focused on keeping her thoughts guarded and the walls of her inner fortress strong.

"Why are you here?"

His smile was small and not particularly kind. "I thought you might need me."

Tilting her head to the side, she returned his smile. "If I had, it would be too late by now. I managed without you."

"Is that so?"

"Yes, it is."

Damon stepped forward. "Let me in, Arowyn," he said harshly. "I would know what I have missed."

She sighed and shook her head, but didn't step back. "No." Turning to walk away, he grabbed her arm, his fingers grasping her so tightly she gasped in pain.

"You do not walk away from me, human."

Anger rose within her and she glared up at him, not surprised to find his strange eyes boring into hers and swirling in anger. Shaking off his arm, she turned back to him, clenching her fists in an attempt to control her rising fury. "You want to see? Very well."

Raising her chin, she kept her eyes locked on his and entered her own mind, pulling forth the memories he so wanted to see. She began with a rolling stream of nothing important; eating, traveling, setting up camp.

He grasped her shoulders, a low growl rumbling from his chest. "That is not what I want to see."

"How about this?" She flung her encounter with the Fey at him, the fighting, her taking their fury, giving it to Prince. She stopped the memory then, skipping how Prince reacted, how he'd kissed her.

His mind pushed at hers, demanding more. She pushed back, gritting her teeth with the effort.

*Do not fight me. You never win.*

*I don't belong to you! My thoughts are my own!*

A dark laugh echoed through her mind. *You bow to those who are stronger than you. That is the way of it. Now show me more.*

Heart hammering in her chest, she struggled to control her rapid breathing and temper. Her temper won and she lashed out at him. "This?" She sent him their fight with the Vor and the pressure on her mind eased. "And this?" Her. Staring down at the wound on her side. The blood and guts. She forced her memories of her panic and her pain into him. Her boys gathering around her, Prince trying to keep her guts in. The pain the pain the pain. Awakening in Rhee-En's settlement. She thrust at him her few memories of the fever, of her knowing she would die.

"Enough, Arowyn."

"But you wanted to see," she whispered. Pressing her hands on his chest, she continued to share her memories. The

Fey coming to give her power. The unrelenting agony of her healing.

Grabbing her wrists, he held them tightly, staring down into her eyes with a look she couldn't at all decipher. His mind crashed into hers, and she let the memories fade.

"You've grown stronger."

"I have." She stared him down, pulling at the wrists he still held trapped between them.

He chuckled, releasing her. "Such a fierce little thing you are."

"I don't have a choice."

"You always have a choice." His eyes left hers, finding someone behind her. "Isn't that right?"

An arm slipped around her waist, pulling her back against a hard warm chest.

"One last rescue, Shael?"

"Princes are supposed to save the beautiful ladies in distress," he replied wryly from behind her. Despite his light reply, his arm tightened around her.

"I wasn't in distress," she muttered. His words caught up to her and her breath lodged in her throat. He'd called her beautiful? A lady? Her anger returned however, he'd been avoiding her since she healed and now decided to come back?

"You are looking better," the Dragos commented. "I would speak with you." He tilted his head to the side, indicating they go elsewhere.

Prince paused, and then nodded. *Will you be–*

*I'm fine. He didn't hurt me.*

*I will not be long.* He left her side, following the Dragos into the trees.

The absence of his warmth sent a shiver along her spine.

"Arowyn."

She turned and froze, surprised to see Rhee-En, and all the other Were, watching her.

He grinned and shook his head. "My people cannot decide if you are stronger than you look, or insane."

She frowned and shook her head, not understanding what he meant.

"You stood up to a Dragos."

"I don't like him in my head."

His lips twisted as he tried not to laugh. "No one does. But it just is not done."

"Never? But surely–"

"Let me rephrase. No one crosses a Dragos and ever lives to speak of it. They are a temperamental sort."

"I've noticed."

He held out his arm. "Come, let us eat."

Slipping her arm through his, she kept her head high, staring straight ahead, as he walked them through the still staring pack.

Eating proved difficult to do. Prince hadn't returned from his talk with Damon. She should never have let them go off alone. Ignoring the food, she chewed on her thumbnail instead.

Going over and over Prince's behavior the last few days didn't help. She understood some of what he must have been thinking, but not why he'd now been avoiding her, or his sudden reappearance and show of affection.

"Are you feeling well?"

She looked up at Rhee-En in surprise and quickly hid her chewed thumbnail. "Yes, I'm fine. Just worried about Prince."

Bo moved over and the alpha sat down beside her. "There is no need to worry. It is doubtful the Dragos will harm an Elven prince."

"They've fought before," she said quietly. "It was Damon who tore off his glamor."

Rhee-En stared at her, clearly shocked and at a loss for words. "That is…disturbing."

She snorted at the understatement and then flushed when he looked at her in surprise.

Chuckling softly, he shook his head in amusement. "Are you still planning on leaving tomorrow?"

"I think so. Everything seems to be in order."

"You should reach the wardwall before evening. If you want to push on, you could rest and then leave when darkness falls. You would avoid any human notice then."

His plan seemed sound and she nodded her agreement. "We will try that then."

"I will have some of my pack stay close while you remain in the forest. Just as a precaution."

Normally, such a statement would have angered her. She'd learned her lesson. "I appreciate that, thank you again."

He stared down at his hands for a moment before looking back over at her with a small, forced smile. "Have you decided what you will do after?"

"No, actually. Not at all," she admitted ruefully. "I've just been so focused on actually getting him home alive."

He paused before speaking again. "You are always welcome with us. If you would like to return," he continued quickly. He flashed her smile, his scars twisting along his face. "You do have to return my horse."

His words, and their apparent meaning, left her flustered for a moment. "Yes, I do," she finally managed. "Whatever we decide, we'll return to the forest first."

"I would like that."

*Be careful,* Garen cautioned. *You have impressed him, with your healing and standing up against the Dragos. You would be an asset to any pack.*

Heat began a slow rise from her neck to her cheeks. *Kei, help me here.*

Kei leaned forward so he could talk around her. "Aro can let you know, whatever is decided."

Rhee-En nodded and stood, smiling at her once more. "We have a feast planned for tonight, perhaps some dancing. We will not keep you up too late though." His smile faded as he caught sight of something behind her.

She turned and saw Prince coming out of the trees. Smiling in relief, it faded when he didn't acknowledge them, but instead disappeared into the building they slept in. Apparently, he'd gone back to ignoring her. Again.

Rhee-En and his Were put on a fun and lively evening event for them. Pushing Prince from her mind, she enjoyed it immensely. She kept telling herself she had to get used to him not being around. There was no lack of friendship or partners for dancing. Kei, Bo, and Garen remained close to her side. Though Rhee-En paid her much attention, she was able to divert any conversation she worried would go down paths she didn't want to visit.

They all rose early the next morning and packed up the horses. The Were circled them, assisting now and then and waved as they departed with the slowly rising sun.

Aro found they'd all been given a cloak and even Kei wore his in the chill early morning air. Fall had descended quickly, though whether it was early or late she couldn't tell.

As they left she walked with Kei and Garen while Bo and Prince took the horses. She watched Prince's stiff back as he rode off into the trees, her heart clenching in her chest. She only had two more days with him and he ignored her. The urge to shake some sense into him just kept growing. Either that or break into tears. She much preferred the first idea.

"We've far to go today," Kei said, bumping her shoulder with his. "Can you keep up?"

"Of course," she sputtered, glaring at him.

He laughed and took off after the horses. With a grin, she sprinted after him.

She'd worried her near death and sickness would have sapped her strength. Thankfully she discovered her body was only a little weaker than before. Perhaps it had been the healing magic, or even the full meals and soft bed. Whatever the reason, she managed to keep pace with Kei and the horses.

Garen roamed around them and many times she caught sight of other Were through the trees. Rhee-En had kept his promise to watch out for them and she found herself starting to like the scarred alpha Were.

When they finally stopped for lunch she plopped down on a log with a groan. Taking slow, even breaths, she slowly calmed her heart rate. While Bo readied their food, Kei and Prince took care of the horses. Her muscles began to protest and she stood, pacing slowly and doing some of the stretches Cassia had shown her.

"Be careful you do not tire yourself."

Rising from a stretch, she placed her hands on her hips and stared at Prince. "You're talking to me now?"

"You are angry."

"Angry? Yes. Confused. Yes. Hurt. Yes."

With each word he jerked as if she slapped him. "Arowyn, I…" He shook his head, lowering his eyes.

"Of course, don't answer," she snapped bitterly. Hands clenching in frustration and anger, she struggled to keep from screaming at him. "Look away. Walk away next. Just keep walking and don't look back."

His head shot up, his lips in a thin, angry line. "Is that what you want?"

She stared at him incredulously. "Of course not," she yelled, not caring that Bo and Kei were trying very hard not to

323

notice their exchange. "I want you to look at me, to see me! I want you next to me, by my side for the time we have left!"

"But then I will be gone," he said softly.

"And?" Shaking her head, she let out a weary sigh. "I almost died. If I learned one thing, it's to live while I'm alive, to cherish the ones I love and let them know I love them."

She knew immediately she'd said the wrong thing. The cold, stony mask slipped over his face as he frowned. "We have discussed this."

Pressing her lips tightly together, she managed to hide their sudden quivering. Remarkably, her eyes remained free of tears. Perhaps because despite the shattering of her heart once again, her anger remained stronger.

"We have," she finally said. "But I know you love me, even if it isn't the type of love I have for you. How can you deny that? What about our friendship? Everything we've been through together this past year? Doesn't all of that mean anything to you?"

"I do not…know what I feel."

His words shocked her. Her brow furrowed as she tried to figure out what he meant. "Come morning, you'll be home. I hope you can figure it out by then."

"As do I."

Before she could continue the conversation, he turned and walked away.

She wanted very much to hit something.

# Chapter 35:
## The Last Night

As the afternoon went on, Aro found herself straining to keep up. Pride kept her from asking Bo or Prince for a ride. Her anger at Prince helped to fight her growing fatigue. She didn't understand him, or what he felt or thought. She didn't understand why he acted like he did.

Garen slipped from the trees to her right to pace her and Kei. *The wardwall is just ahead. Watch your nose,* he said with a mental laugh.

Kei slowed, but curiosity got the better of her and she kept going…and slammed into an invisible wall.

Garen laughed again as she rubbed her forehead.

"Not funny," she grumbled. Raising her hands, she pushed them out until they hit the wardwall. Pushing as hard as she could did nothing.

"Nothing goes in or out," Prince said quietly behind her.

Turning, she saw he and Bo had ridden up behind them. "I can't see it."

"It isn't hard," Kei said before Prince could reply. "I'll teach you."

Patting the wall once, she smiled at Kei. "We should find a spot to camp then."

She didn't look at Prince. She didn't want to start another fight with him. To her, ignoring won over fighting. She headed east along the wall with Garen and Kei spreading out, searching for a suitable site.

Unable to help herself, she did glance back once and then stopped under the shadows of the trees.

Prince had dismounted and stood next to the wall, hands and forehead resting against it. Eyes closed, the quiet longing on his face made her breath catch.

Turning quickly on her heel, she ran. Find a site. Sleep. Travel to the gates of Rivenward. The sooner she could make these happen, the quicker Prince would be home again. The sooner he'd be happy again.

They hadn't found any water, but the site they eventually chose contained a thick grove so shadowed she hoped they'd be able to sleep even during the day. After eating some packed food quickly, she found a promising spot and spread out a small blanket. Curling up on it, she tucked her cloak around her as a blanket and waited for Kei.

It didn't take long for him to return from checking the horses once more. Kei dropped down beside her, though he didn't cuddle into his cloak like she did.

"It's cold today. Why do only my eyes change? Why can't something useful happen like I can stay warm like you?"

He grinned over at her. "You should stop asking for such things. They might happen."

"You're right," she admitted. If she actually did grow pointy ears and claws she didn't know how she'd react.

"Go to sleep, we'll be travelling through the night."

"I know! I'm not tired though." She sniffled and rubbed her chilly nose. Wiggling more into her cloak, she closed her eyes and tried to think sleepy thoughts.

Instead she just listened to the birds, the horses and odd sound the other boys made as they tried to sleep.

*Prince is coming.*

Cracking an eye open, she saw Kei trying not to smile. *I don't know if I want to talk to him or not.*

*Would you regret it if you didn't?*

*True.* With a sigh she rolled over to face the sound of the approaching footsteps. As he neared she pushed herself up with one arm.

Stopping beside her, he dropped down into a crouch. The darkness of the shadows hid most of him from her, but she saw he had the hood of his cloak up against the chill as well. She worried then, over how much the last few days had taken out of him. At least he'd be home soon, and then he could get better. He'd have his family and friends and magic back.

A lump formed in her throat and she swallowed, staring up into his face and trying to see what mood he was in. Her sight suddenly blurred and refocused. She jerked back in surprise.

"Wither me!"

He leaned away slightly in surprise at her outburst. "What is it?"

She blinked rapidly. "I can see you. In the dark. I can…wither me!" She swiveled around to face Kei. "These eyes actually work!"

Kei had sat up at her apparent distress, with a laugh, he flopped back down. "I told you to stop asking."

She grinned. "You did."

"Arowyn."

Her smile faded at Prince's solemn tone. Slowly, she turned back to face him.

Staring down at the ground, he refused to meet her eyes. "I have thought, on what you said. I am sorry for my actions the last few days."

She didn't know what to say. The standard "it's fine" just wouldn't leave her lips…because it wasn't.

When she didn't answer, he looked up at her, his expression determined. "May I have the honor of sleeping next to you tonight? Like we used to?"

Her mouth opened and closed in surprise, but words refused to form for fear she'd say something wrong again and he'd leave. Lowering her eyes, she nodded slowly.

Kei shifted next to her and she turned her head in surprise as he got up. "Where are you going?"

He squeezed her shoulder. "You need some time."

Leaving her with those cryptic words, she stared after him for a moment before turning back to Prince. He continued to watch her, and she felt heat rising to her cheeks. "Well, come on then. We're supposed to be getting some sleep."

Wordlessly, he settled down beside her. She hesitated, uncertain how close he wanted to be. Seeing her confusion, he reached out and grasped her arms, pulling her to him.

She stiffened as his arms wrapped around her, pulling her close. A hand reached up, gently guiding her head to his shoulder.

A slow breath shuddered out of her. They'd never slept like this, her curled up against him. So close. Nervous butterflies tickled through her stomach.

She had no idea how she was possibly going to sleep. "Did you want to talk?"

"I just want to hold you," he whispered against her hair.

She closed her eyes tightly, took one last deep breath, and then melted against him. Shifting slightly so she was closer, she tentatively slipped her hand into the folds of his cloak and rested it on his chest. His hand rose to cover hers, while his other arm squeezed her against him.

She had the sudden urge to mention it wasn't night, but such a thing would surely ruin the moment. A small smile tugged at her lips and she wiggled closer to him, sucking in his warmth.

"Thank you," she murmured.

"My pleasure."

She tilted her head up, trying to see his face. Had his tone just been teasing? From the curve of his lips, yes it had.

Smiling again, she found the comfy nook between his arm and chest. Being in his arms, everything seemed perfect.

The hand at her waist slowly moved, gently gliding from waist to hip and back. His thumb traced lazy circles across the back of her hand for a while and then slipped along her arm. She held her breath, not believing he was touching her like this.

Fingers slid over her shoulder, along her neck and up to cup her jaw. Tilting her head up, she tried to see his face. He shifted slightly onto his side, his head dipping to press his cheek against the top of her head. Every movement occurred slowly, gently. Perhaps he didn't want to frighten her, or tried to give her ample opportunity to ask him to stop.

Stopping was the last thing she wanted him to do. Her lips parted, her mind wanting to ask him what he was doing, but her heart quite firmly said to stay quiet. His thumb moving softly back and forth along her jaw distracted her terribly. His fingers curled, the backs of them running down her neck and under her chin, turning to rise and trail across her lips so very softly she wondered if she imagined it.

Cautiously, she moved the hand on his chest higher. When he didn't try to stop her, she continued until she felt the soft skin of his neck. Her fingers swept up his neck, along his jaw, and strayed by his ear. They wandered; learning, exploring, and touching him as softly as a feather.

Heart thumping rapidly in her chest, she struggled to keep her breathing light and even. His warmth enveloped her, not that she even needed it now. His simple touch lit a fire inside her, demanding more, begging for more.

"Sleep well," he whispered.

She blinked in surprise. A resigned sigh escaped her lips before she could stop it. Closing her eyes, she concentrated on feeling the continuing gentle caresses of his hands on her face and side.

Despite wanting to enjoy every moment of it, the sound of his heartbeat sent her into a peaceful, dreamless slumber.

# Chapter 36:
# Bittersweet Goodbyes

The rumble of a chuckle under her head woke her.

"You need to get up, Aro," Prince whispered, jiggling the arm beneath her.

"Mmm, I don't want to." She snuggled closer against him, smiling. He hadn't left. His arms remained around her. It hadn't all been a dream.

"Up, up!"

The reality of why they were getting up hit her hard. The last leg of their journey. "I'm awake," she grumbled, suddenly not in as good of a mood.

As they gathered their few belongings they'd unpacked and prepared the horses Kei drew her aside.

"So? How did it go?"

Ducking her head to hide a sudden blush, she shrugged.

"Did he tell you?"

She really didn't want to have this conversation. "No. He didn't even kiss me." Kei waited expectantly. "He just held me all night. That's it."

The Fey snorted in annoyance.

She raised her eyebrows. "You wanted him to kiss me?"

"I remember what you said, that he wasn't to do it again unless he loved you. So, yes. I was hoping he would."

331

"Well, I doubt he ever will," she said crossly. "He likely doesn't want you to punch him in the face again."

Kei's laugh wasn't loud, but it had a decidedly wicked tone to it. Narrowing her eyes, she scowled at him. "You're too protective," she complained.

Prince appeared by her side. "There is nothing wrong with that."

Of course he would think so, but then he hadn't heard the whole conversation.

"Ride with me."

She looked up at him in surprise. "I…yes."

He grinned, the boyish look crossing his face startling her. Who was this Prince?

Kei laughed in delight and ran off before she could hit him.

She rode in front of Prince as usual. The wind picked up and clouds rolled by, often blocking out the little light of the stars and moon. In such darkness, this slowed them as they let the horses pick their way along at their own pace.

It didn't take long for them to leave the forest. Once again in human lands, she didn't have to try to see the wardwall. Pastureland ended abruptly and forest began, a clean line running ahead of them.

The rolling walk of their mount and Prince's warm body behind her made her drowsy. More than once, she found herself starting awake.

"You can sleep. I would never let you fall."

Holding the reins around her, his arms brushed against hers and kept her safe. "I know, but I don't want to sleep. I want to be with you. Talk to you."

"Then we will talk," he answered.

They did, about nothing at all. It was wonderful, perfect. Time passed too quickly, and before she knew it the stars faded and the sun began to rise behind them.

They smiled and laughed and…little parts of her broke inside. With every word, every step, he was leaving her.

Yet he had given her this, for whatever reason. She would not spoil it. One day it would be a memory she treasured.

They crested the top of what turned out to be the last of a long series of rolling hills. The rising sun had cleared the clouds away and sunlight lit the lowlands before them. In the distance she saw a small stream crossing to the forest, beyond that, the faint brown mark of a road. Focusing hard, she thought she could see the glitter of the sunlit sea on the horizon.

Taking the reins in one hand, Prince leaned forward, tucking his chin over her shoulder, his face next to hers. He pointed ahead. "Look, Aro. Can you see it?"

Her eyes slipped along the tree-line and then stopped, locking onto two towering structures amidst the forest border in the distance. "What is that?"

"The Guardians of the Gate."

"Statues?"

"Yes, of our first king and queen. The gate is between them. They are impressive, yes?"

She nodded quickly, even though she couldn't make out more than their size. "They're certainly big."

He chuckled. "They are, and quite beautiful as well."

His face remained so close to hers, she couldn't keep from tipping her head against his. For a moment, she felt the soft pressure of him returning the gesture before he leaned back. The tenderness of his action left her warm and happy, a soft smile coming to her face all on its own.

Craning her head around, he surprised her with his boyish grin again. His eyes met hers and then he laughed, shaking his head. "I am not used to your eyes."

Quickly, she lowered her lashes and turned away. "I'm sorry," she whispered.

Fingers caught her chin, turning her head back to face him. "Do not be. They are a part of you now."

Looking up, she met his gaze again and forced herself not to look away as he stared at her strange new golden eyes.

"They suit you." Releasing her chin, he tucked a strand of hair behind her ear.

Behind them, she heard a rumbling laugh. Making a face, she refused to turn and see the boys' reactions to her and Prince.

Though the gates to his home were in sight, Prince kept the horse at a leisurely walk. She didn't complain, the more moments she had with him the better, yet she did wonder once again at his sudden change. Maybe he just wanted her to be happy.

They reached the lowlands and the horse slowed, its hooves making muted sucking noises as it sank into oversaturated soil.

"We will have to go around. It will only get worse." Prince pointed to how the land continued to dip until it reached the small stream she'd seen before rising again. Her eyes settled on the road, which apparently lead to the gates.

As Prince guided the horse north around the wet ground she tried to figure out why there even was a road. Finally, she just asked.

"We do some trade with the humans. Most believe we have humans working for us who buy and sell and move the goods, though in truth we simply wear a glamor and do it ourselves."

"You don't have everything you need in Rivenward?"

"We do, for the most part. We trade for gems and some metals that are brought in from overseas. Human art is collected by some. Mainly it is just that your items are different and it is an excuse for some to travel. Life can easily become tedious."

# Broken Prince

They stopped at the stream to water the horses and wash up. It didn't escape her notice Prince took extra care to get the dirt from his hands and face, to smooth down his clothes and he even ran his fingers through his hair.

Her heart lodged in her throat, but she smiled and chatted with Bo about nothing even as her eyes kept straying to the ever closer gates.

"They're impressive. It's rather amazing we've never heard stories of them."

She nodded her agreement, taking in the details of the two statues. Two beautiful Elves in armor, swords in their hands, crowns upon their heads, their stony eyes locked on something far in the distance. Though beautiful, she also found them frightening.

The horses finished and they mounted and continued on, keeping to their slow pace. Bo moved his horse up next to them, Kei and Garen moving about around them, almost as if they were playing some game. She smiled slightly, perhaps they were.

They reached the road too soon, and she found it harder and harder to breath.

"Will I be able to still talk to you?"

"I...do not know," he replied. "I am not sure if the wardwall will disrupt it, or even how far apart we can be. Our pack is small and the bond really not that strong." He hesitated before continuing quietly, "Do you know where you will be?"

"I don't know. Back to the forest first, to return Rhee-En's horse. Maybe we'll try to winter in one of the cities though. If we can find some work."

"I would suggest Westport," he offered. "It is the second city north of here."

"The one with the quarry?"

"Yes, and partly east of Rhee-En's lands, should you need to return there. They also have the largest human port of the city states. Perhaps you will hear word of your family."

"Then yes, we will try there."

"Arowyn."

She turned at the sudden change in his tone.

His head tilted solemnly as he pulled the horse to a stop. "I think this is far enough."

Swinging around, she saw they'd almost reached the massive gates. Prince slipped off the horse as she stared at them. She hadn't realized the gates themselves were so huge. The statues had made her think them smaller. Beautiful carvings etched every part of them, so many, her eyes darted back and forth trying to see them all.

Something thumped, making the ground shake and the horses shift nervously. With a mighty groan, the massive gates began to slowly swing open.

With a squeak of surprise she dismounted quickly, turning wide eyes on Prince, who chuckled at her sudden panic.

"Apparently the seer is getting better. It seems they know I am here."

She nodded once and turned back to watch them magically open. Behind her, she heard Prince quietly say his farewells to the others.

Light trembles spread through her body. She didn't want her turn to come. The perfect words still eluded her. How did you say goodbye to the one you loved? How did you put all of your feelings and hopes and fears into a few simple sentences?

Her sullen thoughts suddenly stopped short as Elven knights walked two abreast through the gate. Armor gleaming in the sun, they marched in perfect unison. Her eyes widened at the drawn blades each held.

"Prince," she whispered harshly, not daring to turn around.

He stepped up beside her and she risked a look at him. A small smile curved his lips. He didn't look worried at all. Glancing down at her, he finally noticed her distress. "A welcome." His head snapped up suddenly. "That is unexpected."

Following his look, she watched the knights split, three going to stand on either side of the gate. As the last pair parted, a woman strode into view, hands outstretched at her sides, holding the reins of two mounts.

"I will return," Prince said quietly before striding forward to meet her.

Aro stared in shock, wondering what was going on. Her eyes focused on the woman as she drew closer. The lady was, quite simply, the most gorgeous creature she'd ever seen. From her perfectly done hair to the tips of her sparkling shoes, every part of her, every curve and piece of clothing, radiated perfection and beauty.

Closing her eyes, she tried to control the sudden feelings of worthlessness assaulting her. No wonder Prince wasn't in love with her if the women looked like this at home.

She kept her eyes shut until she managed to control the fiery burning of unshed tears. Prince still talked with the beauty, though he now had the reins of both horses in one hand. The woman handed him a small pouch, and Prince nodded, his face intent upon hers.

Finally he turned and made his way back to them. Aro didn't watch him though, her eyes locked with the woman's. The Elf regarded her thoughtfully until Prince reached her side, and then she turned on her heel and walked regally back to the gates.

"Who was that?"

Prince raised his eyebrows at her snappish tone. "Aeriella. Our seer."

"I see she grew up," Aro muttered.

Prince frowned. "She has made your life much easier. She saw my return, and that I wished to repay you for bringing me home." He held out a set of reins to her, the other to Bo.

"These are for you. Not our best stock, they cannot leave Rivenward, but you will not find better horses in these lands."

He turned to Kei and stepped to the side of one mount. "You rarely ride, so I have something special for you here." He patted a large pack. "She has marked other gifts and there are a few bags of coins and gems." His eyes found hers. "You never need to work again," he said softly. "You can buy a house, a bed, whatever you might want."

Bo thanked him loudly, and profusely, while she just stood there in shock. She'd never expected anything from him. Had she thought he'd allow it, she would have refused it all.

He turned to her, a small expectant smile on his face.

"Thank you so much," she said breathlessly. "I–"

"A moment, Aro," he said gently. "I have one more gift to give." He pulled the small pouch from his belt and walked over to Garen. "I have not known you long, but you have become family as well." Opening the bag, he pulled forth a small glowing sphere. "This is an Elven glamor rune. If you agree, I can set it upon you." He paused, apparently listening to Garen.

"No, it would make you appear as a large dog, it would encourage people to avoid you." He listened again. "With this you could enter cities and travel amongst humans unnoticed."

Finally he nodded and crouched down. Garen sat and for some reason opened his mouth. Aro watched in fascinated horror as Prince set the sphere in Garen's mouth and then sat back quickly.

Garen snapped his jaws shut. Color erupted, shooting out from between his teeth as he snorted and pranced about, shaking his head. With a final shake the lights faded away.

*Did that hurt?*

*It was…unpleasant,* he answered her.

He sat before Prince and, tilting his massive head back, opened his mouth again. Before he snapped it shut, she vaguely saw a tattoo on the roof of his mouth.

# Broken Prince

*Now I can protect you anywhere.*

*Garen, you didn't have to do that.*

*Yes, I did. It was the perfect gift.* With another snort he padded over to meet the new horses. They didn't appear disturbed by him at all.

"Arowyn."

Her stomach twisted. The time had come.

Tearing her eyes away from the others, she found Prince standing before her, staring down into her eyes. His hand rose to cup her cheek, his thumb tracing back and forth across her skin.

Refusing to close her eyes to savor the feel of his touch, she kept her gaze on him. After this, she'd never see him again. She wanted to, needed to, remember every detail.

"I'll miss you," she whispered finally.

His eyes lowered for a moment, pain crossing his face, marring his beautiful features. Looking up, a sad smile crossed his lips. "I will see you again. One day."

The tears were suddenly so very persistent. Blinking rapidly, she hardened herself against them. "One day," she repeated. Her answering smile wavered, but it was the best she could do.

His hand dropped from her face. "Thank you, for bringing me home."

A nod was all she could manage. She wanted so very much to pull him to her and beg him to stay. He couldn't, and she knew it, just as she couldn't go with him. It tore her apart.

Forcing one more small smile, he turned…and walked away.

That was all?

Eyes burning, she clenched her fists and struggled to keep breathing. This wasn't how it she'd imagined their parting, but it was done, the moment over.

Staring after him, watching him slowly walk away from her, broke her down into little pieces. Inhaling a slow breath, she held it, and then let it out just as slowly. This was how it had to be. It hurt, but she would survive, and so would he.

*I love you,* she whispered into his mind. She would have no regrets.

At first, she wasn't sure he'd heard her as he continued to walk toward the gates. Then he stopped suddenly, motionlessly staring straight ahead.

She sucked in a startled breath as he spun on his heel and came charging toward her. Had she made him angry saying it one last time? Steeling herself for a fight, she tensed as he quickly reached her.

Sweeping her up into his arms, his lips found hers. He kissed her, firmly and deeply, leaving no doubt in her mind he was quite serious.

She pressed her hands against his chest, weakly trying to push him away. His pity was the last thing she wanted. She refused to let him play games with her. *I told you not to kiss me unless–*

*I know.*

Her heart stuttered at his answer and she gasped against his lips. Taking advantage of the moment, his tongue slid across her lower lip before gently dipping inside. A tremble rolled through her as she melted in his arms. Slipping her hands up his arms, she twined them around his neck, into his hair, pulling him closer as his mouth devoured hers.

Dipping over her, his hair fell around her face as he held her ever tighter. She pushed up against him, wanting to be closer. Their kiss turned frantic, demanding. Heat and longing and need coursed through her veins and along every nerve. They kissed as though they'd never kiss again.

Hearts pounding, both gasping for breath, he reluctantly pulled back. Stunned, she stared up at him, her lips slightly parted in wonder.

Placing a slow kiss to her lips, he then rested his forehead against hers. They stood quietly for a moment, hearts still racing, before she felt his sigh on her skin.

"I must go."

"I know."

"Please, be safe, my Arowyn," he said quietly.

She tilted her head up. "I will. Be safe, my prince," she whispered. *Be safe, Shael.*

*I will.*

It seemed so sudden when he pulled away, leaving her cold despite her flushed face and racing heart. Again, she watched him turn and walk away, though his steps were much quicker this time. Watching him leave again was torture. She supposed, she hoped, it wasn't any easier on him to go.

As he reached the opened gates her eyes caught the rows of Elven warriors and her face burned again. "Wither me." She'd forgotten they were there. They'd seen…

Her tender lips pressed into a firm line and she raised her chin and straightened her shoulders. They would not think her some weak human woman. If they gave Prince any trouble…they better hope she never heard of it.

Prince did not look back as he crossed into his land. The other Elves filed in to either side of him and then the beautiful, massive gates glided silently closed.

The boom of their closing made her jump, but she continued to stare at them, wishing she could see through them.

Truly, she *was* stronger now. After all, she'd just lost another of her boys, her love, and she wasn't even crying. The man she loved had kissed her, he returned her love, and still she didn't cry as he walked away from her.

Aro stared at the gates for another moment and then lifted her chin and turned to her grinning boys. "Let's head out. We have a horse to return."

She might have "One Day" to wait for, but she still had a life to live.

341

Jen Wylie

# Other Works by Jen Wylie

The Broken Ones
  -Broken Aro
  -Broken Prince

Flashy Fiction and Other Insane Tales (anthology with Sean Hayden)
  -Volumes 1 & 2

Sweet Light (novel)

Ring Around the Rosie (short story)

Jump (short story)

Immortal Echoes
  -The Forgotten Echo (novella)
  -The Untouchable Echo (short story)

Tales of Ever (YA novella series)
  -Banished
  -Fire Girl
  -Shadow Boy
  -The Lost Tree
  -Dragon Rising
  -Sanctuary

# About the Author

Jen Wylie resides in rural Ontario, Canada with her two boys, Australian shepherd and a disagreeable amount of wildlife. In a cosmic twist of fate she dislikes the snow and cold.

Before settling down to raise a family, she attained a BA from Queens University and worked in retail and sales.

Thanks to her mother she acquired a love of books at an early age and began writing in public school. She constantly has stories floating around in her head, and finds it amazing most people don't. Jennifer writes various forms of fantasy, both novels and short stories. She loves to hear from her readers!

How to connect with Jen:
Goodreads: Jen Wylie
Twitter: @jen_wylie
Facebook: Jennifer Wylie (page)
Website: jenwylie.com
Email: jenniferw2mail@gmail.com